Hallie Bernhardt,
Bernhardt Bridals,
Boston, Mass.

<u>Checklist for Brewster wedding</u>

1. Confirm delivery date of orchids for la

2. Confirm wedding cake with Chef Jacqu
   with Mallomars. Do not offer more tha

3. Pacify Babs Brewster. Do not let her get to you.

4. Watch weather report. Do not panic.

5. Buy aspirin. What was in that umbrella drink,
   anyway?

6. Have Mr. Aloha measure Rik Austin, best man, for
   tux. Do NOT offer to do it yourself.

7. Meet Rik Austin for dinner. Just dinner. Do not
   have a good time.

8. Reassure Babs Brewster. Again. Do not strangle
   her.

9. Deny rumors of doing rumba in lobby. Do not
   meet Rik for dinner again.

10. Find out what Rik is up to…. Do not panic.

11. Watch weather report. Stay calm.

12. Cancel orchids.   Very.

13. Cancel lanai.   Very.

14. Cancel wedding.   Calm.

15. DO NOT FALL IN LOVE WITH RIK AUSTIN!!!!!

Dear Reader,

We're so glad you could join us in beautiful Hawaii for what promises to be another perfect wedding! But wait—let's hear it from the mother-of-the-bride herself, Babs Brewster:

"Weddings, schmeddings! I can't take any more! First my daughter Stephanie misses her own wedding, then Bentley, my other daughter, introduces me to her phantom husband we'd only seen in photos. But as soon as I ask about grandchildren she goes into a tizzy. And now there's that fool wedding coordinator, Hallie. Is it too much to ask that the very expensive professional—and proper Boston girl, I might add— not be seen slung over the best man's shoulder like a bad lounge singer? And if that's not enough, there's that blasted hurricane coming and we'll probably all be washed out to sea! I ask you, what's a mother to do?"

You're about to find out as we bring you the third book of THREE WEDDINGS & A HURRICANE, a hilarious trilogy from friends Debbi Rawlins, Jo Leigh and Karen Toller Whittenburg. We hope you haven't missed a single moment of the fun!

Happy reading!

Debra Matteucci
Senior Editor & Editorial Coordinator
Harlequin
300 East 42nd Street
New York, NY 10017

Karen Toller Whittenburg

PLEASE SAY "I DO"

Harlequin Books

TORONTO • NEW YORK • LONDON
AMSTERDAM • PARIS • SYDNEY • HAMBURG
STOCKHOLM • ATHENS • TOKYO • MILAN
MADRID • WARSAW • BUDAPEST • AUCKLAND

ISBN 0-373-16698-2

PLEASE SAY "I DO"

Chapter One

Hallie Bernhardt settled her glasses on the tip of her nose and stared over the round pewter frames until the hotel clerk's welcome-to-the-Islands smile and Hawaiian-print shirt blurred into a slightly less annoying brilliance. "I'm afraid you've made a mistake," she said, tapping the registration form on the counter between them. "This can't be my room."

He glanced at the number beneath her pink-tipped fingernail, then checked the computer screen again. "Ms. Bernhardt?" he asked. "You're with the Brewster wedding, right?"

"Yes."

He tapped more keys, frowned, tapped a few more, then flashed that bright white smile again. "No, ma'am, no mistake. Room 1413 has been reserved for you. It's one of our Love Nest rooms and is normally used for newlyweds, but Mrs. Brewster insisted you have an ocean view."

Ocean View? Oh, jeez. "No, no," she said. "You don't understand. I'm the wedding coordinator, Hallie Bernhardt. *B-e-r-n-h-a-r-d-t*. I specifically requested a single room on the ground floor."

His smile didn't waver. "There are no guest rooms on the ground floor, Ms. Bernhardt."

"The next floor up, then."

He shook his head without even checking the computer first. "I'm afraid we're overbooked this week as it is, and Mrs. Brewster did go to a great deal of trouble in trying to move everyone to the same floor."

Hallie shuddered, imagining the entire Brewster clan surrounding her on every side. "There has to be another room," she said a little desperately. "I cannot spend an entire week in *this* room on *that* floor with *them!*"

"This is peak honeymoon season. I wouldn't know where else to put you."

"Switch me with someone. Stephanie Brewster won't be here until later in the week. Give me her room."

"I'm sorry, but that room is already occupied by Ms. Brewster's fiancé, Mr. Keaton." He delivered that information as if he was sure she'd be pleased to hear it. "There's a possibility a room on the twelfth floor could become available later, but I'm sure you wouldn't want to be separated from the family."

Oh, yes, she would. She really would. "I'll take it," she said. "The Brewsters will never miss me."

"It's nothing definite, Ms. Bernhardt. The room is reserved for the rest of the week. I wouldn't want you to count on it."

Flattening her palms on the counter, Hallie leaned forward, just managing to control the impulse to grasp his floral-print collar and yank him across the desk to face her. Tilting up her chin so she could see through the lenses of her glasses, she read the name Kimo, on his gold badge, then shoved the glasses onto the bridge of her nose so she could keep him in focus.

"Look, Kimo, I don't mean to be difficult, but I've

been on a plane so long I thought I was going to have to have the seat belt surgically removed from my hips. Flying makes me nervous, and when I'm nervous, I eat. So I ate everything I could beg from the flight attendants and even embarrassed myself by swiping food from my neighbor's tray. Then we hit bad weather and I spent the rest of the trip holding a little paper sack over my face, in case the turmoil in my stomach stopped going around and around and headed upward.

"The woman in front of me insisted I take a couple of her motion-sickness pills, which I accepted to be polite and had no intention of taking, except I dropped them into my pocket with my vitamin C, and just before the plane landed—the most bone-jarring landing I've ever experienced—I swallowed all of the tablets before I remembered they weren't all vitamins. The pills *looked* like Tic Tacs and I honestly believe she gave them to me hoping they'd have a placebo effect. I'm only telling you that so you'll understand this was no ordinary trip across the Pacific and I'm still a little shaken by it.

"On top of that, I'd hardly set foot on the island before I discovered my luggage never even made it onto the plane with me and is now somewhere on its way to Argentina. As if that isn't enough, this is—beginning to end—the worst hair day of my entire adult life. Normally, I'm a very nice person, Kimo, but I can't promise continued civilized behavior if you keep insisting that the only room available is the thirteenth room on the thirteenth floor!"

His smile barely drooped before it made a dramatic comeback. "The hotel doesn't have a thirteenth floor," he said brightly. "We skip that number because some people think it's bad luck."

She was sorry now she hadn't grabbed his collar and given it a good yank. "Give me a different room, Kimo. I need one very badly."

"But this is a lovely room," he assured her. "With a spectacular ocean view."

She cringed at the thought, took off her glasses, folded the earpieces across each other and tucked them into the outside pocket of her small leather briefcase. Then she took a deep breath and focused on the blur that was Kimo's face. "I'm afraid of heights, okay? And I get seasick just thinking about watching waves erode the shoreline. So I don't need a room with a view. I *need* to be as close to the ground as possible, in a room with even numbers. That's what I requested and that's the room I expect you to give me." Hallie pushed the card across the counter. "Consider it your random act of kindness for the decade."

With a nod of wary confusion, Kimo took her registration and eased a step away from the desk. "I'll do my best, Ms. Bernhardt."

"Thank you, Kimo."

"It's Kee-mo," he said. "Not Ky-mo."

"Whatever," she muttered under her breath, before crooking her head politely and correcting her mispronunciation. "Thank you, Kee-mo."

He smiled broadly, apparently thrilled by this sign of cooperation. A sweet-smelling breeze zipped through the open lobby, ruffling the fronds of the plants and rudely flipping up the hem of Hallie's gored skirt. She slapped at the fabric and wished she'd gone with her first instinct and worn a straight-skirted suit instead of this flibbertigibbet of a dress. The suit would have been hideously uncomfortable on the trip, but at least now she'd look professionally wrinkled instead of dismally rumpled, and her skirt wouldn't be swirling around her thighs.

A second gust of wind lifted her skirt and she batted it down, but the trickster breeze flipped it up from behind. With a gasp, Hallie spun around to protect her backside from further exposure and spied a cool, dark cave of a bar. Normally, she steered clear of alcoholic beverages—no point in killing off brain cells before their time—but one of those icy drinks with the little umbrellas was suddenly very appealing. After all, she was in Hawaii, and considering the day she'd had and the week she was facing, a few brain cells seemed a small price to pay for a few minutes of relaxation. She was absolutely certain she couldn't feel worse.

"I'll just wait in the bar until you find a room for me." She offered the information to Kimo with a backward glance, clamped a restrictive hold on her immodest skirt and headed for the cabanalike bar. Paradise Bay was spelled out in some sort of ropelike material over the grass-hut entrance. Inside, the decor was strictly island eclectic, and outside, the wind danced a mean hula, setting the canvas canopies of the tables sashaying like a dancer's grass skirt.

Dropping her briefcase flat on the bar, Hallie set her hips on one of the stools with a flippant little swivel. The bar was nearly deserted—which she thought was unusual, considering Kimo's assertion that the hotel was overbooked. On the other hand, Paradise Bay was a honeymoon hotel that catered to newlyweds, who undoubtedly preferred the privacy of their suite to all other diversions. Honeymooners, she'd heard, slept late, stayed up late and got drunk on love. On her own disastrous honeymoon—six long years ago—Brad had just gotten drunk.

Looking around for the bartender, Hallie caught the eye of the man sitting at the other end of the bar. He watched her with a benign, but purely sexual, admiration, assessing her *ass*-ets in that annoying way of men who had passed the impulse of youth and wanted women to believe they could afford to be ever so much more selective. Lifting her chin and clasping her hands together on the bar—just shy of a bowl of peanuts— she pretended to be unaware of his presence. Above the bar, a television screen displayed a scene of verdant grass with the kind of hushed commentary common to televised golf. At least golf was a quiet game. No crunching of bones. No blasts from the referee's whistle. Just the nice crack of a club striking a harmless little ball. Steepling her hands, she tapped the two index fingers together and waited for the bartender to return to his post.

Patience wasn't her strong suit, though, and she swiveled the bar stool around to face the empty tables. Propping her elbows on the counter, she leaned back and tapped her foot against the rung of the stool. She tossed her head, flipping her long, honey brown hair into a cascade down her back...at least it would have been a cascade two days ago. She kept forgetting she'd had it cut in its current trendy, frivolous, barely shoulder-length and very shaggy style. How long before she stopped tossing her head like some horse shaking its mane, she wondered. She must look like an idiot.

Her glance slid to the man at the bar...and recognized the curve of his lips as amused interest. All right, so he probably thought she was flirting with him. Ha! Fat chance. Not that he wasn't attractive, if one liked the rugged-individualist type. Even in the festive, Hawaiian-print shirt, he looked ready to run out and climb a mountain on the off chance someone should challenge his masculinity. His hair was black with a few strands of silver tossed in for contrast, his skin was a rich, deep tan.... Obviously an outdoorsman, although she'd have to see more than his muscular upper half to decide if he looked capable of scaling mountains.

He lifted his glass in mute acknowledgment of her appraisal and she jerked her gaze to the front. She wasn't interested, no matter what he thought. He obviously believed he was invincible, which was the only reason she could think of to explain why some people ignored the warnings of countless dermatologists and exposed their skin to too much sun. There was no excuse for playing ultraviolet-ray roulette these days. *She* had been careful to pack plenty of sunscreen, long-sleeved shirts and no less than three large-brimmed hats. Of course, all her foresight wasn't going to do her much good if her luggage didn't show up soon.

"If I get sunburned," she said aloud, "I'm suing the airline, the hotel and the guy who gave me this haircut."

Rugged Individualist looked up. "Bad flight?"

His voice was deep, smooth and pleasant. Why didn't handsome men ever have high-pitched, squeaky voices? She turned her head slowly with eyebrows lifted. "Excuse me?"

He swiveled to face her, his beer clutched in his hand, his smile lazy and so inherently sexy she nearly slid off her stool. "I said," he repeated, blatantly ignoring her discouraging tone, "did you have a bad flight?"

Ordinarily, she would have ignored him, but pent-up frustration pushed the words right out of her mouth. "The worst...*and* they lost my luggage. Then when I finally get here, the hotel wants to put me in the thirteenth room on the thirteenth floor!''

"I didn't think hotels had thirteenth floors."

"My point exactly. You've been lulled into that perception. But if you think about it, skipping a number doesn't make it disappear. So no matter what they call it, the floor after twelve is still the thirteenth floor."

"Can't say I ever thought about it that way."

"It amazes me that more people don't."

He sipped his beer and his gaze slid away from her.

Hallie had seen that reaction before, although usually not quite so early in a conversation. *High-maintenance female,* he was thinking. *Trouble. Steer clear.* In another couple of minutes, he'd finish his beer and leave the room. Not that she minded. She wasn't interested in starting anything with Mr. Individualist...or anyone else. She had far too much to do, far too much riding on this one wedding, far too many other things to think about. Her brief marriage had been more than enough exposure to relationships, anyway, thank you very much.

"So, what's wrong with the haircut?"

His question startled her, and from across the distance of five bar stools, she felt a singe of heated awareness when her eyes met his. He had vivid blue eyes, expressive eyes, and she sent up a mental note of thanks that she had excellent distance vision. If he were any closer, she'd have to put her glasses back on and then he'd leave the room for sure. "I'm sorry," she said politely. "What did you say?"

"I said, 'What's wrong with the haircut?'"

The haircut. She'd almost forgotten. "Oh, please, don't be patronizing," she said on a sigh. "I've had a miserable day and I don't need some stranger trying to tell me this isn't the worst haircut he's ever seen.''

He regarded her thoughtfully, then set his beer bottle on the bar. "I believe you could use a drink, Ms.—"

"Bernhardt," she supplied testily. "Not that it's any of your business. And there isn't a bartender here to fix a drink *if* I wanted one, which I did when I first walked in, but now I don't."

He slid to his feet and strolled toward her. Okay, so he probably did scale mountains on his coffee break. But just because he was tall and good-looking and had a slow, sexy walk was no reason to let him labor under the illusion he would get anywhere near first base with her. Luckily, the closer he got, the fuzzier he looked, and by the time he stood next to her, he had acquired a nicely blurred quality.

"I'm Rik." He extended a hand.

Hallie did her best not to squint and bring him into sharper focus. "Yes?"

"It's very nice to meet you, Ms. Bernhardt," he said pointedly, picking up her hand in his warm, solid clasp and giving it a shake. "And now that we're no longer strangers, I'd like to know what's wrong with your haircut. Personally, I think it's cute."

Cute. Oh, great. As if she needed to hear that! She withdrew her hand from his. "You're wasting your time, Rik. I may be alone, but I'm not available." She swiveled to face the bar and give him the full benefit of a cold shoulder, even though her palm tingled from the heat of his touch and she couldn't keep from rubbing it briskly up and down her leg.

"As it happens, Ms. Bernhardt, I'm also alone but unavailable. Let's drink to that happy circumstance, shall we?'' He was suddenly on the other side of the bar across from her. "What will you have?"

"Do you work here?"

"Nope. I'm merely a guest who doesn't mind lending a hand when needed."

"There are rules about that sort of thing, you know."

He cocked an eyebrow in a disarmingly attractive disregard for authority. "Rules don't scare me much, Ms. Bernhardt. Now, what can I get for you?"

"Something refreshing, maybe with one of those little parasols. Any suggestions?"

"A mai-tai, maybe. Or a tequila sunrise. That's very popular around here. So is Sex on the Beach."

Hallie's gaze flew to his and her hand dived for the peanuts. She wondered if his significant other realized he was on the loose. "Sounds too gritty for me. I'll have that middle thing," she said, then, not wanting to appear totally unsophisticated, added, "on the rocks."

"One tequila sunrise coming up."

He set a slender glass on the counter and she watched with interest as he added ice and a small measure of tequila. Not much alcohol in this drink, she thought, doubly pleased with her choice...until she saw him pick up a bottle of bright red liquid. "Oh, don't put that in."

He looked at her, then at the bottle. "But this is grenadine. The drink won't taste right without it."

"I'm allergic to red dye," she told him. "The drink will be just as good without adding that."

"Red dye," he repeated, and set the grenadine aside before retrieving a container of orange juice from below the counter.

"Whoops," she said. "Better hold the juice, too." His quick look of surprise made her uncomfortable and she scooted the bowl of peanuts closer.

"Are you allergic to oranges, too?"

He didn't have to make her sound like a hypochondriac. "No, of course not. Citric acid upsets my stomach sometimes, that's all."

He stared at her for a moment, then put the juice away, picked up the slender glass and set it in front of her. "One tequila sunrise, minus red dye and citric acid."

She regarded the innocuous appearance of the drink and wished she'd admitted her ignorance straight-out. At least there wasn't much in the glass. She could handle that piddling amount. Resolutely, she lifted the glass in a smart salute. "Down the hatch," she said, and swallowed the tequila in a single gulp.

An unholy fire ripped down her throat and burned like an inferno in her chest. Scalding tears pooled in her eyes, but she couldn't blink for fear of singeing her eyelashes. She coughed, choked and coughed again, ending in a hacking gasp and a pathetic wheeze. "Water," she gasped. "Water."

The water was in her hand almost before the whisper was out and she gulped it down. The fire in her belly sizzled and she let her head drop back, hoping to God that smoke wasn't pouring out of her nose.

"Are you all right?"

His voice floated to her through a misty heat that oddly, gently pooled into pleasure. "Fine," she whispered raggedly. "Never better."

He frowned and looked—it was difficult to discern his expression without her glasses, but she thought he looked concerned. "Tequila should come with a warning label," he said. "Want some more water?"

She shook her head and picked up another handful of peanuts. "I've always thought it came with a worm."

"In this case, I guess that would be me. I shouldn't have let you drink straight tequila...on the rocks or otherwise. It's obvious you're a novice."

Novice? He thought she was a *novice?* "Honestly, you sound like somebody's reverend uncle. I choked, that's all." She pushed the glass toward him. "I'll have another drink, Mr. Unavailable. Just like the last one."

His eyebrows rose. "Don't you think you ought to pace yourself?"

"I'm not running the Boston Marathon." Hallie tossed a peanut into the air and caught it in her mouth. Amazing. She'd never done that before in her life. Catching his eye, she felt a little foolish and a whole lot daring. "You didn't think I could do that, did you?"

"Can't say that I did." He recapped the tequila after pouring a little in her glass. "You're one surprise after another."

She nodded...although she wasn't entirely clear on why she was agreeing with him. "You'd be amazed at the things I can do." Hallie looked at the peanuts that kept mysteriously collecting in her palm. "Efficiency is my middle name."

"And what comes before Efficiency?"

"Organization."

"That's quite a name. What do your friends call you?"

"Hallie." She picked up the glass and turned it in her hand. "Short *a*, long *e*, silent *i*." Sucking in a breath, she downed the tequila in a gulp, ready for anything except the sudden high-pitched beeping that seemed to surround her on all sides. She looked cautiously at—his name eluded her at the moment—and realized he had turned his head to see the television. Something was going on at the golf game, she decided, but even with a determined squint, she couldn't make out the words scrolling across the bottom of the screen. "What happened?" she whispered.

"It's a weather advisory." He tossed the information over his shoulder. "An update on the hurricane."

"What hurricane?"

"The one that's been building in the Pacific for the past couple of days."

"The Pacific *Ocean?*"

His glance was sharp, as if he was checking to see if she expected an answer. She knew, of course, that Pacific was shorthand for the Pacific Ocean and that the expanse of deep blue water visible not a quarter mile from where she was sitting was, indeed, the Pacific Ocean. But if there was a hurricane out there, someone should have told her. "Impossible," she said. "I checked the weather channel before I left Boston and there was not a single mention of a hurricane."

"It must have been a really long flight."

She narrowed her eyes at the television, but the words remained fuzzy. "Tell me what it says."

She felt his glance but was too busy searching through her briefcase to look up. "I have excellent distance vision," she explained. "The television is just a little too close for me to get in focus. Now, what does it say about a hurricane?"

"'The National Weather Service has upgraded the tropical storm in the Pacific to a hurricane,'" he read for her. "'With winds approaching seventy miles an hour, Hurricane Bonnie is moving in a southeasterly direction and, on its current path, will pass to the south of the Hawaiian Islands late Thursday. Residents are advised to prepare for high winds, heavy rain and possible swells. Stay tuned to this station for further updates.'"" He turned back to her. "That's the same bulletin they've been giving since yesterday."

Hallie found the glasses and put them on, no longer caring that, since the haircut, she looked like a studious Cabbage Patch Kid in them. "Well, all I can say is they're flat-out wrong about the rain, because there is no way I'm going to let bad weather ruin Stephanie's wedding."

"Stephanie? You're here for Stephanie Brewster's wedding?"

He sounded incredulous and, with her glasses on, she got a full dose of the question in his gorgeous blue eyes. "I'm the wedding coordinator. Bernhardt Bridal of Boston. That's me. I've been planning this wedding for months, which is not nearly enough time to arrange the kind of ceremony Babs Brewster expects, but I've managed to put together something very nice...even though it all had to be done by telephone and despite the fact that I've yet to speak with the bride. Do you know her?"

"We've met," he said crisply. "I'm the best man."

"*You're* the best man? In Stephanie Brewster's wedding?" Her voice bounced inside her head in a funny kind of echo. "No, you're not. I personally sent in the measurements to Mr. Aloha Formalwear and you weren't on the list."

"You didn't have my name?"

"I don't know, but I'm positive your measurements weren't on there..." The echo was getting worse, but she hung doggedly to her train of thought. "I'm a professional and I would have remembered the size of this." Reaching across the bar, she put her hand on his biceps and squeezed. His hand came over hers, engulfing, electrifying, and she tried to recall what the hell she'd been thinking. She brought up her chin. "I'll bet you're wondering what I'm doing, aren't you?"

His smile was entirely too sexy and her glasses made focusing on him entirely too easy. "Why don't you tell me?" he suggested in a soft, insinuating tone of voice.

"I'm measuring your arm," she said, as if it should have been obvious and as if her fingers weren't itching to give his arm just a brief massage. "Of course."

"Of course," he repeated. "And did you reach a conclusion?"

She wished she could reach the peanuts. "Just as I suspected, you weren't on the list I mailed to Mr. Aloha."

His fingers stroked the back of her hand. "You can tell that by copping a feel of my arm?"

"I did no such thing." Jerking her hand from his touch, she grabbed the bottle of tequila. "I don't 'cop' feels, as you so inelegantly put it. Your arm is not that extraordinary, and besides, I don't even know your full name." With that, she poured another drink and tossed it back as if she'd been doing it for decades.

He moved his face closer, altogether too close for comfort. "Rik Austin," he said. "That's Rik. Short *i*, no *c*. Austin, as in Texas."

Austin, Texas, buzzed through her brain like a pesky mosquito, and Hallie frowned as she tried to remember the point she wanted to make. "This is Hawaii." *That* wasn't it. "You can't be the best man because he's from the same place as the groom is...and it isn't Texas."

"Jack and I worked together in South America and his arm is approximately the same size as mine."

Hallie looked at him. "Are you trying to confuse me?"

"No, but I can't think it would be very difficult to do at the moment."

"Well, you're wrong," she told him with feeling. "Because I know exactly what I'm doing." To prove it, she ate another handful of peanuts and washed them down with more tequila.

"You should go slow with that stuff." He reached for the bottle, but she moved it out of the way.

"Uh-uh-uh. I'll have you know I take my vitamins every day, rain or shine, and I feel perfectly fine, thank you, Uncle Rik." Hallie was amazed at the purling laugh that floated past her lips and right over the lovely buzz inside her head. "I never knew a tequila sunrise would taste so good."

"You should see what I can do with a screwdriver."

She wrinkled her nose. "I had that once. On my honeymoon. It made me sick."

"The drink or the honeymoon?" His smile faded as she frowned at him. "Sorry," he said. "Bad joke."

"To be honest, I can't remember." Her frown deepened. "It must have been the drink. Honeymoons don't make people sick."

"That would depend on whose honeymoon it is."

She wanted to consider that, but the thought sort of wisped away. "You know, Rik, I don't usually drink anything except bottled water. But I *like* tequila."

"The feeling will pass, believe me." He clasped the bottle of tequila, preparing to put it away, but divining his intention, Hallie closed her hand over his. She liked the warmth and shape of his fingers under hers, and she told him so in a smile. "You know, Rik, someone said they put worms in this stuff." Lifting the bottle, Hallie laid her head on the bar and looked up at the concave glass bottom. "You know what I think, Rik? I think

Stephanie should have planned her own wedding, instead of letting her mother do it for her.''

"Maybe she doesn't want to get married."

There was a distinct interest in his expression that Hallie didn't miss, despite the distortion of the thick glass bottle. "Naturally she wants to get married. The money's already spent, the arrangements are all made, the ceremony is set, Babs Brewster has rounded up the whole family and herded them over here. The wedding will be perfect. So, of course Stephanie wants to get married."

Rik looked pointedly at the palm trees outside, which were swaying dramatically with each new breeze. Taking off her glasses, Hallie followed his gaze, then poured a bit more liquor into her glass, set the bottle on the bar and tossed back the drink. "Stephanie is getting married Saturday if I have to kayak out into the Pacific and personally tie a knot in Hurricane Bonnie's tail."

Rik's eyebrows went up in that wickedly sensual arch. "You're a braver man than I."

"That's because I'm a woman. It's easy to be brave when your entire future comes down to one wedding."

"I hope you're exaggerating, because a future is a lot to risk on a simple ceremony."

"Simple?" Her laughter sounded too loud in her ears and it occurred to her, with woozy clarity, that maybe those funny little white pills hadn't been Tic Tacs after all. "Simple," she repeated, shaking her head. "Weddings are never simple. Even simple weddings aren't simple. Even small family weddings aren't simple. Out-of-town weddings aren't simple. Weddings like Stephanie Brewster's definitely aren't simple. Just perfect. They have to be perfect, you know. All of them. And that's my job. That's why the Brewsters hired me. To make this wedding perfect. And I will. Or my name isn't—'' She paused and waited for the answer to click into place. "Hallie Bernhardt," she finished, tapping the counter for emphasis. "That's me."

He leaned his elbows on the counter and clasped his hands only inches away from the peanut bowl and her restless fingers. "What difference does it make if the ceremony's perfect? The couple's just as married no matter what happens during the actual wedding."

"You're wrong," she stated emphatically, wanting more than anything to dip into the dwindling mound of peanuts. "Dead wrong. I can tell you for a fact that what happens during the wedding can make or break the marriage."

"I'd be more inclined to believe that Babs Brewster has threatened murder if the wedding doesn't come off as perfectly as she's planned."

"The way things have gone so far, murder is a distinct possibility." Hallie wished she could lay her head on the bar and close her eyes for just a minute. There seemed to be a Grand Canyon-size cavern inside her head, where all the words she said and all the words he said collided and split into a million echoes. "At the moment, I think it's a toss-up whether her hit man gets to me before I get to her. On the other hand, maybe I'll just wait here and let him come to me. Madame Sally warned me that I'd meet someone dangerous."

"I'm not dangerous," Rik said with showy deference. "Just a touch uncivilized."

Hallie looked up at him and decided that if Babs Brewster knew how susceptible she was to dark-haired men with blue eyes, Rik would be the perfect choice of hired gun. "Madame Sally must have been talking about Jose Cuervo. She's always told me I don't have the aura to attract dangerous men.''

"I think you're attractive.''

"But you're not dangerous, are you? Just uncivilized. And for the record, there's a big difference between being attractive and being attracted. Besides, you're just being nice because you know I have really bad hair.''

"I like your hair.'' He slipped the tequila bottle out of her reach and under the counter, but she didn't try to stop him. Her skin felt strangely elastic, and she thought that if she stretched out her hand, it might snap back and hit her in the nose.

"Do I look okay to you?'' she asked.

"You look fine to me...which is a lot better than okay.''

"I mean, my face isn't sagging or anything?''

His smile was easy on her eyes. "No sags, wrinkles or makeup lines.'' He stroked the furrows of her forehead, smoothing out the frown, and she wished he would keep touching her that way until she fell asleep. "There,'' he said. "Perfect.''

She sighed, knowing that if she could figure out how, she'd wrap herself around him and purr. Definitely time to move on. Putting her hands on the bar, she pushed herself upright. "I think I'll see if they've found another room for me yet. I'm feeling a little jet-lagged suddenly.'' Slipping off the bar stool, she teetered and caught her balance with a hand on the countertop. She licked her lips, wondering why her mouth suddenly had such a dry-roasted feeling. How many drinks had she had? Two? Three at the most. And there hadn't been more than a drop of tequila in each one. Still, she wasn't used to drinking at all and she probably shouldn't have combined alcohol and all those salty peanuts. Some things just weren't meant to be together. She knew that for a fact, and now she knew she'd have been better off to wait in the restaurant with a glass of water and a bowl of papayas. But then she wouldn't have met Rik and found out she needed to take his measurements.

Which was a good thing, because how could anyone have a perfect wedding if the best man wore khaki shorts and a Hawaiian shirt during the ceremony? But she'd take care of it. There was always some last-minute detail to handle at a Bernhardt Bridal wedding. Nothing big, just some little thing overlooked. And little things could ruin a wedding...and her reputation. She would write herself a reminder in her Day-Timer. Call Mr. Aloha, she mentally noted. Get him to come over and measure the best man. Walking slowly but steadily, she reached the doorway and batted what seemed like an acre of dried grass out of her face. The lobby stretched before her in a shiny expanse of sea green, like a mirage on summer pavement. With a blink, she adjusted her focus and started toward the distant front desk.

RIK WATCHED HALLIE Bernhardt walk into the arch of dried grass at the entrance of the bar. She slapped the grass away, then paused to straighten her shoulders before she took the first confident—if slightly wobbly— step across the lobby. Unless he missed his guess, she was ten minutes or less from passing out, and when she woke up, she was going to wish she'd never heard of Jose Cuervo or a tequila sunrise. She probably wasn't going to remember him too fondly, either.

What a package of problems she was, he thought as he picked up her forgotten briefcase. It would take a man years just to figure out everything she was allergic to. And she had that clipped Boston accent. Nothing like Stephanie's softer tones, mellowed by years away from the city of her birth but still reserved and quiet. No, Hallie Bernhardt talked like a Bostonian, and had told him more than she realized.

Until she'd sashayed in, Rik had been enjoying the quiet dusk of the open bar. He'd savored the rapid crashing and ebbing of the tide, inhaled the fragrant wind and appreciated the shelter of a real roof over his head. Hallie obviously didn't enjoy quiet, didn't know how to listen to the pounding surf, didn't know how to hear the sound of the wind as it tried and failed to find her. Over the course of his years in the Amazon, he'd learned a healthy respect for nature as well as an admiration for her unpredictability. And here, in this ridiculously luxurious hotel, he met an unpredictable woman who, despite the image she tried to project, was about as sophisticated as a chimpanzee in a fashion show, a woman who prided herself on her organization and efficiency and walked off without her briefcase.

Setting the leather satchel behind the bar, Rik smiled at her threat to tie a knot in the tail of a hurricane. She was interesting. No, more than that. She was fate.

He believed in allowing the forces that be to direct his energy and to deliver whatever he needed to his doorstep. And, just as he'd been wondering if that philosophy could survive outside the jungle he had called home for thirteen years, Hallie had walked in to prove it once again. She was Bernhardt Bridal, the ringleader of the committee that had planned Stephanie's wedding. The wedding he had been sitting here quietly plotting to sabotage. Just as he was coming up empty on ideas about how to stop the woman he loved from marrying the wrong man, the wedding coordinator walked in and started talking. If he could have chosen a better person to meet at this particular moment, he couldn't think who it might have been. Stephanie wasn't here yet. Wouldn't arrive until Friday, just before the Saturday ceremony. Jack, the groom, and Rik's best friend in the world, was here but not talking. Jack thought he was committed to this marriage already, thought it would hurt Stephanie if he bowed out, gracefully or otherwise. Rik hadn't been able to talk a grain of sense into that hard head of his.

But here, suddenly, was the answer. A woman who knew every detail of the upcoming wedding, who had access to and influence over problems Rik couldn't possibly create. And unless his signal decoder was seriously out of whack, she wasn't as unavailable as she wanted him to believe. He felt a momentary pang of conscience at deliberately using her for his own purpose, but it passed. Stopping this ill-conceived wedding was worth whatever deception, whatever ruse, whatever scheme it cost...up to and including his hotel room.

Chapter Two

Rik reached the front desk just as Hallie gave the pretty, dark-haired clerk a perturbed look. "No, I don't understand," she was saying. "If I needed more bad luck today, I'd smash a mirror. All I'm asking is to change from one room to another room on a different floor. That can't be so difficult."

The clerk shook her head, her long, straight hair swinging behind her shoulders with brisk apology. "I'm sorry, Ms. Bernhardt, but there's nothing I can do."

"Where's the other reservation clerk? Where's Kimo?"

"Kimo doesn't work the front desk." The clerk turned to answer the persistent ringing of the phone. "Paradise Bay," she said. "This is Earlette. May I help you?"

"You can help *me*," Hallie persisted. "Kimo does work the front desk because he took my registration and put me in room 1313."

"Fourteen-thirteen," Rik corrected, leaning casually against the counter beside her. "You're in room 1413."

Hallie glanced at him and frowned as if she couldn't quite recall where she'd met him. She was wearing her glasses, but behind the pewter rims, her hazel eyes reflected anxiety, exasperation and the rising fog of too much tequila. "I *know* what room I'm in." With a dismissive toss of her head, she leaned across the counter and waved her hand to gain Earlette's attention again. "Yoo-hoo," she said in an exaggerated whisper. "Can we talk?"

Earlette held up her index finger and tried to continue her phone conversation. But Hallie bent further across the counter and grasped the opposite edge, bringing her body into an intriguing alignment with the desk. Rik made it a point never to question a gift from the gods, and his appreciative gaze dropped from her slender shoulders to the curve of her hips and the softly sloped hollows behind her knees. He wondered, idly, what sort of erotic noises she made when a man kissed her there.

"Kimo made a big mistake," she whispered loudly. "He put me in the wrong room. So if you'll just put me in another one, that will fix everything."

Earlette covered the mouthpiece. "Please, Ms. Bernhardt, I'll be with you in a moment."

"But this is important," Hallie persisted, as Earlette turned away to finish her conversation. "My feet hurt and I'm not feeling too good myself."

"You can lie down in my room." Rik dangled the offer like a shiny red ribbon. "I'm on the tenth floor."

Hallie looked over her shoulder and sighed. "I don't suppose you'd want to trade."

Rik arched his brows in what he hoped was a *Eureka!* expression. "Why didn't I think of that? Of course I'll swap rooms with you."

"You will?"

He nodded, hoping the sudden, astonished look on her face was one of gratitude.

"Aw, shucks."

He had expected something in the way of thanks, but that wasn't it. "What?"

"I'm stuck," she repeated, her eyes cutting to the far side of the counter. "Stuck!"

In a glance, Rik noted her white-knuckled grasp on the countertop and realized the tequila was responsible for her softly blended consonants and her distress. She was not only a novice, she probably had never had a drink of liquor before in her life. When the full effect of the tequila hit her, he could only imagine what else she might get *schtuck* to. Feeling more than a slight twinge of responsibility for her present condition, he reached across and pried her fingers loose. Drawing her hands into his, he helped her straighten. "There," he said. "Un-schtuck."

She looked at him, then at her hands, the counter and her hands again. "Thank you." She spoke carefully, with only an enchanting blush to reveal her embarrassment.

"You're welcome." He gave her an it-could-have-happened-to-anyone shrug. "So, are we trading rooms?"

The creases reappeared on Hallie's forehead as she formed her next words with distinct concentration. "I thought Mrs. Brewster wanted the wedding party on the same floor."

"She didn't want me," Rik declared. "She thinks I'm a bad influence on her prospective son-in-law."

"Are you?"

"I do my best."

Hallie's lips curved in a smile Rik found completely charming, if a bit slack.

Earlette hung up the phone and turned her attention to Hallie, and then by default to Rik. "Hello, Mr. Austin," she said warmly. "Is there anything I can do for you?"

"Hello, Earlette. Don't tell me you're having another day like yesterday?"

"Worse, I'm afraid. What can I do for you?"

Hallie's gaze swiveled from him to Earlette, but not before she took the precaution of planting her hands on the counter for balance. "That's not what you said to me."

Rik slipped his arm around her shoulders as backup support. "Earlette, Ms. Bernhardt and I are switching rooms. Can you arrange that for us?"

"But, Mr. Austin—"

"Give me his room." Hallie seconded Rik's solution with a nod that brought her hand up to steady her head. "He can have mine."

"It's all right," Rik assured Earlette. "I don't mind moving upstairs."

"As I've been trying to tell Ms. Bernhardt," Earlette explained, "the computer is down, and until it's up and running again, I can't make any changes."

Hallie looked at Rik. "*That's* what she said to me."

"Hmm," he said.

"Can't you change just one teeny-weeny room?" Hallie coaxed.

Earlette shook her head. "The best I can offer is to store your luggage."

"I don't have any ludge...lug-gage." A slur swam in Hallie's voice and she paused to correct it. "My clothes could be somewhere in Rio de Janeiro by now." She shook her head sadly. "I have to work and my clothes are off on their own little vacation. Now I ask you, what kind of justice is that?"

Rik gauged the situation and gave Earlette a persuasive smile. "Give me the key to room 1413," he said. "I'll take care of the swap." Drawing the key card to his own room from the pocket of his khaki shorts, he placed it on the counter in front of Hallie and took the key card Earlette held out to him. "You can do the paperwork and reprogram the keys when the computer comes back on. How does that sound?"

"Perfect." Hallie leaned down and took off her shoe, wobbling a little as she straightened. "It's terribly warm in here, don't you think?" Dropping her high-heeled sandal on the counter, she drew the back of her hand across her forehead and closed her eyes.

Rik's palm hovered near her elbow, anticipating the moment when she'd fall flat on her face. "Let's walk outside," he suggested. "There's a nice breeze."

"Nice breeze? Did you say *nice breeze?*" Hallie slapped the counter for emphasis, then slung her hand around to shake off the sting. "Well, let me tell you something. *I* listen to the weather reports and it's not a nice breeze, it's a hurricane. And a damn hot one, too!"

Earlette's dark eyes met his and Rik knew it was up to him to get Hallie upstairs and into his room before she passed out. Tucking his old room key into her hand, he guided her in a smooth turn away from the desk. "Let's have some coffee."

"Never touch the stuff." Hallie hobbled forward and Rik grabbed for her shoe...which was just out of his reach. "Caffeine ruins your sleep. Didn't you know that?"

"We'll get decaf," he promised, making another effort to hold on to her elbow and rescue her sandal.

She pulled away from his grasp and limped toward a cluster of chairs, seemingly unaware that she was wearing only one shoe. "That's even worse. Don't you pay any attention to the health reports on the news?"

"I've been out of touch for a few years." Rik tucked the lost sandal into his pocket and turned back in time to see Hallie kick her other shoe into the air. After a halfhearted swipe at catching it, she left the shoe where it landed and kept walking. She was going to have one hell of a hangover tomorrow, he thought as he swept the second shoe off the floor and into his other pocket before catching up with her again. "Where are you headed?" he asked.

"Somewhere cool." She fanned her flushed cheeks. "Aren't you hot?"

"No. You're just feeling the effect of the alcohol."

"I don't drink alcohol. It's these clothes I'm wearing. There're too many of them." She reached for the buttons at the bodice of her dress and Rik grabbed her hand.

"We're still in the lobby," he said. "Probably not the best place to undress."

"I'm only taking off my jacket." She shook off his hand. "That's not against the law here, is it?"

"Only if you're not wearing a jacket."

"I beg your pardon. I'm a professionable. I always wear a jacket." Her speech was uncertain and careful, in the manner of someone who realizes they're not feeling quite normal but thinks if they talk slowly enough, no one will notice.

"Okay, you're wearing a jacket," Rik said to appease her. "But you really shouldn't take it off in the lobby."

"Maybe I should and maybe I shouldn't." She stopped walking and faced him, her mouth sliding into an angled smile as she peeled off her glasses and let them dangle from her fingertips like a limp thread. "You aren't going to try to stop me, are you?"

"Wouldn't dream of it." He crossed his arms but kept ready in case she swayed off balance.

"Do you see this?" She held up the key card. "It's the key to Paradise. Now you see it—" she dropped it down the front of her dress and showed him her empty palm "—and now you don't."

At times, in the jungle, he'd fantasized about moments like this. A luxury hotel. Tropical breezes. A provocative woman, teasing him with her sexuality. Somehow, though, he'd never imagined it would take place in the lobby...and it had never once occurred to him that the woman would be skunked. "Let's go upstairs," he suggested. "I'll show you my room."

"You're pretty fresh for an old guy, Rik Austin Texas." She nodded, obviously pleased by her ability to remember his name. "Why don't you ask me to dance?"

"There's no music. I'd have to sing and you wouldn't like that." He reached for her arm, but she slipped aside.

"Uh-uh-uh. No touching allowed on the first dance."

She was losing inhibitions faster than he could count. Rik glanced at the few other people in or near the lobby, but no one seemed to be paying much attention. One of the benefits of being in a honeymoon hotel, he supposed. "Let's go upstairs, Hallie."

Her answer was a long, sensual stretch. Eyes closed, glasses swinging from her fingertips, arms swaying above her head like a supple young tree, she moved to the rhythm of a melody only she could hear. Rik watched her for a moment of purely virile enjoyment before he reluctantly stepped forward to stop the show.

"Hallie?" he said softly. "You should go upstairs and lie down."

Her answer was a right-left tilt of her head, a one-two swing of her hips and a resonating clap of her hands, which caught her glasses and crumpled them into uneven, ungangly thirds. Unconcerned, she threw them aside like a stripper tossing the first glove and belted out a remarkably tuneful, *"Blame it on the bossa nova!"*

Rik stroked his chin, debating his responsibility to remove her from the lobby and further embarrassment. True, he was thoroughly enjoying the slinky movement of her body, and on a strictly ethical note, he believed in the golden rule of allowing everyone the unchallenged opportunity to make a fool of themselves when they chose. He certainly didn't want to be rescued on those few occasions when he crossed the line between acceptable and obnoxious behavior.

Not that Hallie was obnoxious. On the contrary, he found her unleashed inhibitions a charming surprise. If anyone had asked him when she first came into the bar, he'd have said that Ms. Bernhardt didn't know how to relax, was afraid of anything she couldn't control and was scared to death of her own sexuality. But now... Well, Jack always told him he was too quick to make up his mind about people.

A bronzed young man, holding tightly to the hand of a bronzed young woman, stopped within earshot of Rik.

"Who's the boss of Nova?" she asked.

"Not who, what," her partner answered in a self-important, patient tone that all but flashed a neon sign proclaiming them to be newlyweds. "The Bossof Nova. It's a star named for Clyde Bossof. I read about it in *Science Digest*."

"Oh." She sounded impressed by his reading material. "And he's a songwriter, too? That's pretty cool."

Rik felt a flicker of anxiety about the future leaders of the good ol' U.S. of A., but he didn't have time to brood over it. Across the lobby, he saw the unmistakable swing of Babs Brewster's unmistakable pageboy and the equally unmistakable look of recognition on her Donna Reed face. Rik figured she had spotted him even before she stepped out of the elevator and wanted to remind him—once again—that the bachelor party on Friday night was not to turn into an orgy and that she expected him to deliver Jack, bright-eyed, bushy-tailed, tuxedoed and on time, to the ceremony on Saturday. It was too late to make a clean getaway. Hallie, blissfully unaware of everything except the song in her heart and the rhythm in her feet, bossa-novaed right in the path of the woman Rik intended one day to call Mom.

Hallie. One glance confirmed his gut feeling that she was in no condition to discuss the wedding. At the moment, he doubted she could remember who was getting married. But Babs had a long memory and she would not be forgiving of any embarrassment caused by the wedding coordinator she, personally, had hired. There was only one thing to do under the circumstances.

"Hey!" Hallie demanded as he wrapped his arms around her thighs and hoisted her over his shoulder like a worn-out, rolled-up carpet. "Didn't anyone ever teach you how to dance?"

"This is how we do it in the jungle," he said, and headed straight for the elevator, passing Babs in her impeccable beach attire and her husband, Danforth, in his yachting cap and sailor suit. Rik nodded cordially. "Hello, Mrs. Brewster. Mr. Brewster."

"Rik, there's an important matter I'd like to discuss with you."

Whirling smoothly, Rik kept his face toward Babs and Dan and walked backward to keep Hallie's face out of view. "I'm kind of occupied right now." Giving Hallie a playful swat on the butt, he winked at Babs. "You understand."

From the look on her artfully beautiful, perfectly made-up face, she appeared to understand all too well.

"Who do you think you are, you big gorilla?" Hallie demanded. "Tarzan, the monkey man?"

He managed, somehow, to keep her from wiggling off his shoulder, and kept smiling as he moved steadily backward toward those elevators. "She's crazy about me."

"So it seems." Babs took a few steps after him, clearly intent on getting a look at the woman slung over his shoulder. "Someone you met in the jungle, no doubt."

Rik jabbed the elevator button and maneuvered like a toreador to keep the two women from coming face-to-face. "She was raised by hyenas," he said. "She isn't accustomed to civilization yet."

"Hyenas, you say." Danny sounded intrigued. "What do you feed her?"

"Kahlúa pig. It's all she'll eat."

"Ha! For your information, I'm a strict vegetablearian. I don't eat pig—and especially not if it's been Kahlúaed." Hallie's flutter kick caught Rik in the ribs and he thought about saving himself a great deal of trouble and putting her on her feet so she could square off against Babs Brewster.

"There's something familiar about her voice." Babs

leaned to one side in an effort to see around him. "I'm sure I've heard it somewhere before."

The elevator chimed its arrival and Rik shuffled sideways as the doors slid open. "'National Geographic,'" he supplied. "It's the call of the wild."

"I hear a Kahlúa pig sandwich calling my name," Danny announced.

His inspired tone was given short shrift by Babs's aggrieved and perfectly audible response. "It frightens me to think Jack spent all those years in the jungle with that man."

Rik smiled weakly as the elevator doors closed. This little escapade was going to be a setback in the son-in-law and mother-in-law relationship he envisioned. On the other hand, if he didn't stop Stephanie's wedding, there wouldn't be a relationship at all. Better to protect the reputation of the wedding coordinator and prevent the marriage from taking place than to let Hallie take the fall and leave the wedding arrangements completely in Babs's controlling hands. Later, he'd worry about convincing the Brewsters he was an all-around nice guy.

"I thought hyenas lived in the desert." Hallie walked her hands up his back and pushed upright. Some perverse impulse kept his arms around her as she slid to the floor. Her skirt bunched about her waist and he felt the tantalizing rub of her legs against his, the sweetly curved shape of her pressed close to his chest. A warm, compelling awareness stroked his consciousness like Pachelbel's music, sharp and scintillating, and for a long moment, they stood like partners at the end of a dance, breathing hard, yet hardly breathing at all.

Hallie pulled away and his arms fell empty at his sides. She braced her hands on the rail that circled three sides of the elevator and eyed him with bleary suspicion. "You're acting very strangely."

He smiled. "Who, me?"

She nodded. "Yes, and you don't have to take me to my room. I'm quite capa—capapapab—" A frown crumpled the smooth skin of her forehead. "I can get there by myself."

"My things are still in the tenth-floor room. I'll need to pack."

"Oh." She pressed her fingertips against both temples as if she could clear her thoughts if she could only keep her head steady. "Thanks."

"For...?"

"Whatever." Her hand waved like a prima donna gathering roses at the close of a performance, and then, without so much as a sigh of warning, she fell forward.

Rik caught her, but just barely. If he'd been holding a bowl of soup, her face would be smack in the middle of it. So much for gratitude, he thought. He had a feeling that when she woke up, thanking him was going to be the last thing on her mind.

The elevator stopped on the tenth floor and Rik half carried, half dragged Hallie into the hallway. She was deadweight and he didn't think he could toss her over his shoulder again without risking permanent disk damage. He grappled with her skirt, batting at the material as he tried to get one arm under her knees while still supporting her weight. Finally, in a less-than-suave move, he hiked up her skirt, leaned her against the wall and held her there by benefit of hip and shoulder while he maneuvered himself in front of her. Then he draped her arms around his neck, looped his arms around her knees and hoisted her onto his back.

Feeling a little like Trigger trying to rescue a comatose Roy Rogers, Rik jostled his burden a bit higher on his back and took a step toward the faraway door of his hotel room. Hallie's arm slipped, her head lolled to the side, and her weight shifted, throwing off his center of gravity. Struggling to keep balanced, he half stumbled, half ran down the hall. He was past his door before he could get stopped. He paused long enough to catch his breath and readjust her position...and in the closeness of the hall, the quiet fragrance of gardenias sneaked up on him, unaware. Without meaning to, his nose followed the scent to the underside of her elbow and the creamy white skin, which, he suspected, could entice a man to bury his lips in its satin smoothness over any and all objections.

In the curve of his shoulder, Hallie's warm sigh tickled the back of his neck, setting off a fine network of unsettling responses he'd just as soon not recognize. His heart was set on winning the heart of Stephanie Brewster, had been since Jack had introduced them several months ago during her visit to their tour headquarters in the Amazon. If he'd had more time to spend with her then, Rik was confident she wouldn't be planning to marry Jack on Saturday. She didn't love Jack and he didn't love her and Rik knew he could have changed her mind for good about trophy husbands. But no matter. He'd already mapped out the future he wanted. Stephanie was the perfect woman for him, no doubt about it.

Reaching his door at last, Rik braced Hallie against the wall and lowered her to the floor. When she was sitting by the door, leaning like the Tower of Pisa against the narrow doorjamb, he straightened and shoved his hand into his pocket to retrieve his room key.

The card slipped into the slot and the red light flashed before he remembered that he had the key to Hallie's room on the fourteenth floor. She had dropped the key to his room down the front of her dress. He looked at her, limp as a rag doll at his feet, her honey brown hair only a shade darker than his sun gold skin. His gaze slipped to the rounded slope of her breasts and the hint of cleavage visible just below the demure neckline of her dress. With a guilty glance up and down the hall, he stooped in front of her and eased his hand beneath the row of buttons on her bodice. The things a regular guy had to do to be a hero, he thought. Sometimes it was hell, but once in a while, it wasn't too bad.

It was just a crying shame he was too much of a gentleman to tell Jack about this. Over their years together, first in the NFL and then in the Amazon, he and Keaton had swapped a lot of tales. Some true, some not. Their friendship had been forged from common goals and uncommon trust. Neither one of them ever felt the obligation to confess he lied through his teeth about sexual conquests. They'd both known that under the circumstances—jungle humidity, infrequent female companionship and a clientele too often composed of raunchy, adventure-seeking men—honesty was admirable but didn't do a thing for the male ego.

So, here he was, his hand moving cautiously between a very nice pair of breasts, and there wasn't a man anywhere on the island, least of all his best friend, who'd ever believe he was simply searching for a credit-card-size key. A key, he realized a moment later, that was not where he'd seen her put it.

Rik sat back on his heels and frowned at the disheveled state of Hallie's dress, the smudge of a shadow where her lashes touched her cheek, and the sweetly discontented pout on her lips. This was getting damn embarrassing, he thought, and pushed his hand further down the front of her dress. Where in the hell was that key?

At the far end of the hall, a door opened and a housekeeping cart trundled into view, pushed by a young woman who looked about twelve but was undoubtedly older. Her long brown ponytail swung freely as she pushed the cart down the carpeted hall toward Rik and Hallie. Guiltily, Rik jerked his hand back, trying to get free of Hallie's bosom, but a string of some kind snagged on his fingernail. He flicked at it with his thumb, aware of the approach of the housekeeping cart and the odd appearance he was certain he presented. Grabbing Hallie's elbow, he hauled her against him as if he were giving her a hug. She roused enough to flop her arm over his shoulder before her head fell forward onto his chest. The cart rolled to a stop a few feet away.

Hoping the housekeeper wouldn't notice that his hand was buried awkwardly between Hallie's breasts, Rik looked over his shoulder as the brown ponytail swayed toward a door on the other side of the hall. "We're locked out," he said conversationally. "Could you open the door for us?"

Ponytail turned, her brown eyes openly skeptical, her dubious smile revealing a gap between her front teeth. "Ten-twelve?" she asked.

He nodded, thinking if she'd just help him get Hallie inside, he'd tuck a fifty-dollar bill under that ponytail holder. "My, uh…she…" He patted Hallie's back as if the girl might not know who he meant. "She forgot where she put the key."

"Don't you have one?"

Valid question. "Can't get to it," he answered,

knowing exactly how lame that sounded. "To tell the truth, she's not feeling very well. Not enough sleep last night, you know, and I really hate to wake her."

The brown eyes gauged the situation and Rik hoped it didn't look as bad from her angle as it did from his. "I can't open a room for you, but I can call security," she said. "I'll warn you, though, we're very short-handed, and with the computers down, it might be faster to get another key at the desk." She picked up a stack of fluffy white towels and placed them below the Do Not Disturb sign hanging from the doorknob of the room across the hall. Then she took hold of the cart's handle and pushed past Hallie's outstretched legs. "Newlyweds," she muttered as she passed, her ponytail bobbing in a nothing-surprises-me-anymore message.

"So much for diplomacy." Rik waited until the cart turned at the far corner of the hall before easing Hallie into her Raggedy Ann slump against the doorjamb again. He glanced up and down the hall before making another attempt to disengage his snagged hand and locate the card key. She sighed in her sleep, and the arm still draped over his shoulder curled companionably around his neck. His fingers fumbled beneath the satin-soft fabric of her bra, and her low, throaty growl startled him. He drew back, but her eyes were still closed and her breathing slow and deep. Whatever her dreams, he thought, she seemed satisfied with them. He'd be satisfied, too, if only he could get his hands on that key and get out of this hallway.

Planting his body weight on his knees, Rik thrust his hand further down the opening of her dress until he reached the smooth, even surface of her stomach. Nothing there, obviously. But he should probably run his palm over her skin a couple more times, just to make sure. Conscience slapped him on the wrist the way his fifth-grade teacher had when she caught him with his dad's *Sports Illustrated* swimsuit edition.

Never mind the fact that he had a perfectly legitimate reason to have his hand down Hallie's dress. Never mind that if he didn't find the key, they were both going to end up in the hotel security office, trying to explain this public display of affection. Never mind, even, that she was sound asleep and would never know if he took advantage of this tempting opportunity to "cop a feel." He still felt guilty for having thought about it and he *hated* feeling guilty. It wasn't as if he were doing anything wrong, after all. He was trying to save Hallie's reputation. Get her into a room where she could sleep off the effects of the tequila and stay out of Babs Brewster's firing range. Sinking back on his heels, he began slowly to wiggle his hand in a renewed and ninety-eight-percent-impersonal search.

When the lock clicked on the door across the hall, Rik jumped a foot and twisted around—whacking his elbow against the door frame, sending a sharp pain from his funny bone into his shoulder and causing a jerk that ripped every button from the front of Hallie's bodice. He grasped the edges of her dress to preserve her dignity—and his own—but by the time he got situated and prepared to explain his predicament if necessary, the door behind him closed again. He glanced back to see the Do Not Disturb sign swinging back and forth on the doorknob. The stack of clean towels had disappeared, leaving in their place a round, room service tray on which sat a champagne bottle, three-quarters full, and four foil-wrapped chocolates, unopened.

A sudden pressure on his neck brought him back to the problem in his arms. Hallie was awake, the irises of her hazel eyes dilated, her lids drooping sleepily. "Hello there, handsome," she said in a husky whisper. "I'd like a kiss, please."

Rik blinked, his gaze drawn to the seductive curve of her lips. "A kiss?"

Her corroborating nod was damned certain and, under the circumstances, it seemed pointless to argue, so he bent his head and kissed her. Her soft "Oh!" might have been surprise or pleasure. He couldn't tell and was frankly too surprised himself to care. Her pouty lips translated into a delightful, wholly kissable mouth, and while he'd meant to leave her with a peck, he found it wasn't that simple to pull away. With her arms looped around his neck, and the entirely unexpected sweetness of her hesitant response, he thoroughly enjoyed the moment and was in no hurry to have it end. So it was something of a jolt when she shoved him back, rocking him off balance and sending him scooting on his butt to the middle of the hallway.

"What kind of thank-you is that?" he demanded.

"An I'll-thank-you-to-keep-your-lips-to-yourself," she said with a dusting of her hands.

"You asked for it."

She frowned at him. "I asked for a piece of candy and you took ad—advantage."

"You *asked* for a kiss."

"Yes." Her answer slid right in the direction she pointed—to the tray beneath the Do Not Disturb sign. "A candy kiss."

He couldn't believe she had looked into his eyes so seductively and asked for a piece of candy. "You wanted chocolate?"

"I'm hungry."

"You're hungry," he repeated, more irritated than he cared to admit. "And you want someone else's candy?"

She just looked at him, obviously confused about everything except those four foil-wrapped candy kisses. With a sigh, he pushed the tray across the carpet to her and watched as she meticulously, laboriously unwrapped each bit of chocolate and lined them up on her palm. "My tongue feels funny," she said. "I think I ate too many peanuts." She put two of the candies in her mouth at once and chewed them thoughtfully. "You didn't slip a mickey in my drink, did you?"

"I gave you exactly what you asked for."

"I asked for water."

"And that's what I gave you."

She frowned, and Rik could all but see the wheels of her brain trying to concoct a lucid memory. Leaning her head back against the doorjamb, she picked up the champagne bottle, swiped her palm across the open mouth of it and took a swig. She choked, coughed and coughed some more, until he moved closer and thumped her between the shoulder blades. "That isn't water," he said.

"I *know* that."

"Do you also know where the room key is?"

"What room key? My room key? I would think it's in my briefcase." She glanced around. "Where is my briefcase?"

"You left it in the bar, but I wouldn't go down there now if I were you. Besides, I happen to know your room key isn't there."

"Then where is it, if you're so smart?"

"You put it down your bra."

Sputtering a little, she wobbled her head from side to side. "I did no such a…such thing."

Far down the hall and around a corner, the elevator dinged, announcing its arrival on the tenth floor. "I don't see how you can think about your stomach at a time like this, Dan. There was something very familiar about that woman Rik had slung over his shoulder and I mean to find out who she is."

The voice belonged to Babs Brewster. Rik recognized it right off, even though he'd only just become acquainted with that clipped, regal style and unmistakably determined tone. Hell, he thought, the only thing between Hallie and certain disaster was the laundry cart and maybe two minutes. "We've got to get out of sight," he whispered urgently as he looked for a means of escape.

"I'm not moving until I feel better," Hallie stated as she ate the third candy kiss. Holding the champagne bottle at a distance, she squinted and read aloud, "Made from the finest grapes in the Napa Valley, this sparkling champagne is our finest—" With a gasp, she clutched the bottle to her chest. "This is champagne," she said, aghast. "I took a drink of champagne."

"Don't worry. I doubt your stomach will notice." In one dedicated movement, he was on his feet and bending to lift her into his arms, chocolate kiss, champagne bottle and all.

"What are you doing?" she asked as he scooped her up and headed for the red Exit sign at the end of the hallway.

"Trying to save you from disaster." He shouldered his way into the stairwell and started up the stairs.

"My hero," Hallie said on a sigh. "What kind of disaster is it? A dragon on the loose? A hurricane out of control?"

"Just plain old disaster, spelled *B-a-b-s*."

"Babs? Babs Brewster?"

"Ah, I see you remember her."

"What's she doing in here? I thought I was just having a bad dream."

That rankled, but Rik kept moving...past the eleventh-floor landing and the twelfth. His breathing was getting faster and harder to control, and Hallie wasn't even heavy. As a hero, he was sadly out of shape.

"Did we...did I...did you kiss me?" she asked uncertainly.

He paused to look at her. "You're confusing me with your appetite for chocolate candy kisses."

Her gaze stayed with his for a moment before she shook her head. "I never eat chocolate," she told him as she popped the last piece of candy into her mouth. "It's addictive."

"Really." He adjusted her weight in his arms and headed up the final flight of stairs to the fourteenth-floor landing. "I suppose you never drink champagne, either."

"Of course not." She held up the bottle and admired its sparkle. "I bathe in it," she said, before upending the bottle and dousing them both in champagne.

Chapter Three

The best Hallie could tell, she'd swallowed poison, she was dead, and this was hell.

Even if there hadn't been something covering her eyes, she didn't think she wanted to open them and confirm her suspicions...as if the awful taste in her mouth wasn't confirmation enough. A look around would mean moving her head, and she was absolutely certain that wouldn't be wise. There was an unholy pounding in her brain and she couldn't feel her feet or her hands. Wait, maybe that prickly tingling in her fingers meant they were still at the end of her hands. Lifting the little finger of her right hand, she rubbed it against something smooth and soft. That was good. Her tactile senses were still operative. She could smell, too. A rather delicate overall scent of flowers. Gardenias, she thought. Her favorite. And other exotic, beautiful fragrances...which pretty much ruled out the hell theory. There was the unmistakably perky scent of coffee, too.

Okay, so she wasn't dead. Moving very, *very* slowly, she trailed her hand toward her head, trying to use as few muscles as possible on the journey. Her fingertips brushed her thigh, hip, stomach, breast, neck—naked all, beneath a cover as smooth and soft as the one beneath her. The name wound its way through the pounding surf inside her brain. Sheets.

Hallie exhaled softly. She was in bed. The floral bouquet of scents must mean she was in bed in Hawaii, because her Boston apartment didn't smell like this. She struggled to identify the sounds around her, but the constant roar of the ocean defeated her efforts. Wait a minute. Ocean? She was supposed to have a room on the other side of the hotel. She'd called ahead specifically to make sure of that. But there it was. Waves crashing, beating the shore senseless. Had the hotel booked her into the wrong room?

In a collage of indiscriminate and oddly shaped images, she remembered...Kimo, bad hair, lost luggage, the Paradise Bar, peanuts, vitamins and tequila. Not necessarily in that order, and with no clue as to how she'd gotten her clothes off and herself into this bed. Lifting the corner of the pillow covering her eyes, she forced her eyelids up. Light burst through her skull as if from an interrogation lamp, and with a groan she slapped the pillow back into place.

"Good, you're awake."

There was nothing good about hearing voices that trumpeted, disembodied, out of a blinding light. Hallie struggled against the throbbing ache in her head, knowing there was something she should recall about that voice, something out of place about it. Keeping the pillow pinned across the upper half of her face with one arm, she licked her dry lips, gathered her meager resources and demanded in a raspy whisper, "If I'd known I was going to wake up like this, I would never have gone to sleep."

"Headache?"

"That's a major understatement."

"I could get a damp cloth to put on your forehead." The voice boomed closer, and a moment later, she felt a tug on the pillowcase.

"Touch this pillow and you're a dead man," she said in no uncertain whisper. "I don't see how a damp cloth is going to help. My head hurts inside, not out."

"Do you want some coffee?"

She shook her head beneath the pillow and winced. "Is that my only choice? A damp cloth or hot coffee?"

"I can see if there's a brain surgeon in the hotel, if that will make you feel better."

"I'm not sure dying would make me feel better." With a tremendous effort, she slid the pillow off her face and took a first, cautious, squinted peek at the morning. She was in bed…a huge four-poster iron bed with fancy scrollwork and draped with soft green gauze and artificial palm fronds. The room beyond was a soothing blend of green and beige. When she could bear to open her eyes, she was sure she'd see palm-frond patterns in the wall covering and in the upholstery of the lone chair pushed close to the open window. In a billow of palm-frond green, the gauze curtains blew in and out, like the puffy cheeks of a tuba player. The sound of surf surged in and out, in and out, making her stomach churn with its nauseating roll. She squeezed her eyes tightly shut, but the sound kept pouring into the room. Rolling out. Rolling in. Rolling…

"Where's the bathroom?" she asked, grappling with the covers and trying to get out of the bed in a hurry without moving any faster than she absolutely had to.

"There." He pointed the way. Not that Hallie actually looked. She just slid out of the soft, smooth sheets and followed her instincts to the bathroom.

RIK ADMIRED Hallie's naked backside until she vanished behind the definitive click of the bathroom door. As a way to start the day, sharing a room with a naked woman had its good points...and from what he'd seen so far, he had no complaints. On the other hand, he'd gotten very little sleep, crunched as he'd been in the chair. And for all his trouble, all his arguing with the hotel staff, all his persuasive techniques with Earlette, he'd accomplished nothing except to establish himself as a fixture in the life of Hallie Bernhardt, wedding coordinator for Stephanie Brewster's upcoming nuptials. Oh, yes, he'd been all too successful in accomplishing that. Wait until Hallie found out the two of them were sharing this thirteenth room on the thirteenth floor.

"Aaaaaack!"

Rik reached for his socks and shoes, figuring that no matter how the next few minutes evolved, he ought to be ready. The door opened and he glanced up to see Hallie wrapped in a bath towel, the ends tucked modestly—and very seductively—into place above her breasts, leaving her shoulders beautifully bare beneath the cautious, angry expression on her face.

"What are you doing in my room?" she asked crisply, despite the way she winced after each word. "And what is your stuff in my bathroom doing?" She frowned. "What's it doing here?"

Pulling his gaze from her shoulders, he allowed himself an appreciative glance at the length of shapely legs below the towel. The glance lingered, and he reminded himself that this particular pair of legs were high maintenance. Extremely high maintenance. He tied the laces of one athletic shoe and then the other before he settled back in the chair. "I believe you're under a slight misapprehension," he said. "This is *my* room and my stuff belongs here."

She processed that information with pursed lips. "Then why am I here?"

"You don't remember?"

With a shake of her head and the accompanying wince, she captured not only his sympathy but his interest. In that one act, she seemed both courageous and vulnerable and, for an instant, he wanted to take her in his arms and feel the weight of her head on his shoulder. Not that she'd allow that. Not that he'd actually consider initiating such a move.

"As it turns out," he said conversationally, "this is your room, too."

She stared at him while her fingers compulsively checked the tucked end of the towel. "You're going to have to talk slower. I thought you said—"

"This is our room," he volunteered. "Yours and mine. If you had any…stuff…it would have just as much claim to the bathroom counter as mine."

"The airline lost my luggage," she said.

"And the hotel gave you a room on the fourteenth floor."

"They wouldn't change it for me."

"You went into the bar…"

"I went into the bar."

"We started talking…"

"Bad haircut."

"Rough flight."

"Hurricane Bonnie."

"No one to tend bar."

Her eyes squinched shut in painful recollection. "Tequila sunrise."

"Tequila sunrise," he confirmed.

She shielded her eyes against the light and shifted from one foot to the other. "Is this a hangover?"

"That would be my guess."

"I don't drink, normally."

"Or eat chocolate."

She shuddered. "I ate chocolate, too?"

"Four little kisses, but you barely tasted the champagne before you poured it over your head."

"Champagne?"

He nodded, oddly pleased to be able to confirm her worst fears.

Sagging against the door frame, she contemplated her toes. "The last thing I remember is asking someone at the front desk to change rooms with me." She looked up, comprehending. "That was you."

"That was me."

"So how did we end up in the same room?"

"Computer glitch."

"I thought the computers were down."

"When they came up, I got moved into your room, but you never got moved into mine."

"So all I need to do is call the front desk and ask to be switched."

Rik shook his head, trying to ease her into reality a little at a time. "They gave the room to a trio of weather chasers."

"Someone gave away my room?"

"Technically, it was never your room. The minute I was checked out of it, the weather team was checked in."

"But don't you have a key?"

He fought a sensual rush of memory. "It disappeared somewhere between…"

"Between…?"

He chose the high road. "The lobby and the tenth floor."

"Tenth floor?" She paled, her fair skin turning a shade lighter. "Then we're…this is…? Please don't tell me we're on the—"

"Fourteenth floor. Thirteenth room. Ocean view."

Hallie's eyes closed as a groan escaped her clenched lips. "There has to be another room somewhere."

"If there is, the staff is keeping it under padlock and key. With the hurricane taking a path so close to the Islands, travel in and out is being discouraged."

"So, I'm stuck here with you?"

"And I'm *schtuck* here with you."

She eyed him suspiciously and he could almost hear her thoughts. "No, I'm not lying," he answered her unspoken accusation. "I don't like this arrangement any more than you do. And, no, we didn't sleep together."

"That thought certainly never occurred to me," she denied too quickly and too vehemenently.

He arched a dubious brow and doubt flickered momentarily in her eyes. "I may have a hangover," she said firmly, "but I know for a fact nothing happened in that bed last night except some really bad dreams." And with that, she closed the door.

THE MIRROR BATHED HER in good lighting. Most hotels had too few lightbulbs and too many harsh, yellow-tinted bulbs. Usually, putting on makeup was an exercise in frustration, leaving a face with foundation smudges, eye-shadow streaks and unevenly plucked eyebrows. Not this hotel. Oh, no, Hallie thought in disgust. This hotel had to have soft white light, perfect for seeing the red eyes, purple shadows and cracked lips of the morning after her first and only binge. She couldn't believe it. She never consumed alcohol, never imbibed champagne, never allowed herself a bite of unadulterated chocolate. And in one night, she'd apparently tried to make up for a lifetime of restraint. If, of course, Rik Austin could be believed.

She squinted at her reflected image. Why would Rik lie to her? He couldn't want to be stuck—*schtuck,* why did that slurred syllable sound so embarrassingly familiar?—in the same room with her. She looked like warmed-over death with a froo-froo haircut. Lifting the scattered layers of her hair, she wondered how she'd landed herself in this predicament...sharing her head with a killer headache, sharing her bathroom with a man's shaving cream and razor, sharing a one-bed hotel room with an attractive stranger. Whoops! Better strike that adjective. Not that he wasn't attractive. He had bedroom eyes that could probably seduce women across a crowded room, and under that overly bright Hawaiian shirt, she was certain he had strong, broad shoulders and a well-exercised and muscular chest. Exactly why she was certain seemed a touchy area, so she skirted past it and continued her original train of thought, which was that Rik Austin was attractive, but she had no business noticing such things.

She had to pull herself together, get down to work and show Babs Brewster and the hotel staff that she was a professional who didn't allow personal problems to interfere with her duties. At least, she would if she could just find something to wear.

She jerked open the door. "What did you do with my clothes?"

Rik turned from staring out the window to look at her. "I hung them outside to dry."

She blinked. "You did *what?*"

"Everything was soaked in champagne, so I hung them outside to dry."

"Don't they have a cleaning service in the hotel?"

He had the grace to look embarrassed. "I'm afraid that thought never occurred to me."

"Wait a minute." Despite the annoying drumbeat inside her head, she was beginning to regain her confidence. "Let me get this straight. You brought me to this room, stripped off my champagne-soaked clothes, and instead of sending them out to be cleaned or simply hanging them up in the bathroom, you hung them *outside* to dry?"

He shrugged. "I'm not accustomed to sending my clothes to a dry cleaner's."

"Are you accustomed to drying them outside?" She indicated the window with a nod. "In a brisk wind?"

"It wasn't that brisk last night."

Hallie was beginning to get a bad feeling about this. "Where are my clothes now?"

With a rueful frown, he pulled back the curtain and motioned her to join him at the window. "See that tree?"

From where she stood, she could see several trees, but even with her hand shading her eyes against the sunlight, her gaze settled on the one he pointed out. Maybe it was the peach-colored dress draped across the green-and-brown palm fronds that caught her eye. And then she noticed the dangling nylon foot of a pair of panty hose that dipped and danced from the balcony rail with every hefty breath of wind. But what ultimately drew her attention was the full-blown cups of her pricey, peach-hued brassiere, flying like a double-pointed flag from the tip of the closest palm branch.

The word that fell from her lips into the silence was

succinct, and successful in drawing Rik's attention. "I guess I owe you an apology," he said.

She couldn't wear an apology. "I'd settle for something to wear and a full bottle of aspirin. No. Never mind. No aspirin." With a frustrated sigh, she muttered her mantra of positive thinking under her breath. *Anything that keeps me from fulfilling my professional obligations is unacceptable. If I can't fix a problem, I'll look for another solution. If I can't find another solution, I'll discover a way around the problem. If I have nothing to wear, I'll make a muumuu out of the shower curtain. Anything that keeps me from fulfilling my professional obligations is unacceptable.*

Which was all well and good, if only her head would stop throbbing so she could think. If only she could figure out what had happened between her last lucid moment at the front desk and waking up in that bed. She hadn't slept with Rik, that much she knew, but she could have told him things she didn't want anyone else to know. No, of course she hadn't. Even at their worst, people didn't betray their true nature, didn't bypass their normal restraint. He knew no more about her than she did about him...except he'd seen her naked.

The ache in her head worsened at the idea and she promised herself she'd deal with that thought—and all its ramifications—later. As soon as she had something other than a bath towel to wear. Steadying herself with a hand on the partially opened door, she took a deep breath. "Could you go downstairs and get me something to wear? There must be a dress or gift shop in the hotel somewhere."

"There's at least one shop I know of. What do you want?"

"A suit."

"A swimsuit?"

She cringed. "You don't have to shout."

"I'm not," he denied, although he did have the courtesy to lower his voice. "You're just overly sensitive this morning."

"Thank you for pointing that out."

"No problem. So, do you want a two-piece or a bikini?"

"I want a suit," she repeated. "Skirt, blouse and jacket."

"Don't you want something a bit more…Hawaiian?"

"No. I want a suit. No frills, no ruffles and definitely no floral prints."

"I'm not sure the shops here carry that sort of thing."

"Of course they do."

He shrugged. "Okay, if you say so. Black, blue or pin-striped?"

"Black, preferably, but blue will do, if that's all they have." She frowned, then grimaced as the pounding in her head increased in direct proportion to the furrows in her brow. "What did you do with my shoes?"

Rik started across the room and Hallie grasped the edge of the door, taking an involuntary step back into the bathroom, in case he made a move toward her. He didn't. He simply walked across the room and returned with her impractical white sandals looped over his thumbs. "You kicked them off downstairs in the lobby and I carried them up here in my pocket."

"I *kicked* off my shoes?" she asked, positive he was making that up. "In the lobby?"

"You tried to take off your jacket, too."

Aha, she thought. "I wasn't wearing a jacket yesterday," she said, in a pale shadow of her usual *so-there* tone of voice.

He started to say something, then stopped and merely smiled...which made her all the more uneasy. "I'll be back."

"Where are you going?"

"Downstairs. To get you something to wear." He came closer and she wondered if he'd been this tall yesterday. He held out her shoes, and without having to release her protective hold on the towel, she caught the heel straps on her index finger.

"Thank you."

"You're welcome." His confident smile was too sexy for her comfort. "You know, I'd be better off if you gave me your measurements."

Well, of all the nerve. "If I were feeling more myself this morning, I'd pop you in the nose for that bit of impertinence."

He raised an eyebrow in amusement. "Aren't you a little short to be using big words like that?"

"As you've just demonstrated, height has nothing to do with being impertinent. You may have gotten me out of my clothes while I was unconscious, but you can forget any ideas you might have about scoring a touchdown this morning."

"A touchdown?" he repeated, stroking his thumb across his jaw.

"Don't pretend you don't know what we're discussing here."

"I'm going to take a wild stab at this and guess *you're* talking about sex."

"For your information, I don't discuss intimate topics with strangers and I definitely never give out my measurements!"

"There seems to be a lot of things you don't do, Ms.

Bernhardt. And getting clothes that fit is about to become one of them.''

He hadn't been asking for her bust, waist and hip measurements, she realized, only for the jacket, blouse and skirt sizes she normally wore. The blush stole over her like an unexpected spring shower. ''You wanted to know what size suit to get,'' she whispered self-consciously. ''I misunderstood.''

''Forget it.'' He shrugged off her meager apology. ''Just call the dress shop and let them know you're sending a man to do a woman's job. That way, you can give them your measurements in the strictest confidence and my nose won't get popped for asking impertinent questions about what size undergarments you wear.''

''I would have thought you'd have checked that out when you had the chance,'' she said.

He smiled, revealing a slight cleft in one lean cheek. ''A gentleman would never do such a thing, Ms. Bernhardt, and if he did, he certainly wouldn't admit to it.''

As he walked to the door, Hallie watched, somewhat bemused at the thought of sharing a hotel room with a man who seemed so confident, so assured, so nicely put together. And he had quite a nice butt, too. What was wrong with her? As if she didn't have enough to think about already. The last thing she needed was to share a room with anyone, least of all a man. The moment, the very moment he was gone, she would pick up the phone, call the front desk and raise as much hell as her headache allowed. Then she'd call the airline and find out when she could expect her errant luggage to arrive. After that...well, maybe her first call would be to the dress shop. No point in taking chances with her best shot at getting something to wear.

Rik cleared his throat and Hallie realized he was

waiting for her to look up. With his hand on the doorknob, he regarded her with a raised eyebrow. "Just for
the record, I think you should know you were never
unconscious last night. Asleep, yes, but not unconscious."

Before she could process that information, there was
a brisk *rap-a-tap-tap* on the door and the knock echoed
like a Chinese gong inside her head. Rik frowned over
his shoulder at her and she shrugged her ignorance as
to who might be visiting at this hour. With a glance at
the bedside alarm clock, she realized the hour wasn't
so unreasonable. It was only her brain that was lagging
behind. The knocking came again, pounding so loudly
she thought her head would split. "Whoever it is," she
said, "I'm not here."

"It could be for me, you know."

"One can only hope." With that, she closed the bathroom door and leaned her head against it. This was a
bad dream. It had to be. She couldn't be nursing a hangover. There hadn't been more than an ounce or two of
liquor in that drink she'd had. But it hadn't been only
one drink, she recalled with grudging clarity and a
heartfelt groan. A groan that strangled in her throat as
she heard the ringing, articulate vowels of Babs Brewster's unmistakable voice.

"Rik? What are you doing in Ms. Bernhardt's
room?"

"Whose room?"

"Hallie Bernhardt. I booked it for her myself."

"Oh. Her. We traded rooms."

Hallie knew she was in trouble, and all she could do
was stay out of sight and listen to the conversation taking place in the next room.

"Why ever for?" Babs asked. "This is one of the

best rooms in the hotel. Certainly, it's costing me a fortune. The hotel believes the view is worth— What is *that?*"

"A window?" Rik's voice suggested.

"Don't be obtuse. What is that pink thing hanging on the tree branch?"

Hallie squeezed her eyes shut, praying for some small miracle to occur and block Babs's view. A total eclipse of the sun would be good.

"It looks like women's underwear," Rik answered, his voice dipping as if he were moving across the room, then gaining strength as he came closer to the bathroom door. "Probably one of those New Age artists experimenting with palm tree art."

Babs's skeptical "Humph" was as resonant as a doorbell. "Is Jack here with you?"

"No, he isn't. But you know, now that you mention him, that does look like his underwear out there."

"You, Mr. Austin, have been in the jungle too long. And that goes double for the dancer you had slung over your shoulder in the lobby last night."

Hallie laid her forehead against the door. Rik and a *dancer?* And he'd had the gall to insinuate that he'd spent the entire evening with her, Hallie.

"Appearances are sometimes deceptive, Mrs. Brewster. I was merely attempting a rescue."

"Yes," Mrs. B. answered, her voice going one decibel below sarcasm. "Of course you were. When you see Jack, please tell him I have a message for him from Stephanie."

"Stephanie?" Rik's tone softened like a scoop of vanilla ice cream on top of hot apple pie. "When is she going to arrive at the hotel?"

"Not a moment too soon for my peace of mind. The

weather forecasts are none too good, and I've told her to catch the next flight from Honolulu.''

"Good.'' He sounded excessively pleased at that bit of information, Hallie thought. "I mean, you're absolutely right,'' Rik continued. "We don't want anything to interfere with Saturday's wedding, do we?''

"Even the weather wouldn't dare,'' Babs said with absolute conviction. "Now, what room did you say Ms. Bernhardt is in?''

"I didn't say.''

"But you traded rooms with her. You surely know the room number.''

"I have an atrocious memory. Jungle fever, you know.''

"Indeed. I suppose I'll find her one way or another. Goodbye, Rik.''

"Goodbye, Mrs. Brewster. Say hello to Mr. Brewster for me.''

The door hadn't even clicked shut behind Babs when Hallie cracked open the bathroom door. "I have to get out of this room. Thirteen is bad lu—''

"I almost forgot, Rik…'' Babs pushed into the room again and Hallie slammed the bathroom door and leaned against it, breathing hard.

"I was just on my way out,'' she heard Rik say. "Why don't you ride down on the elevator with me? We haven't had much chance to get acquainted and I'd really like to hear your plans for the wedding. Jack doesn't seem to know what he's in for and I thought I might be able to—'' His words were clipped off by the sturdy click of the lock as it snapped shut behind him.

Hallie leaned over the sink, turned on the faucet and splashed her face with cool water. When she raised her head and faced the mirror, she grimaced at the sight in front of her. And to think when she'd gotten out of bed yesterday, she'd actually believed the worst thing about this trip was going to be her haircut.

Chapter Four

"What do you mean the dress shop wasn't open?" Hallie asked as she watched Rik dump three sacks, a box and two plastic-wrapped bundles onto the bed.

"I mean, the door was locked, the place was dark, and there was a sign that said Closed. Was someone there when you called?"

"I couldn't even reach the hotel operator. Just a recorded message saying all the lines were currently busy and I should try my call again later." She pursed her lips. "Why would a retail store be closed on a workday in the middle of the week?"

"Couldn't tell you. According to Earlette, the proprietor is a retired accountant from the mainland who doesn't depend on the shop for her income, so she works pretty much when and if she wants to."

"That's a ridiculous way to run a business. She should hire someone to be there when she isn't."

Rik stopped unwrapping one of the bundles and looked up. "I'll bet she never thought of that," he said dryly.

"I just can't believe it was closed."

His eyes seemed bluer somehow than she remembered. Or maybe the cold shower she'd taken had

cleared away some of the fog from her head and she
could actually see better. Or maybe her lingering hangover just made her farsightedness more sensitive than
normal. Either way, he had very expressive eyes. And
right now, they were expressing a slight impatience.

"The dress shop was *closed,* so I got what I could
from the gift shop." He unwrapped the plastic from the
bundles and laid out several articles for her inspection.
"Toiletries," he said, touching each in turn. "Your
choice of straight or angled toothbrush, soft or medium
bristles. Dental floss, mouthwash, eyedrops, hairbrush,
comb, magnifying mirror, bath gels in four fragrances—
I couldn't decide which you'd prefer, so I bought all of
them. Twin-edged razors, moisturizing soap, an assort-
ment of deodorants, colognes—not much to choose
from in that line, I'm afraid. Hairspray, safety pins,
straight pins and—" he tossed the last item in the air
and caught it with a triumphant sweep of his hand
"—the supereconomy pack of extra-strength, nonacidic
pain reliever."

Hallie approached the bed with a mixture of astonishment, appreciation and awe. "Did you buy out the
entire gift shop?"

"Only the clothing section." He reached for one of
the sacks and upended it next to the displayed toiletries.
"Unfortunately, there wasn't a suit to be found in black,
navy or pinstripe, so I hope you like bright colors." He
whisked away the sack, leaving a cluster of brilliant-
hued spandex behind.

Hesitantly touching the swimwear, she sorted out two
modest bikinis, one a sea green floral, one a solid neon
pink, four maillots in various shades of blue, one in all-
American red, white and navy with matching cover-up,
and the last a vastly immodest, gold mesh with high-

cut legs, low-cut neckline and more material cut out than left in. Hallie let the swimsuits dribble from her fingers into a resplendent heap on the bed before she raised her gaze to Rik's. "What am I supposed to do with these?"

"Wear them," he suggested, a trifle offhandedly for true nonchalance. "In place of your, uh, intimate apparel."

She looked at the mound of swimsuits again. "In case you haven't noticed, these are a little obvious for intimacy. No one would need X-ray vision to see my underwear, now would they?"

"That would depend on what else you were wearing." He reached for another sack and a brilliant mix of tropical colors streamed from inside. "Feast your eyes on these Hawaiian muumuus." He pulled out one after another after another. "Guaranteed to disguise a variety of personal problems, including an abundance of bright underwear or, in some cases, a lack of underwear altogether."

"This is it?" she asked, panic rising like a bread dough seasoned with too much yeast. "I'm here on business, you know. Not a vacation. I can't wear muumuus. They're completely unprofessional and so... colorful. In my line of work, I'm supposed to blend into the background, not stand out like a tiger lily surrounded by orchids."

"Everyone will understand, Hallie. It isn't your fault the airline lost your luggage."

"And it isn't my fault that what little I had left is gone with the wind, either, but I don't want to have to explain that to Babs Brewster. It won't matter to her whose fault it is."

"She isn't totally unreasonable."

"How long have *you* known her?" Hallie sank onto the edge of the mattress and fingered one of the muumuus while making a supreme effort to quell complete hysteria. "She expects perfection. All the Brewsters do, in one way or another, it seems. This wedding has to be flawless down to the last grain of birdseed. Babs and Danny Brewster wield a great deal of influence in Boston society circles and I could gain or lose a lot of future business depending on the outcome of this one wedding." She picked up one of the muumuus and shook it out to full volume. "Forget I said that. This wedding will be perfect. All my weddings are. Do you think there's any other way to get into the boutique?"

"Other than waiting until it's open?" He frowned at her. "You're not thinking about knocking over the dress shop, are you?"

She supposed it was pointless to discuss this with a man who thought a bikini was an adequate substitute for lingerie. "I'm thinking about getting something decent to wear." With a frustrated glance at the paraphernalia scattered over the bed, she tossed the muumuu on top of the heap and set her hands on her hips. "Didn't you bring anything else?"

"As a matter of fact…" There was a flash of irritation in his blue eyes as he picked up the last sack and handed it across the bed. "Try this on for size. I think it could be just the style you need to make a lasting impression."

She took the sack, opened it and pulled out a grass skirt and a bra made of coconut shells. "This room isn't big enough for me and your sense of humor," she said. "So, thanks very much, but you can take your things and leave anytime now."

He came around the bed so fast she didn't even have

time to back away. For a moment, he stood perfectly still, towering over her in attitude as well as intimidating height. Hallie's heart began a fast, arrhythmic beat and she wondered vaguely what she'd done with her glasses. Not that she really wanted a more focused look at him just now. Even fuzzy, he was altogether too attractive and she was altogether too alone with him. Alone, nearly naked and entirely too mouthy for her own best interests.

It was this room, she thought, searching for a scapegoat. The thirteenth room on the thirteenth floor. What in hell had she been thinking? Asking *him* to leave? She ought to beat a path to the door...except she couldn't move. Not beneath the blurred force of his penetrating and angry gaze.

"Look, you," he said, and for a second, Hallie thought he was going to thump her chest with an accusing fingertip. He didn't, though, and she realized she half wished he would so she'd have an excuse to thump his chest in return. "I don't know who you think you are," he continued. "I've done my best to help from the minute you walked into the bar yesterday. I didn't have to. I didn't really even want to. But you looked as if you didn't have a friend in the world, and I've always been a sucker for the underdog.

"However, now I'm stuck with you, so we'd better get a few things straight. This is my room, and if anybody's leaving, it's going to be you. I have my own agenda for this wedding, my own future to worry about, and frankly, I don't give a damn if you want to strut naked through the lobby to satisfy your suspicious little mind that the dress shop is indeed closed. You can wear the clothing I spent both time and money getting for you or you can climb out on that tree limb and make a stab at getting your own clothes back. I'm washing my hands of your troubles, here and now. Since the room mix-up wasn't entirely your fault, I'm willing to negotiate on sharing, but that's as far as I'll go. You're welcome to find another room, get yourself more suitable clothes and irritate the devil out of some other poor male, but I'm out of it. Understand?"

Well, Hallie thought, taken aback. How long had he had to practice that speech? "I understand, all right. Now that you've backed me into the proverbial corner, you're trying to blame me for the whole situation. Well, it isn't your underwear swinging from the branch of that palm tree." She pointed in the direction of the window. "It isn't your luggage that's lost. It isn't your future on the line. It isn't your neck Babs Brewster is breathing down. And it certainly isn't you who's going to have to coordinate a very important wedding while wearing spandex and a floral tent!"

His lips tightened into an irritated smile. "You're right. My luggage is here." He indicated a duffel bag by the closet. "My future is planned to perfection. I can handle a dozen Babs Brewsters. And, best of all, I look really cute in my Speedo and Hawaiian shirt. So why am I worrying about you?"

The knock at the door was brisk and businesslike. "Room service."

Hallie smelled the distracting, delicious aroma of freshly prepared food. And her attitude made a U-turn. "You ordered breakfast?" she asked hopefully. "For me?"

With a scowl that seemed more self-directed than not, Rik strode across the room and opened the door. By the time the tray had been placed on the table and the waiter tipped and gone, the scent of bacon had filled the room with an enticing aroma and Hallie conceded she wasn't up to a standoff. At least, not until after she'd satisfied the empty rumbling in her stomach. "Truce?" she suggested. "I apologize for fussing at you. I apologize for the fussing I'll probably do after I've eaten. But for now, could I please, please, have a cup of coffee?"

"You said you never touch caffeine. You said it ruins your sleep."

"I don't and it does...which is exactly the reason I'm touching it this morning. Coffee is the only thing standing between me and crawling back into that bed, burying my head under the covers and sleeping until I can go home." She took a step toward the table, glancing back at him. "You don't mind, do you?"

He shrugged. "Be my guest."

The irony wasn't lost on her, it was just wasted. She couldn't remember the last time she'd been so hungry. Ravenous, really. Her headache clamored for a distraction. Her nerves were on edge from the cropped and shaggy ends of her hair to the tips of her toes. She felt truly awful, but her sense of smell sat up and took notice as she poured the coffee and her mood perked up at the sight of soft-boiled eggs, toast, jellies, marmalade, bagels, cream cheese in three flavors, bacon, ham and half a dozen fluffy, golden brown biscuits. She would have agreed to wear the grass skirt and coconut shells for the duration of her stay in Hawaii if Rik had demanded she do so as compensation for what she was about to eat.

Luckily for her, he didn't demand anything at all, not even her attention. She was halfway through her second bagel before it occurred to her that she was still wrapped in the towel. Rik probably thought she had no inhibitions whatsoever. Not that he seemed to notice what she was—or, more accurately, wasn't—wearing. She should have been the one to notice. How could she be so comfortable with a complete stranger that she had sat across from him, bare-shouldered, with nothing more than a tuck between her and total humiliation, and she hadn't even realized it until just now. Obviously, food had been her highest priority.

With a surreptitious glance at Rik, his stoic focus on breakfast, she started to slide out of the chair, bagel in hand, intent on casually scooping a muumuu from the stack on the bed and slipping into the bathroom to change. It was possible, she thought, that he'd never even notice she was gone.

Possible, but not likely. Not when she tripped on the chair leg and stumbled across the room like one of the Flying Wallendas. She corrected her balance, kept her towel on and peeled the cream cheese side of the bagel off her chin before she risked a look at Rik, who watched her with interest while munching on a bacon strip. He didn't have to look so complacent, she thought. Or so amused.

"Don't get up," she snapped as she wiped cream-cheese residue off her lips. "I'm fine. No damage done. No need to worry."

"I wasn't worried." He dolloped orange marmalade onto yet another biscuit and smiled—attractively—at her. "Roomie."

She did not like the tone of that, but she couldn't exactly say why. Maybe it was just that the body count of her embarrassments kept rising. Or maybe it was the idea that he knew things she couldn't remember. She wanted to ask a few discreet questions about last night. She wanted to know how she'd gotten to this room…and into that bed. And she'd sort of like to know the circumstances leading up to the removal of her clothes. After that, she was pretty sure she didn't want any details.

"I'm going to change clothes," she announced, as if it were an earthshaking decision and he shouldn't even consider trying to stop her. "Do you, by any chance, know what happened to my glasses?"

"Top drawer of the chest." He used the biscuit as a pointer. "They suffered a major blow last night, but I straightened them out for you."

Apprehension wedged its way past her headache. She had one pair of glasses until her luggage arrived, and if he'd broken them... Hallie jerked open the dresser drawer and lifted out the pewter frames. The lenses were still intact, which was good, but the frames...well, they weren't so good. "How am I supposed to wear these?"

One—just one—of Rik's eyebrows lifted, giving him an are-you-talking-to-*me?* expression. "On your nose?"

"Don't get cute. You broke my glasses and now you expect—"

"Hold on there, Quicksilver." He set the remainder of the biscuit on his plate and rested his hands, palm down, on the table. "*I* had nothing to do with breaking your spectacles. You did that yourself during a particularly rowdy segment of your dance routine. I, being the nice guy I am, retrieved the broken pieces and meticulously taped them back together. Now, I understand that hangovers don't make good bedfellows, but I'll be damned if you're going to ruin my breakfast with unfounded indictments."

Hallie stared at him, her belligerence fading, her apprehension growing as rapidly as the magic bean stalk. "*Dance?*" she whispered. "*I'm* the dancer? The one

Babs accused you of slinging over your shoulder last night?"

"It wasn't an accusation." His nod was reluctant, his shrug apologetic. "More like a statement of fact."

She sagged onto the edge of the mattress, processing the information, the implications and... When she looked up, he met her eyes, and for no good reason she felt there might still be hope, after all. "But Babs didn't recognize me?"

"To be honest, you weren't facing her. You might want to avoid bending over when she's around, though. She got a really good look at your, uh, derriere."

Hallie closed her eyes. "I mooned Babs Brewster," she said dismally, and then her eyelids flew up with another horrifying thought. "Please tell me I was still wearing clothes at the time."

"Your butt was covered. The clothes didn't come off until later."

"How much later?"

"Not until we were alone in our room."

That sounded terribly intimate and Hallie decided she did not want to go there, did not want to know the details, did *not* want to ask if he'd shared any part of the bed with her during any part of the night. Of course, nothing had happened. She knew that.

Well, something obviously *had* happened. It was the *what* she didn't want to know. She met Rik's gaze again, uncomfortably aware this time that she was in his debt. "Thank you," she said.

"For...?"

"Rescuing me from a potentially disastrous evening."

"I only saved you from getting fired and catching a cold, both of which probably would have happened if I hadn't, one, gotten you out of the lobby when I did, and, two, gotten you out of your soaked clothes before you took a chill.''

"Well, I'm grateful, although I can't believe it was necessary to remove every stitch of clothing I had on.''

He popped the last bite of the biscuit into his mouth and chewed with a very male kind of smile. ''You know, you could be right. For some reason, that possibility just never crossed my mind.''

Hallie jumped up. So he'd enjoyed seeing her naked, had he? Enjoyed taking advantage of her defenseless state. Enjoyed taking off her clothes and staring at her body and maybe touching her breasts and maybe putting his lips... The images flipping through her overly sensitive brain bathed her in a tingling heat. From her toes to her sticky chin, she felt hot and restless and embarrassed. Well, she'd teach him a lesson. She'd get dressed. He wasn't going to have the opportunity to enjoy himself at her expense any longer.

Setting her crimped and patched glasses on the dresser, she tossed the crumpled, cheesy bagel into the trash, dusted her hands on her terry-cloth-covered hips and scooped as much as she could hold from the bed into her arms. The hairbrush fell and clonked her on the toe, but she didn't wince or slow down. "I'll just change in the bathroom," she said, not caring if he cared one way or the other.

Just then someone knocked at the door and Rik looked up. "Would you mind?" he asked. "It's probably the waiter returning to pick up the tray."

Since she was practically in front of the door anyway, it seemed petty to refuse, so she juggled the shifting lump of toiletries, box, bags and muumuus in her arms, grasped the doorknob and pulled open the door. "We're not quite finished," she said as she opened the door. "We'll just set the tray outside when we're—"

Except it wasn't the room service waiter, she realized too late. It was Danforth Brewster.

RIK HAD NEVER LEFT a table so fast. He was on his feet, across the room and slamming the door on Dan's astonished face before the coffee cup he'd hastily set on its saucer stopped rattling. "Be with you in a minute," he called through the door to Dan as he tried to figure out what to do with Hallie. And how he was ever going to convince his future in-laws that he was actually a man of very high morals. He looked down into her startled eyes and knew she didn't want to be found with him any more than he wanted to get caught with her. "Quick," he whispered. "The bathroom."

She nodded and dashed inside, scattering toiletries in her wake. Rik quickly retrieved what she dropped and tossed them into the bathroom after her. The moment she closed the door, he brushed back his hair, inhaled sharply and opened the door.

"Mr. Brewster," he said, edging his body into the opening between the door of the hotel room and the hallway, where Dan Brewster shifted from one long foot to the other. Stephanie's father was tall, lean and perpetually in motion, and Rik had a pretty good idea that this visit was not his idea. "How nice to see you. All set for Saturday's wedding?"

"I am. I am." Dan's gaze slid past Rik's face in an effort to see past him and into the room. "Who answered the door?"

Rik grinned. "I didn't hear the door ask a question."

"Now, there's an oldie but a goodie," Dan said as he craned his neck a little farther to the left. "What are you doing in there, Rik? Auditioning some local bathing beauties for the bachelor party?''

"You know better than to ask the best man a question like that, sir. You're the father of the bride.''

"Which means I ought to be in on the selection process.''

"I can't believe Mrs. Brewster would be happy about that.''

"Well, of course she wouldn't.'' Dan stepped forward, and Rik had to either slam the door in his face a second time or step back. He stepped back…against his better judgment. "But she's not going to know about it, is she?''

"Wives have a way of finding out these things. It might be best if you just admitted you didn't see anything at all.''

"I saw someone in a towel… Oh, I see.'' Dan nodded, apparently coming to a belated understanding. "I didn't *see* anyone. I only *imagined* I did.'' With a broad, conspiratorial wink, he continued to look for the someone who was merely a figment of his imagination. "I do that all the time…think I see someone or something when I don't. I'm outnumbered by women, you know. What with Babs and my two daughters. But you know Stephanie, of course. Like mother, like daughter, I say. Daughters, I suppose I should say. Like mother, like daughters. The other one's already married, though. You probably know about that. Mrs. DeHaven. That's our Bentley.''

Danforth Brewster wasn't the world's greatest conversationalist, but under the circumstances, Rik was having a little trouble keeping his mind on the subject, too. "Well, it was thoughtful of you to drop by.'' He began to close the door. "I'll see you at the rehearsal dinner Friday night."

"Yes, yes, of course you will." He smiled, nodded and turned away. But Rik's sigh of relief was short-lived as Dan turned immediately back. "Now, Rik, you can't expect to get rid of me that easily. As it happens, Babs sent me here to discuss a highly-confidential matter with you. And since I didn't really see a beautiful exotic dancer wearing only a towel, I think it's perfectly all right for you to invite me in."

"But this isn't a good—"

"It's important," Dan interrupted. "Otherwise, I wouldn't have come so soon after breakfast." His long face creased with a smile as he glanced into the room, his gaze settling on the room service tray. "You're still eating. Well, I'll be damned. There's enough for two. Now, that's what I call planning. I mean timing, good timing. To tell the truth, I wouldn't mind having a little bite of that ham to tide me over until lunch."

"There's not much left," Rik began, but his objection was overridden by Dan's good-humored laugh as the older man strong-armed the door open and barrelled across the room to take Hallie's vacated seat at the table.

"Now, there's plenty here for the two of us. I'll just have a couple of bites of that ham. Sit down, Rik. Finish your breakfast. I don't want to interrupt your meal." Dan picked up a muffin. "Or whatever else you were doing."

A tall order, considering the proximity of bathing suits and female folderol still strung out on the bed, the intimate apparel still waving from the balcony and the fact that he was harboring a hungover Hallie while entertaining his future father-in-law. All of which supported, rather than contradicted, Dan's notion of what was going on in this hotel room this morning.

Not exactly the situation a prospective son-in-law wanted to get caught in. But there was nothing he could do to prevent Dan's "little bite of ham" from turning into a feast. And there was even less he could do to keep from shuffling crumbs nervously from one side of his own plate to the other. What in the hell was he doing? Sitting at a table with Stephanie's father while a woman he barely knew lounged in a bath towel in the bathroom behind him. Why was he protecting Hallie to his own detriment? And how was he going to get Dan Brewster to leave?

"What did you want to discuss?" he asked finally, in growing desperation.

Dan put down his fork and picked up the last biscuit. "You didn't want this, did you?" He was spooning marmalade before Rik could concede that he wouldn't dream of taking the last biscuit. "Yes," Dan said with a crisp, clean Boston accent despite the mouthful of Southern-style biscuit he was chewing. "Babs sent me to ask you about Jack."

"Ask me what?"

"I'll get to that in a minute. Babs is the most insistent woman, you know, and to my shame, I can never find the heart to say no to her."

Rik didn't think the *heart* was the organ that couldn't contemplate facing Babs's displeasure. "Maybe you should try it sometime," he suggested. "See what happens."

"Hmm." Dan settled back in his chair and rubbed a belly that looked too flat to hold the amount of food he'd just consumed. "I don't see much point in it. Babs and I have been married a long time. No need to throw

my weight around and risk rocking the boat at this stage
of the game...if you know what I mean."

Rik didn't know exactly what one thing had to do
with the other, but he was more concerned about the
gusts of wind whipping the palm fronds into a rhythmic
wave. He watched as the wind loosed Hallie's panty
hose from their knotted hold on the railing and plastered
them against the patio door—crotch first.

"Babs is a hell of a woman, you know," Dan continued, oblivious for the moment to the scenic view on
his right. "Oh, she's a bit stubborn at times, I'll admit,
but all in all, a hell of a woman."

"I'll take your word for it, sir."

"No need, no need. You'll discover it soon enough
for yourself. Like mother, like daughter, I always say."
Dan frowned slightly, seemingly confused. "Well, no,
I suppose you won't be making that discovery, will
you? I was daydreaming again, thinking I was talking
to Jack. But, of course, Jack knows Babs already. He
and Stephanie are getting married, you know."

"Yes," Rik agreed. "So I understand."

"Well, that's the reason I'm here. To discuss Friday
night's bachelor party. Babs wants your personal guarantee that nothing will go on at the party that shouldn't
go on, if you know what I mean." Dan leaned back in
the chair. "Basically, Babs wants your assurance that
no big-busted broad jumps out of a cake during the
party."

"That idea never even crossed my mind." Rik stood,
hoping to encourage his uninvited guest to do the same.
"I understand perfectly, and you can assure Mrs. Brewster that nothing is going to happen at Jack's bachelor
party that she wouldn't approve of wholeheartedly."

"Sit down, sit down." Dan waved him back into the

chair. "For a man who's lived his whole life in the jungle, you're a jumpy kind of fellow."

"Thirteen years," Rik corrected. "And it pays to be on edge...in or out of the jungle."

"I guess you never know when something might drop from a tree branch and..." Dan's words drifted away as his gaze drifted to the window. Hallie's clothes had been rearranged on the palm tree and the balcony door. Dan took a considerable amount of time to visually examine the evidence before he looked back at Rik with a pleased smile. "Looks like Sheena of the Jungle is somewhere in the neighborhood," he said. "Auditioning, is she?"

"I wouldn't think she'd do that, no." Rik wished he'd had the foresight to close the drapes. "I don't even know her."

"Sure, sure, I understand." Dan winked, smiled and stood, his pencil-thin legs unfolding like a carpenter's ruler. "Your memory's as bad as my eyesight."

Rik didn't know how he was ever going to explain away this conversation once he and Stephanie were married. Providing, of course, that he could prevent Stephanie from marrying Jack in the first place and convince her that *he* was, in fact, the best man. "Thanks for dropping by," he said. "You and Mrs. Brewster have nothing to worry about. I'll make sure Jack's bachelor party is in the best of taste."

"I like the sound of that." Dan strolled toward the door. "Just have one question. What 'flavor' of cake are we going to get a taste of? Blonde, brunette or redhead?" He laughed at his own joke and Rik tried hard to join in, although he sounded more like Foghorn Leghorn, strangling on a grain of humor.

"The cake isn't my department," Rik said. "That's the hotel chef's department."

"Right, right. Well, I'll reassure Babs that you are a man after my own heart in regard to proper etiquette and all. She'll be happy to hear it." He nudged Rik with a conspiratorial elbow. "Put my name down on Sheena's dance card. Don't forget!"

Oh, hell, Rik thought as he followed Dan to the door. "Thanks for stopping by. I'm sure we'll see each other again during the next couple of days."

"No doubt about it, considering we're practically neighbors. Babs and I are in the suite next door." Dan glanced at the bed. "Looks like you've been shopping."

"Gifts for my nieces and nephews," Rik replied without missing a beat.

"You must have dozens of them."

"Dozens." One, actually. Sam, who wasn't even a year old yet and whose daddy would never let him wear a muumuu, no matter what the color.

Dan held up one of the adult-size bathing suits. "Must be darn near grown."

"They're big kids," Rik added hastily.

"Hmm. I guess you know what size they are."

"Oh, I do. I do."

Dan grinned. "Watch out now. 'I do' is Jack's line."

Not if Rik could do anything about it. "You can return to Mrs. Brewster and reassure her that Jack's future is in capable hands. I'll take good care of him."

"Never doubted it for a minute. Thanks for the snack. I'd better get back before the little woman comes looking for me."

"I thought she sent you."

Dan smiled, pleased. "So she did." He stopped at

the door and glanced again at the clothes on the bed, then at the panty hose pressed against the glass. "Some days I'd give anything to be thirty again."

"Take my word for it, sir. Some days it doesn't pay to get out of bed, no matter what age you are."

Rik locked the door behind Brewster, then knocked on the bathroom door. "Coast is clear. You can come out now."

Hallie opened the door and stepped out, dressed in the only piece of clothing he hadn't intended for her. The pareu hugged her body in a slim, exotic line. Its colors were just as brilliant as the swimsuits and muu-muus, but he couldn't imagine that they would look even half so spectacular when worn. He couldn't imagine Stephanie in the pareu, either. Even though he'd bought it with her in mind. He shouldn't have bought it at all. It had been an impulse. Nothing more. A gift for Stephanie. But the impulse had now given way to something else, something to do with Hallie. What was the old saw? If you can't be with the one you love, then love the one you're with?

Now where had that come from? He wasn't fickle. Hadn't he known the minute he laid eyes on Stephanie that she was the perfect woman for him? And hadn't he known just as surely that Hallie was trouble? But staring at her now, her sandy brown hair feathered around her face in flattering disarray, her eyes shimmering with what was probably half a bottle of Red-out, her hands displaying her self-consciousness in an uncertain brushing against the poppy red flowers in the fabric of the pareu, he had a feeling his world was shifting.

"Is it really that bad?" she asked. "I mean, it's the only thing that looked sort of…well, you know…"

He did know. To his own surprise. "You look—"

Beautiful? She did, but he couldn't say so. They were sharing the room, for Pete's sake, and he didn't want her to get the idea he wanted to share anything else. "You look—" *Sexy?* He certainly wasn't going to say that aloud. He cleared his throat of an annoying huskiness. "You look—okay. Of course, I've seen you naked."

She slammed the bathroom door, leaving him wondering what had gotten into him, why he'd said something so ungentlemanly and how he was going to manage to apologize without admitting some other most ungentlemanly desires. He glanced at the demolished breakfast he'd ordered with the thought in mind that they'd sit and talk and he'd ask questions about Saturday's wedding and make mental notes about ways to sabotage the whole project. It would have worked, too, if Danforth Brewster hadn't popped in with a thinly veiled excuse and an appetite he didn't bother to hide. Babs wanted to know whose clothes were outside the window. She wanted to know who Rik had slung over his shoulder last night and carried out of the lobby.

Keeping Hallie's identity under wraps and her reputation as pristine and pure as driven snow was turning out to be a challenge. But he wasn't going to let Babs discover any excuse to fire Hallie. She was his one solid link to the information he needed to sabotage Saturday's wedding, and come hell or hurricane, Rik was going to stop Stephanie from marrying Jack, even if he had to blackmail Hallie into helping him do it. He wasn't going to let himself get distracted. No matter how great she looked dressed. No matter how much concentration it took to forget how great she looked undressed, too.

He had a mission.
He had a moral obligation.
He had to persuade ''Sheena'' to come out of the bathroom....

Chapter Five

Hallie bolstered her courage with the thought that she had something to wear and she looked damn good in it—no matter what Rik thought. *Okay*, he'd said in that annoying, pseudoreassuring tone. *You look okay*. As if she had chicken pox or measles or some other rash and that was his polite way of saying she looked like hell, but she'd get over it eventually. He could have said she looked presentable. Or pale. Or positively awful.

But *okay?* That was apathy, pure and simple.

It had been a long night. She was having a difficult awakening this morning. There was a roaring inside her brain that resembled the sound of a half-dozen Mack trucks playing dueling engines. The least Rik could have done was offer her a compliment. No matter how insincere. She needed confidence, words like *professional*, *pretty*, even *passable*, would have gone a long way toward mollifying her insecurities. She needed self-confidence, not apathy. She needed to know that he'd looked at her naked body and felt something akin to attraction. Even if it was only because she was the nearest female. Even if it was merely a fleeting thought.

Checking her appearance one more time in the bathroom mirror, Hallie frowned. Six years. Seventy-two

months since Brad had turned his back and walked out
on her, ending their short-lived marriage and taking
every ounce of her self-esteem with him. Six years, and
she was still looking for male approval. Seventy-two
months of rebuilding her self-confidence, and still when
a man saw her naked she reverted to that needy twenty-
two-year-old she'd been on her wedding day.

Well, to hell with men and their opinions. No matter
what she was wearing, she was still *the* Bernhardt of
Bernhardt Bridal of Boston. With a final glance in the
mirror, she wrinkled her nose and said, "So there."

Turning, she jerked open the door and announced,
"Rule number one. Whatever happened last night *didn't*
happen. Rule number two. No matter what condition
I'm in, you are not to remove any article of my clothing.
Rule number three. I don't know what rule number
three is, but when I think of something, you'll be the
first to know."

Rik greeted her announcement with impassive silence, and when she peeked around the bathroom door
into the room, she realized the reason. He was gone.
Which was just as well. She only wished he could have
left the room service tray and a little more breakfast. If
hangovers made her hungry—and apparently they did—
she had one more reason never to repeat last night's
fiasco.

Outside the window, the wind thrashed the palm trees
like a mad teamster whipping his mules. Her dress had
blown away long ago, but her bra still flew, high and
haughty, over the terrace. She recognized yesterday's
panty hose, plastered like a nylon suntan to the win-
dowpane. Hallie couldn't decide what bothered her
more...the undignified sprawl of the panty hose on the
glass or the realization that the wind was strong enough

to hold the nearly weightless nylons in place. Probably had something to do with G forces and wind velocity or some other equally inexplicable weather science, she decided. Nothing for her to worry about. Just a passing glance from a hurricane that was far, far out to sea. It would be long gone before Saturday's wedding. Barely even a memory by then.

Now the only thing standing between her and a completely professional demeanor was the knowledge that her underwear was billowing like the Jolly Roger over the Paradise Bay Honeymoon Hotel. So all she had to do was step out onto the little balcony, peel the panty hose off the window, and grab hold of that silly brassiere....

THERE WAS NO SIGN of Hallie when Rik entered room 1413. He set the peace offerings—orange juice in a plastic cup, V8 vegetable juice in a single-serving can, a bag of pretzels and something called VitaBar, the nutritious equivalent of a balanced meal!—on the table next to the ravaged remains of breakfast. The vending machine at the end of the hall was a far cry from the room service meal he and Dan had demolished, but at least Hallie could have a selection from each of the four basic food groups.

A low, keening wail turned his gaze to the window and he promptly forgot sensible eating habits. What in the hell was she doing out there, he wondered as he approached the long plate-glass windows and Hallie, who was stuck to the glass like a two-toned, poppy red and pale pink pressed flower. With her back to the room, her arms extended, her palms flattened snaillike against the window, she looked uncomfortably in need of rescue.

The wind blasted him in the face the moment he slid open the glass door, and the salty, humid smell of sea spray stung his lips and nostrils, clinging to him like sand to wet skin. Wherever Hurricane Bonnie was at the moment, she was too damn close to shore. "Hello," he yelled over the rush of wind and the roar of agitated ocean. "Enjoying a breath of fresh air, are we?"

Hallie's hazel eyes rolled sideways in the briefest of glances, but otherwise she didn't move a muscle. "I...came...out...to...get...my...clothes." Her voice reached him despite the wind. "I...can't...move."

"Sure you can," he yelled. "The wind is rough, but it isn't that bad."

"Not...the...wind." She cut her eyes in his direction again. "Look."

He followed her gaze to the flailing palm fronds of the nearest trees. Beyond the palms, there was an expanse of gray and grumpy sky and an even grayer and grumpier ocean. She was scared, he realized. Scared because she was standing on a thin layer of concrete and steel overlooking a pretty impressive display of Mother Nature in a very bad mood. He somehow didn't think Hallie would feel one iota less uncomfortable, though, if the sky was as clear as a bell and the Pacific as calm as a slice of bologna. "Take my hand," he said, inching nearer. "I won't let you fall."

"I'm...not...moving."

"Okay. We'll just stand here and enjoy the view. It's magnificent, isn't it?"

"This is no...time...for jokes."

"You don't find this view exhilarating?"

"Please. Don't mention...the view."

The tight line around her lips got even whiter and he was torn between feeling sorry for her discomfort and irrationally annoyed by it. "What possessed you to come out here if you're so afraid of heights?"

"I didn't like...my panty hose to be displayed...like some grotesque...piece of artwork." She took a deep, shaky breath. "And I'm not afraid of...heights. The view is...just...intimidating, that's all."

"Then let's go inside."

"I can't."

"Mind over matter, Hallie." He reached her hand and peeled it off the glass. "Come with me."

She shook her head.

"Are you planning to spend the rest of your life out here?" He tugged impatiently on her hand. "Come on."

"Not until my...underwear...is off...that palm branch."

Rik narrowed his gaze on her, wondering if he could possibly have heard her correctly. "What did you say?"

She turned her head, keeping it steady by pressing back against the window. "I said," she repeated, "I'm not going inside until I get *that*—" she briefly raised and lowered her index finger to point at the bra "—unhooked."

"Let me get this straight. You're intimidated to the point of paralysis by this particular view of the ocean. But you won't go inside until you've rescued your underwear?"

"I don't consider it a rescue." She turned her head in his direction again. "It's a matter of principle."

"The principle of insanity?"

"Look, go inside if you want. I'm going to make a grab for it."

Rik looked from her to the dangling strap of the peach-colored bra. "You can't reach it," he said. "Not even if you stood on the balcony rail and held on with your toes. Not a wise course of action on a windless day, much less in a hurricane.''

"I could reach it if I had a *really* long coat hanger," she said. "Would you get some for me from the closet?"

"No. Because you're not going to risk your life for a scrap of polyester, principle or not. If you don't like the thought of wearing swimsuits under your clothes, I'll borrow something for you from Earlette or Stephanie's sister, Bentley. Or *my* sister, for that matter. But you're not going out on a limb to get that bra. The wind is going to rip it off of there eventually, anyway, and you won't have to look at it after that."

Her gaze turned from him to the lingerie on the tree branch and she pursed her lips. "The wind ripping it off is what bothers me. It's bad enough knowing it's dangling outside my hotel room. The thought of it dropping in on someone else's balcony is more than I can stand. So I'm going to get it down...one way or another."

Rik frowned at her underwear. He frowned at her. And then he did the only thing he could under the circumstances. He hauled her into his arms and let the wind tumble them backward onto the hotel-room floor.

He hit the floor and rolled, pulling Hallie with him and landing, with some degree of intention, on top of her. Bracing his weight on his arms, he looked down into her wide eyes and grinned. "That was fun. Want to do it again?"

"There was no call to act like a caveman." Hallie blinked rapidly, trying to bring his face into focus. "I wasn't going to leap off the balcony, you know."

"No, you were going to fall off." Rik discovered a

scar on the smooth, creamy-colored slope of her cheek, just below her right eye. A tiny mark, barely noticeable except for the lighter shade of her skin there. He touched it, exploring. "What happened?"

"What do you mean what happened?" She moved her head away from his fingertip. "You went for the gold medal in the team tumbling event."

"No, how did you get this scar?"

Her hand moved to her cheek and she brushed the mark with her knuckle. A shadow darkened her hazel eyes. "Oh, that. I don't remember."

He didn't know why she lied about it, or how he knew for certain that she had, but the little scar bothered her still. And for no good reason, it bothered him, too. "You couldn't have reached the bra," he said reasonably. "I rescued you from certain disaster for the second time."

The shadow vanished and he allowed himself to relax and enjoy the soft, feminine feel of her body under his. If he wasn't a one-woman kind of guy and if his mind wasn't already set on Stephanie, he might entertain some very lustful thoughts right about now.

"Don't look at me like that," she said.

"Like what?"

"Like that. Like you expect me to dedicate the rest of my natural life to you in gratitude for being rescued."

"I don't expect anything of the sort, although gratitude is seriously underexpressed in this country, in my opinion. Besides, you're only guessing at my expression."

"Why would I do that?"

"Because you're not wearing your glasses and you can't see up close without them."

"Maybe I'm wearing contacts."

"You don't own a pair of contacts because the saline solution they're washed in irritates your eyes and, even if you did own a pair, they'd be tucked in a zippered bag inside the plastic compartment of your luggage—which is still lost—because you wouldn't want to take a chance of having the solution spill on anything else in your suitcase."

"How did you know that?"

"Lucky guess." He realized with a twinge of surprise that he liked Hallie Bernhardt. Liked the way her forehead crinkled, and the way she widened her eyes to keep from squinting at him and the way her nose turned up just a little at the tip. He liked the idea that she had gone out on that balcony for a stupid reason, because otherwise he wouldn't be lying on top of her enjoying the hell out of her predicament.

She struggled to push herself upright, but since he didn't move, she only succeeded in stirring a little mutual attraction, which he could read clearly in her expression and in the way she closed her eyes for a minute, then opened them and lifted her brows in a meaningful arch. "Do you mind?" she asked.

"Heck, no. I've always liked women who wear glasses. There's something inherently sexy about short-sighted females."

"That's farsighted," she said testily. "Not short-sighted."

His smile curved lazily. "My mistake."

"I wasn't asking your opinion on women with glasses. I want you to move, please."

"Sure. I'll even help you up, but you'll have to promise to do something for me in return."

"You're pushing your luck, Rik. I didn't ask to be

rescued. I didn't need to be rescued. And I'm sure as hell not going to be tricked into doing something stupid like promising to kiss you in return for getting a hand up off the floor.''

He curtailed his smile and frowned down at her, noting the belligerent line taken by her lips and the quirk of rebellion that reared its mischievous head in the back of his mind and practically demanded he kiss her now. "I was going to suggest you promise to let me get your bra down from the tree before I let you up, but now that you mention it, a kiss would be a lot less dangerous and a whole lot more desirable.''

The response showed immediately in her eyes... awareness, attraction, apprehension and a sort of appalled excitement. "I'd rather you unhooked my bra, thank you.''

His smile was slow and good-humored. "Last night you said you wanted a kiss, and then you said you didn't. Now you want me to forgo a kiss and put my hands on your underwear, instead. I'd almost forgotten what fickle creatures women are.''

"You're the one who's making up all these options. I only want to get off the floor and out from under you.''

"A noble gesture, but really, I'm quite comfortable as I am.''

She tilted her head and stretched her neck, trying, he knew, to get a more focused look at him. "How long *have* you been away from civilization? And how soon are you going back?''

"The Amazon is a jungle, but it isn't entirely uncivilized. And I'm not going back. I'm staying in Hawaii. I'm starting a tour business here.''

"In that case, you'd better get yourself a book on

how to impress women, because your technique is severely out of date.''

The curtain puffed across his shoulder as the wind blew a fine, hot mist of humidity into the room. Playtime was over, Rik thought with disappointment. He couldn't keep teasing her like this indefinitely. But the next time Hallie offered, he just might take her up on it. If only to prove that kissing was never stupid and that she wasn't quite as immune to his nearness as she'd like for him to believe. She angled her brows an unbelievably impatient degree higher, arching them in a saucy little dare while she waited for him to make a move. Hell, he wished she hadn't done that.

"I don't think much of self-help books," he told her. "Not when hands-on training is available."

He saw the flicker of panic in her eyes, even though he wasn't sure if it was apprehension or comprehension or a simple matter of unfocused vision. But it pleased him to know she realized her mistake and his intention at approximately the same second. Then he was close enough to smell the tropical fragrance that clung to her skin, close enough to feel the moist, warm rush of her breath, close enough to acknowledge that kissing Hallie might possibly hold some small danger for him, as well. Then he covered her lips in a quick and forceful kiss.

At least he intended for it to be quick and forceful, but she tasted of island wind and ocean spray, and her shoulders were bare and soft to the touch of his hand, and her lips parted, ever so invitingly, under his. A pleasantly sensual blend of responses kindled inside his body and he let them have their way, turning the forceful into purposeful and the quick...

Well, one out of two wasn't bad, and there was no way, once the kiss had begun, he could let it end. Not right away. In fact, he could think of any number of reasons this particular kiss should continue indefinitely. The main one being that he hadn't imagined he could enjoy kissing Hallie this much.

Now that he thought about it, though, that was the very best reason he had to back off. Which he did, surprising himself by the strength of willpower it took to leave the warm, parted softness of her lips. Her eyelids remained closed for a moment, her lashes forming a straight, pudgy shadow against her skin. When they drifted upward and her eyes opened, he felt a funny stirring somewhere around his heart, a feeling all too close to desire and decidedly uncomfortable.

He met her gaze with a purposely casual smile and the unbidden hope that her dazed look was a result of his kiss and not just her lack of corrective lenses.

"I guess I should have held out for the book," he said.

"*And* the video." She moved beneath him and he pushed to his feet, leaning down to offer her a hand up.

An offer she ignored as she got her feet under her and stood. "If my brain wasn't so woolly from last night's tequila sunrise, you'd still be on the floor, in pain, and reaching the conclusion that rescues are no longer in your job description." She dusted her hands— of him, he suspected—and moved to close the sliding glass door. The curtains settled with a final puff, and the humidity in the room rose in a stuffy and stale silence. Hands on her hips, she stared out the window at the peach-colored bra, and Rik admired her shoulders and the long, slender drape of the pareu.

Maybe he had been in the jungle too long, because Hallie was looking damn good to him. Kissing her had been better than his first taste of full-bodied red wine, and just the memory of her eyebrows doing that flirty thing sent a streak of rebellious desire through his veins. She was definitely not the woman for him. Stephanie was. Stephanie, with her cool blond sophistication, her sleek, contemplative moods, her quiet, I-know-what-I-want-and-how-to-get-it finesse. She was just the partner for him. He'd thought it through carefully those last months in the Amazon, making an equitable assessment of all the reasons she was wrong for Jack and coming to the inevitable conclusion that, since he and Jack were different in fundamental ways, she was absolutely the right woman for him. Having reached that astounding and factually supported theory, he wasn't going to get sidetracked by a passing attraction to his roommate. Even if the inclination to try that kiss one more time was operating full strength on his willpower.

The ringing of the phone saved him and he picked up the receiver with measurable relief. "Austin," he said out of habit.

"Rik?" It was Babs Brewster, her voice cultured despite the high-pitched edge of her surprise.

He stiffened. "Mrs. Brewster. How nice to hear from you again so soon."

"What are you doing in Ms. Bernhardt's room?"

"This is my room," he answered, grateful for the ability to think on his feet. "What number did you dial?"

"Oh." She clipped the single syllable as if she were cutting off the tip of a cigar. "For operator. Then I asked for Hallie Bernhardt's room and you answered."

"Well, you have the wrong number."

Hallie turned, her forehead creasing with a frown.

Rik shrugged off any concern she might be feeling and listened as Babs informed him, "I do not have the wrong number. How can I have the wrong number? I asked for Hallie Bernhardt. The operator connected me with this room and you answered."

"Probably just a computer glitch," he said, putting a soothing smile into his voice. "This is the first time I've been able to use my phone all morning. Wires must be crossed somewhere in the hotel."

"You're positive this isn't Hallie's room?"

"Now that you mention it, this was her room originally. Maybe the hotel operator doesn't realize we switched rooms." He lifted his shoulder in a don't-know-what-else-I-can-say shrug, and Hallie's eyebrows started to rise in that questioning arch he found sexy and sweet and completely unnerving. "Why don't you try the call again, Mrs. Brewster? I can't imagine that same misconnection would happen twice."

"This is very strange," Babs said, and hung up.

Rik dropped the receiver in the cradle and it rang almost immediately. "It's for you."

Hallie looked at him as the phone rang a second time. "What if it isn't?" she asked. "What if she's calling you, instead? Checking to see if you answer?"

"Why would she do that? She's been in this room once already. She sent Dan to take a look around five minutes after she left. She's trying to call you. Trust me."

An uneasy feeling followed Hallie to the bedside table. "Hello?" she said hesitantly into the phone receiver.

At the other end of the connection, a man cleared his throat. "Either I've got the wrong room or my best man is having a better day than I am. Is Rik there?"

Hooking her finger through the coiled cord, she let the receiver dangle. "It's for you."

"She called me?" Rik barely voiced the words as he stepped over to take the phone and Hallie stepped back, swinging the receiver toward him so their fingers couldn't brush in passing. She didn't want him to touch her, even accidentally, and especially not in passing. She didn't know why he'd had to be so...so *male* this morning. Picking her up, carrying her inside, tumbling her to the floor, kissing her....

A shaky sigh escaped her. She wasn't going to think about that kiss. Or the weight of him pressing down on her. Or the feel of his long, hard body nestled on top of her, pushing her into the soft, but unforgiving, nap of the carpet. Rik wasn't her type. He wasn't even close.

Okay, so he was close enough. It had been a long time since she'd let a man touch her, kiss her, look at her the way Rik just had. And she'd liked the way he did it. And she wished he was still doing it. But this was not the time to start something she couldn't finish. She glanced at him as he stood, holding the phone, looking so virile, so vital, so very male. Admittedly, she felt the yin and yang pull of sexual attraction. But this definitely was not the time. And Rik definitely was not the man.

"I can't believe she'd turn right around and call my room just to satisfy her suspicions," he said almost under his breath. Then he lifted his gaze, caught her staring, and his lips curved in a rueful smile. "What am I saying? Of course I can believe it. How such a compulsive, obsessive mother as Babs Brewster raised a woman as serenely beautiful as Stephanie—"

Putting the receiver to his ear, Rik raised his voice to an audible level and prepared for yet another Brewster onslaught. "This is Austin."

"No, it isn't," Jack stated with good humor. "My

pal Austin wouldn't have a woman in his hotel room first thing in the morning without inviting his best friend up to say hello."

"There's a Do Not Disturb sign on my door, Jack. And it means you."

Jack's chuckle was steady and familiar. "Right. And if you think I'm going to believe there's a perfectly logical...and utterly platonic...reason for a female, whose voice *is* suspiciously husky, to be answering the phone in your room, you're not the defensive lineman I used to push all over the football field during practice. Fess up, Austin, you overtipped the maid so she'd screen your calls for you and try to make people think you're some kind of lothario."

"Voice mail would be simpler," Rik said. "And far more efficient at screening nuisance calls like this one. What do you want, anyway?"

Jack whistled. "A little companionship. A little male bonding. A little distraction to keep me from going crazy before Saturday. Want to take the copter up for a spin?"

"Sure," Rik agreed, knowing neither one of them was crazy enough to fly a kite in this wind, much less the helicopter. "I'll meet you downstairs as soon as the wind velocity hits a hundred miles an hour. No sense in wasting our time on that little bit of breeze out there now. Can't be more than forty, forty-five miles an hour. No challenge in that."

Jack's laughter sounded bored. "You're right. I'm getting overly anxious to risk my neck, as usual. Who's the girl?"

"What girl?"

"The one who answered the phone, smart aleck."

"If I told you, you'd want to meet her. If I don't tell

you, you'll still want to meet her. So, here's the deal, buddy. I'm not going to tell you and you're not going to meet her. There. I've simplified your life for you once again.''

"I share the embarrassing details of my life with you, Rik. It wouldn't hurt you to open up, explore your feelings, tell your best friend who she is and where you found her."

"Not a chance. I know you, Keaton, and exploring feelings isn't your forte."

"You're just jealous because I'm getting married and will no longer have to pretend to be sensitive and open to my feelings in order to get dates. Married men are expected to be insensitive and closed off, you know."

"No, only trophy husbands can get away with that. Married men have to learn to be honest with themselves.''

A stilted pause echoed across the phone line, then Jack eased the tension with a chuckle and a change of topic. "You're never going to believe what flew past my window about an hour ago. A dress. And then, maybe twenty minutes later, I swear I saw a pair of panty hose go by. Someone at this hotel is having a very good time...and it isn't me. Speaking of not having a good time, Dan just dropped by to tell me you're auditioning 'ex-*ah*-tic dancers,' as he phrased it, for Friday night's entertainment. I think I should have some say in the selection, considering it *is* my party. Why should you have all the fun? I'll just come on down to your room and make sure there's real 'ah' in exotic.''

"No." His reply sounded indisputable even to Rik himself. "And don't get your hopes up. I've promised Babs that there will be nothing about your bachelor party she could possibly disapprove of.''

"Oh, gee, now I'm really looking forward to Friday night. Don't let me down, Rik. It's my last night of freedom. I mean to make it memorable."

Rik wanted to offer Jack some heartfelt advice. He wanted to make him see what a mistake he was about to make. He wanted to save Jack from ruining the futures of three people, including his own. "Don't worry," he said instead. "I'll make sure your bachelor party is the most memorable night of your life to date. Have I ever let you down?"

"No, so that must mean you are auditioning and I'll be right there."

"Don't bother, because I won't let you in. I'm keeping Friday's entertainment under wraps. No one gets a glimpse before ten o'clock Friday night."

"Except you."

Rik rubbed the back of his neck, weary of fencing with Jack, weary of trying to figure out a way to stop this ridiculous wedding from happening. "Except me." His gaze connected with Hallie's and some unrecognizable sensation pulled tight across his chest. She was watching him—at a distance that ought to have him squarely in the twenty-twenty range—and there was something intense about her. The sarong had shifted during their roll on the floor and she'd smoothed it back into place. Except the places it had settled were different than before. Looser across her breasts. Tighter around her hips. Seductive all over. The tightness in his chest moved lower.

Since that last kiss, he was looking at her with new awareness. And she was looking back. And...it wasn't going to happen. No way. Not even if she kept staring at him as if she was starving and he was dessert. She sighed. He couldn't hear her, of course, because Jack was talking...and talking. But he could see the rise of her breasts as she breathed in and then the slow movement of the exhale as the sigh escaped. Something was going on here that he couldn't quite put a name to. She was thinking something. Something about him. Something she obviously wished she wasn't thinking. And he, suddenly, didn't want her to stop thinking about him at all. No matter what the context.

"I got you some juice," he said impulsively, gesturing at the peace offerings he'd left on the table, forgetting totally that Jack was on the other end of the phone receiver still pressed against his ear. "You didn't get to finish your breakfast."

"Ah, Rik, that was so sweet of you," Jack said after a moment's pause. "Orange juice and a chorus line. I'll be right down."

Down. Rik jerked to attention. "Okay," he said. "Sure. Come on down. You know the way."

"I do." Jack chuckled, this time without much humor. "I do. I do. See, I'm practicing for the big day. Don't say it. I know what you're thinking and we're not going to discuss it again. I'm marrying Stephanie on Saturday and that's that." He hung up and Rik slowly replaced the receiver, his eyes on Hallie as she peeled back the silver cover on the orange juice. Jack didn't know what the hell he was talking about. He didn't know that his approaching nuptials hadn't even been in the running for first place in Rik's thoughts, and he also didn't know Rik had switched rooms with Hallie and was just down the hall, not three floors down. Rik hoped whoever was occupying room 1012 was friendly.

"You invited him here?" Hallie asked, her pensive expression replaced with one of annoyance. "To meet me?"

"I invited him downstairs...to the tenth floor. There is a difference."

"It won't take him long to figure out his mistake."

"But it will take considerably longer to figure out exactly where I am."

She set the plastic cup back on the table. "Why didn't you just go down to his room? Or meet him in the lobby? You and I are only sharing a room and only by mistake. It's not as if you have to watch over me like I'm a baby and in need of constant attention. I promise I'm not going to make another rescue attempt this morning."

He glanced at the bra flag outside and the perfect idea clicked into place. A baby. By God, *that's* what he needed. A baby. With a grin, he grabbed Hallie by the shoulders and pressed a fleeting kiss to her crinkled forehead. "I'll be back," he said, pushing her to arm's length. "Don't answer the door or the phone. Take a nap or something. Give your hangover a little TLC."

She cocked her head to the side and narrowed a suspicious gaze on him. "What is wrong with you?"

"Nothing," he said as he headed for the door. "Nothing at all."

Chapter Six

The door closed behind him and Rik was gone. Where, Hallie didn't know, couldn't imagine, wasn't entirely certain she cared. Except now that she was alone, she didn't want to be.

Her headache wrapped around her brain like a flannel blanket, muffling her usually crisp, clean morning thoughts. Her stomach growled and she alternately eyed the cup of orange juice and the can of V8 juice and reminded herself that she didn't handle acidic foods well. The pretzels were fat free, but the sodium content was very high, which might be okay if she had a gallon of water to drink with them. There was only tap water, though, and with everything else that had gone wrong on this trip, she hated to take chances with her drinking water.

Too bad she hadn't been more particular about what she poured down her throat last night. Tequila probably wasn't filtered for purity. But then, neither were the random glimpses of last night that ricocheted at odd intervals through her memory, bebopped across her mind's eye and gave her a chill of embarrassing recognition. Not that any singular memory was stand-alone awful, but the whole bundle together was enough to submarine her self-confidence. She *couldn't* have been dancing in the lobby last night. She'd remember doing something so…so out of character.

But already this morning, Babs had mentioned a dancer as if she knew what she was talking about. Dan had mentioned a dancer as if he knew what he was talking about. And Rik had said…

I've seen you naked.

Humph. She'd like to know exactly how he'd managed to justify taking her clothes off.

No, she wouldn't.

Yes, she would.

No. Definitely no. Some things were better left to the imagination.

She only wished the last twenty-four hours had been one of them.

With a groan, Hallie picked up the energy bar, tore open the wrapper and bit off a mouthful. It was actually more like sawing off cardboard with her teeth, but then, food that took effort to chew was usually better for the digestive system.

But what she wouldn't give for a Hershey's candy bar right now.

Hershey's bar. Hershey's Kiss. Rik's kiss. Rik.

She would not think about him. He was no gentleman. Taking advantage of her sorry situation to get her out of her clothes, teasing her, kissing her….

Giving her his room—well, trying to, at any rate—keeping Babs away from her, ordering breakfast, bringing her not just a change of clothes but an abundance. He'd provided necessities she hadn't yet thought about needing. He'd even gotten snacks because she'd been cheated out of breakfast and he thought she might still be hungry. He'd rescued her from the balcony without chiding her for going outside in the first place.

So, okay. Just because his manners were a little on the rough edge was no reason to deny he possessed some gentlemanly traits. He had lived in the jungle, for heaven's sake. *Miss Manners Saves the World* probably didn't make the top ten reading lists there. All of which meant that Rik's behavior wasn't the problem. It was her reaction to his behavior that bothered her.

Gnawing on the energy bar, Hallie decided she owed Rik a measure of gratitude. He shouldn't have kissed her, certainly, but she could have—should have—made it clear she didn't want to be kissed. Instead, she'd enjoyed it, responded to it, liked it. She was fairly certain he knew that, too.

Lord, her head hurt. She would never, ever, for the rest of her life, take another sip of tequila. She'd be a model of propriety from now on. Hawaii wasn't on her short list of preferred places to be. It wasn't even in the top hundred. But since the Brewster wedding had brought her to Paradise, she'd make the best of it, avoid any excess exposure to the island atmosphere and stay as far away from the ocean as possible.

While she was at it, she'd stay as far as possible from the attractive man who just happened to be sharing his room with her.

Recognizing Rik had good points didn't change the basic truth that he had his own agenda. He'd told Jack he was keeping the bachelor party's entertainment under wraps. He'd told her he had a few surprises in store for Jack. Hallie didn't like surprises in conjunction with one of her weddings. If Rik was planning to play some taste-less joke at Friday night's party, he'd have to do it over her dead body. Which, considering how she felt at the moment, wasn't out of the question.

But she'd be better by Friday night, and she'd make certain Rik's silly surprise wouldn't spoil even a single moment for Jack and Stephanie. It was, after all, what the Brewsters were paying her to do.

FROM WHERE HE WAITED by the bank of pay phones, Rik observed the lobby. The woman at the concierge desk reminded him of Stephanie, except she was shorter, darker and rounder and looked nothing like Stephanie at all. Earlette was working the front desk, which must mean someone hadn't shown up for their shift. She was looking a bit frazzled, but her smile still carried a sincerely warm welcome. He was going to like living in Hawaii. He was going to like flying tours between the islands, being married, having kids, putting down roots....

Leaning his shoulder against the booth divider, he wished the woman on the other end of the phone would take him off hold. She was checking on a costume, but the longer it took, the less he was sure this baby idea was a good one. If it worked, Jack would still be single come Sunday morning and Stephanie would be looking at him, Rik, in a new light. Well, it might not be quite that simple, but—

"Sorry to keep you waiting. Barney isn't available, but we do have a nice Big Bird, if you'd want that."

Big Bird. Wasn't that something like a stork? "The bird'll be great," he told her. "You have all the instructions, right? And my credit card number. Anything else you need?"

"Normally, there's an extra charge for making a special delivery along with the singing telegram, but since we couldn't provide the costume you originally requested, I'm going to waive that fee.''

"Thanks, I appreciate your help. You're sure the telegram will arrive as scheduled tomorrow afternoon? Without fail?"

The woman laughed. "Barring complications, Big Bird will be there."

Complications were exactly what Rik hoped would arise from this little escapade. He was beginning to feel a bit uneasy about the whole thing, but damn it, he had to do something to stop Jack from going through with this. There was no other way Rik could see to clobber his buddy's complacent rush into this misconceived state of matrimony. It wasn't as if Rik wouldn't be right here to oversee this small practical joke. He could step in the minute things got out of hand. If they got out of hand. Which they wouldn't. Jack just needed a jolt to open his eyes to the sham his marriage would be, and Rik felt sure this little delivery would do it.

Now, all he had left to do was to check with his sister, Lynn, and make sure she still intended to leave baby Sam with his uncle Rik for a couple of hours tomorrow afternoon. And if this didn't turn the tide, Rik had no idea what else he could do. Except stick to Hallie like a saddle bur and do his damnedest to interfere with the wedding arrangements.

"This is strictly confidential," Rik reminded the woman who'd taken his order. "I don't want my friend to be able to call you and find out I'm the one who set him up. At least, not right away."

"We're very good at keeping secrets here at Patty's Party-Grams, Mr. Austin. Thank you for calling. I believe you'll be very happy with our services."

"I'm counting on it," he said.

THE PHONE SHRILLED and Hallie gave up on the idea of taking a nap. The darn thing hadn't stopped ringing for the past ten minutes, and even with the pillow stuffed on top of it, she could hear every jarring jangle. It no longer mattered to her who was calling whom, or whether she was supposed to answer or not supposed to answer, whether she was supposed to be in this room or another one. She just wanted the ringing to stop, so she stopped it.

"Hello," she said into the mouthpiece.

"Ms. Bernhardt." Babs's voice tapped across the phone line like a redheaded woodpecker on a hollow tree. "I thought I would *never* reach you. Do you know they have *lost* you at the front desk?"

Hallie wasn't surprised to hear it. After yesterday, she wouldn't be surprised to learn her birth certificate had been revoked. "I'm here," she said, as brightly as possible. "On the job."

"I am relieved to hear it. In the last hour, I've been told you were given the wrong room when you arrived, that you checked in, then checked out, and that now they have no record of you in the reservations computer at all. But, as I told Danny, I knew you had to be here and that there was simply an error on the part of the hotel. Frankly, Hallie, I expected a bit more from this hotel. You gave it such a glowing recommendation, I felt comfortable sending that enormous check, sight unseen. I realize we've only been here since yesterday, but I have to tell you I'm bothered by a few things."

Hallie eyed the bed with desperate longing, but there was no escape.

"The orchids." Babs began listing, and Hallie reluctantly, but quickly, picked up a pen and began making notes on a pad of hotel stationery. "Have you checked with the hotel to make certain we can keep them in the restaurant refrigerating unit until the last possible moment? Well, I have, and the kitchen manager was not at all encouraging. He was almost rude. And the chef..."

Those last three words somehow formed a complete sentence that spelled trouble. Big trouble. Hallie said a silent prayer that Jacques hadn't been offended. It had taken her an entire month of phone calls to persuade the chef to agree to make the wedding cake himself. He was touchy, she knew from experience. One wrong word from Babs, much less several words together, and there could be major problems already on tap.

"Jacques," she wrote on the notepad.

"Also," Babs continued, "I think you should call the weather bureau. This wind will ruin the effect of the waterfall and I've invested too much time, energy and money into this wedding to allow it to be ruined by a passing hurricane."

"Weather is one of the variables we discussed, Mrs. Brewster, if you recall. It's always a factor, and since we can't control it, we will simply work around it."

"I hope you can get a commitment from the hotel groundskeeper, because I couldn't. I merely asked him about moving some trees closer to the lanai where the ceremony will be held, and he was quite snippy about refusing."

Hallie didn't know why Babs hadn't just asked him if he'd mind putting up a seawall between now and Saturday. A pretty one, made out of seashells to complement the bridal bouquet. "I'll talk to him," she said, and wrote "Harold" on the pad.

"I do hope you'll call the weather bureau. All these special reports on the television and radio are nerve-racking for a woman of my sensibilities, you know. I'm not sure I can survive this wedding."

A sentiment Hallie had heard repeated any number of times since Babs Brewster first walked into her office. She'd just never really thought about how much easier this wedding would be to carry off if that particular sentiment came true. "I've never lost a mother of the bride yet," Hallie said cheerfully, and added "hitman" to the list. "You hired *me* to worry about these things, remember? I'll take care of everything. You relax and enjoy these couple of days before Stephanie arrives. She'll be here Friday evening, right?"

"That's another thing. I've been calling her, telling her she needs to change her plans and arrive sooner than that." Babs's sigh was heavy with the frustrations of motherhood. "She's so conscientious, you know. Can't leave the office until her desk is cleared. That sort of nonsense. Honestly, I wouldn't be at all surprised if you thought Stephanie wasn't excited about her own wedding. Which she is, of course."

"Of course she is." Hallie had pegged this bride as brilliant from day one. Stephanie Brewster obviously had no illusions about the kind of wedding she would have, whether she wanted it or not. So she'd wisely given her mother carte blanche and stayed as far from the wedding plans as possible. Hallie only wished she could have afforded to do the same. But this was her business, she was damn good at it, and Babs was merely an experience she'd look back on with satisfaction and a ton of relief. "Stephanie will love the orchids. You were absolutely right to insist on having enough to fill the entire staging area in front of the waterfall. It's going to look just gorgeous."

Babs's pleasure flowed through her voice like fine

wine. "Isn't it, though? I'm beside myself with antici- pating the moment Stephanie and Jack see the lanai all covered in orchids on Saturday." Her tone changed. "If this terrible wind doesn't ruin everything. You will talk to the groundskeeper right away, won't you?"

"Right away," Hallie said, and underlined Harold's name.

"And you will inform that dreadful man in the kitchen that we do, indeed, require the entire refrigerator from Friday night until Saturday noon?"

"Consider it done." She circled Jacques's name in ink.

"Wonderful. Now, if you'll just tell me your room number, I'll let you get on with your work." There was the sound of a drawer being opened with a creak. "Wait, let me find a pen so I can write it down."

Not in this lifetime, Hallie thought. "There's some- one at the door, Mrs. Brewster. I'll phone you later."

"No, wait! I nearly forgot the reason I called you. You'll need to contact someone about getting Danny a tuxedo. Can you believe the man cannot locate his pants anywhere? I can't imagine what he's done with them, but I'd rather buy an extra tuxedo than have him fret over those pants. You will take care of that for me, won't you, Hallie?"

"Absolutely," she assured Babs, and wrote down "Dan's pants." Not that she believed Danforth Brew- ster could work up a good fret even if he'd lost every pair of pants in America. "Now, I really must see who's at the door. Goodbye, Mrs. Brewster."

"Keep me informed" were Babs's last words before Hallie cradled the receiver and sank onto the edge of the bed. As if there could be anything Hallie might know that Babs hadn't discovered first. Why had she ever agreed to do this wedding? It had shouted "Headache" from the introductory call. Not just out of town, this wedding had to take place half a world away. Not just an absent bride and groom, neither one had even been available to speak to Hallie about the arrangements. Not just another family, this was the Brewsters, one of the most influential names in all of Boston.

Which was the reason Hallie was here now. Business was business, no matter how much of a nuisance the mother of the bride turned out to be. And Babs was going in the record books...right after Hallie proved she could deliver the perfect wedding, no matter where, no matter who, no matter what the weather. Picking up the notepad, she read over the list of potential hazards and decided to tackle the easy one first. It would drive Babs crazy to have to rent a tux for Dan, but Hallie wasn't about to take him shopping and she didn't see how she could find time to argue about tuxedo pants. If Mr. Aloha Formalwear was good enough for the groom— and it had been Jack's choice—it was good enough for the father of the bride.

And the best man.

Making arrangements to have Rik and Dan measured for a tux would be a simple matter of scheduling, she thought as she found the Honolulu phone number in her briefcase and put in a call to Mr. Aloha. One simple call and her sense of accomplishment was on the rise.

At least it was until the phone failed to produce any more than a busy tone and an oft-repeated message to hang up and try the call again. Okay, she'd move on to the next item on her list and try the call again later.

Jacques, the chef. The arrogant, irritable genius whose own staff referred to him as the Pope of Pastries and Pout. He hadn't taken well to the idea that the

Brewster-Keaton wedding cake had to meet certain standards. Babs's standards. Hallie had had to compromise her principles and promise him a night of secret passion—a rendezvous with a box of Mallomars, his weakness—in order to coax him into saying yes. She did not think she could deal with Jacques and her hangover at the same time. He could wait.

Harold. One glance out the window at the clouds and the peach-bra wind sock told her that Harold had more important matters on his mind right now than weatherproofing the lanai.

Which brought her back to Mr. Aloha. Somewhere in this hotel, sometime today, there would have to be a free phone line that could connect her with Honolulu. She'd try the call again...just as soon as she found that bottle of pain reliever Rik had bought in the pharmacy, just as soon as she washed down a couple of the non-acidic aspirin with the acidic orange juice.

What the hell. This morning was not going to get better, anyway.

THE CONNECTION WAS scratchy at best. "Mr. Aloha Formalwear?" Hallie repeated. "Honolulu?"

"Yeah. What d'ya want?"

This definitely was not the cultured man she'd conducted her business with long-distance not two months ago. "Could I speak with Mr. Reynolds, the owner?"

"Yeah, you could...if he was here, which he ain't."

"When will he return?"

"Didn't say. You wanna leave a message?"

"Is there someone there who can assist me with a rental order?"

"Yeah. Me. What d'ya want to rent?"

She had a bad feeling about this, but she told him anyway.

"YOU'RE SURE YOU WANT to do this?" Rik couldn't believe he'd said that, especially when his sister's laugh echoed over the phone line.

"If you're feeling that apprehensive about baby-sitting your nephew, I can leave Sam home with a sitter," Lynn said. "But last week you said you wanted to watch him while I went to my doctor's appointment. Honestly, Rik, it isn't like you're going to have him for longer than three or four hours at the most. And he still takes long afternoon naps. Besides, you're usually better with him than his own daddy. Keanu is still scared to death that Sam is going to break."

"He isn't, is he? Going to break, I mean?"

She laughed again. "Of course not. Sam is made of sturdy stuff. He's half-Austin, remember? I suspect in another few months, he'll be making even you wish you were in better shape to keep up with him."

"You're sure?" Rik asked, knowing in his heart of hearts that he should not be making plans involving his nephew. "He's barely eight months old. Maybe I shouldn't—"

"If you're trying to tell me you've had a better offer for tomorrow afternoon, you'd better think again. Being uncertain about your baby-sitting skills is one thing. Dumping your nephew for some skinny blonde in a skimpy bikini is another."

"No. Save me from skinny blondes. Plump ones, too, for that matter. I'd rather be with Sam any day. He smiles at my jokes and laughs when I make a face. No blonde has ever come close to liking me as much as he does." Rik was nuts about the little guy and he did want to see him, spend time with him. And maybe he wasn't crazy to think that a couple of hours with a great kid like Sam would squeeze Jack's tough-nut heart and make him realize what he'd be missing if he went through with this wedding. "Of course I want to baby-sit tomorrow. Just tell me where to meet you and what time."

She did.

RIK INSERTED THE KEY CARD into the door of room 1413 and waited for the green light before he reached for the latch.

"Psst!"

He looked over his shoulder at the deserted hallway, looked in the other direction at the same empty view, then pushed open the door with the heel of his hand.

"Psst! Rik!"

This time he knew he hadn't imagined the reedy whisper and he turned around, scanning for the source, as the lock clicked back into place behind him. At the end of the hall nearest his room, the fire escape door opened a crack. A half inch, maybe three-quarters, but not more. And sticking out of the opening was a finger. A woman's finger, crooked and beckoning him down the hall.

Whatever this was about, it ought to be good. "Tell me quickly," he whispered as he stepped into the stairwell and saw Hallie. "Are we on the trail of the elusive lingerie? Or is this a romantic assignation?"

"It's an assignation, all right. Minus the first three syllables."

Her morning obviously wasn't going as well as his. "What are you doing out of the room? I thought you were going to take a nap."

"I had to use the phone." Her hazel eyes seemed brighter, sharper than the last time he'd looked into them like this.

He snapped his fingers, realizing why she looked different, like a little girl with pudgy cheeks and flyaway hair surrounding a serious, studious face. "You're wearing your glasses...and a sweater." Pausing, he stepped back to note the eclectic mix of poppy red sarong and brick red, cotton cardigan. "Your glasses. My sweater. Are you cold?"

"I'm locked out."

"Hmm, usually women lock themselves in my room, not out of it."

She frowned. "Have you been drinking?"

"I must have had three glasses of orange juice already this morning, and it isn't even eleven o'clock."

She wrinkled her nose. "The acid in the juice doesn't bother your stomach?"

"Nothing bothers my stomach."

"It's early yet. Look."

He arched a brow. "At you?"

"No, look down the hall." As he was about to yank open the door and take a look around, she stopped him. "Don't open it all the way, for Pete's sake. Be discreet. He might be out there."

"Who?"

"Mr. Aloha."

"Mr. *Aloha?*"

She peeked under his arm at the scant inch of visible hallway. "Trust me, you don't want to be found."

"I don't?"

"Well, I don't. I suppose you can decide for yourself."

"Which is why you lured me into the fire escape for this little rendezvous?"

Her chin came up and she stepped away from the door. "If I had wanted to *lure* you, Rik, I'd have hung out a neon sign with a big green arrow pointing at the door handle. As it happens, I called you in here to warn you."

He was beginning to like the sound of this. "Okay, here I am. Warn me."

She cocked her head at an angle, and behind the slightly bent, duct-taped pewter frames, her hazel eyes nailed him. "You know, you deserve what's going to happen to you."

"I certainly hope so. I've worked hard all my life to get my just deserts."

"Fine. I wash my hands of you." She demonstrated the effect by dusting her hands. "Just remember when it comes time for Mr. Aloha to measure you, I tried to save you from embarrassment."

"All right, Hallie, I'll bite. Who is this Mr. Aloha and why do you believe he's going to embarrass me?"

"Mr. Aloha Formalwear is the shop I asked to handle the tuxedo rental. You need a tuxedo for Saturday's wedding. Therefore, Mr. Aloha needs your measurements."

"For an Aloha lei?"

She didn't even smile at his joke. "For a standard tux."

"Ah." He nodded sagely. "The standard tuxedo measure. And you thought that would embarrass me?" Rik laughed. "Really, Hallie, that's sweet and all, but believe me, there isn't any part of my anatomy that won't measure up. Certainly nothing I'll be embarrassed about."

She eyed him with tightly pursed lips. "I don't know what I was thinking. You obviously are a man among men and this won't bother you one teeny, tiny bit." Grabbing the door, she jerked it open and then closed it just as quickly with a shove. "He's out there!"

"Mr. Aloha? Let me see."

"Jack." She splayed herself against the door, holding it closed, even though it was under no threat of being opened. "At least, I think it's Jack. He's built like a football player and he's wearing a football jersey."

"Blue or green?"

"What difference does it make?"

"Makes a lot of difference if you're on the opposing team. Let me take a look."

"No." She kept him back with a narrowed gaze. "If he realizes we're in here, you'll just invite him in, and frankly, this is not a good time."

"Speak for yourself. I'm having a heck of a good time."

"You've been in the jungle too long, Rik."

"Several people have said that to me lately. It doesn't offend me, you understand, but it does sound a trifle condescending. Sort of like a polite way of calling me an ape."

"There isn't a polite way to call you an ape. I can't speak for anyone else, but I was merely saying that your idea of a good time needs a serious overhaul."

"Isn't that just like a woman? You've known me less than twenty-four hours and already you're trying to change my spark plugs."

"Men." She rolled her eyes and made a hundred-and-eighty-degree turn, cracking the door once again. Rik tilted his head to the side and glanced over her head.

"He's at our door," she said in a sinking voice. "You'd better go out there and stop him."

"Psst! Jack!" Leaning over her, Rik sent a loud whisper through the door crack before she slammed it closed, almost taking off the tip of his nose.

"What are you doing?" she demanded, wide-eyed.

"You said to stop him."

"I said go out *there* and stop him. Not invite him in here."

"He's a nice guy. I'll vouch for him."

"Sh! Will you keep your voice down? I'd prefer to meet the bridegroom under more positive circumstances."

"Oh, I'm pretty sure he'll enjoy meeting you under any circumstances."

"This is not a good time for me to make Mr. Keaton's acquaintance," she said tightly.

"Why not? He has a sense of humor."

"Considering he's been living with you for the past several years, that isn't reassuring. I'm not taking any chances on him confusing me with the ex-*ah*-tic dancer you've hired for his bachelor party. I have to protect my business and professional reputation, Rik. I can't have Jack Keaton or Dan Brewster or anyone else thinking I'm some sex kitten, sharpening my claws on your bedpost while I wait for Friday night."

The image was a tad overpowering, coming from a woman who had, only an hour ago, responded to his kiss with more primness than purring. "Sex kitten?" he said with a slow grin. "You?"

It was the wrong thing to say. The glint of annoyance in her eyes crystallized into a challenge as she whipped off the pewter-rimmed glasses and stared him down. At least she tried. He knew she couldn't have him in focus at this range and he was pretty certain she preferred it that way. But for a moment, watching her defenses rise like a trout to the fly, he could only admire her self-protective technique. Any man in his right mind would kiss her about now. Before she opened her mouth and gave him what for.

"Mr. Austin," she said crisply. "Regardless of your opinion, there are men who find me quite attractive."

"Wait a minute. There's a broad jump between saying a woman is attractive and referring to her as a sex kitten. I never said you weren't attractive."

She clasped her hands at her breast. "I will carry your so gallant compliment with me to my dying day." The hands returned to guard the door. "In the meantime, please keep in mind that I am a professional. I'm going to do whatever I have to in order to bring off Saturday's wedding with style and good grace. Babs Brewster hired me to ensure that everything goes according to her plan. She won't, and I can't, tolerate any tasteless practical jokes in connection with this wedding."

Rik felt the blood surge to his face. She couldn't know about that. He'd only just gotten off the phone after making the arrangements with Patty's Party-Grams and Lynn. He wasn't even sure he would follow through with the idea of dropping a baby on Jack's doorstep. So how could—

"Whoever you've hired as entertainment for Friday night—and I have no interest in knowing her name, nationality or vital statistics—better keep a low profile. Because I'm on the job and I'll be keeping an eye out for trouble."

The tap on the door behind her came so abruptly it startled her and she jumped up and forward...right into

Rik's arms. He staggered a little with the unexpected-
ness of having his arms full of female, but he recovered
as Jack opened the stairwell door and looked in.

"Excuse me," Jack said. "I was looking for a ninety-
pound weakling. Guy named Austin. You two haven't
seen him, have you?"

Hands locked behind his neck, Hallie stared dismally
at Rik, then at Jack, and whispered a sickly "No."

"See what happens when you keep an eye out for
trouble?" Rik told her. "It walks right up and knocks
on your door." Lowering her carefully to the floor, he
couldn't help thinking Jack usually got the better of him
in moments like this. "Great timing, Jack," he said.
"But wrong stairwell. The ninety-pounder is in the fire
escape at the other end of the hall."

Jack's knock-'em-dead smile turned full strength on
Hallie. "Hello," he said. "I'm Jack Keaton. And you
must be the entertainment—"

"Committee," Rik inserted smoothly.

"Consultant," Jack finished with a you-didn't-really-
think - I - was - going - to - say - what - you - thought-
I-was-going-to-say-did-you look. "I'm so happy to meet
you. Rik was telling me over the phone how extraordinarily *talented* you are."

Hallie's shoulders went back and her chin came up
so fast the top of her head nearly whacked Rik in the
chest. "Really?" Her laugh was two seconds' worth of
pure nerve-racking beauty. "Trust me, he doesn't even
know the extent of my talents. I can be very entertaining. Depends on how much I like you."

Jack blinked, and his wary eyes sought Rik's with a
question, which Rik couldn't have answered even if his
speech mechanism hadn't been held hostage by sur-

prise. The best he could manage was a don't-ask-me shrug.

"Well," Hallie continued in a satisfied, tight little voice, "now that we're all acquainted, let's go to your room, Rik. I think it's time we took a few measurements."

Keaton's gulp was audible in the stairwell and Rik only wished he could swallow his own astonishment. Whatever Hallie was doing, he wished she wouldn't. Although, on the other hand, this was the first time since the wedding announcement he'd seen anything more than a despondent resignation in Jack's eyes. Panic wasn't exactly the substitute he'd hoped for, but it was a start.

If Jack could only meet another woman, someone who could ignite his interest and stake a real claim on his heart, he'd have to give up the idea of marrying Stephanie. Hallie wasn't the woman, of course. She'd drive Jack nuts in a matter of minutes. But she had the advantage of being close and of being the only person in recent memory to get any reaction out of Jack at all. He didn't like the look in her eye, but he'd be damned if he was going into that bedroom with her alone. Whatever she had in mind, he figured he could use a witness. "Sure," he said. "Let's all go to my room. I have the key right here in my pocket."

"You know," Jack said, "I'd really love to join you, but I just remembered I signed up for a tennis lesson."

"There's no charge for no-shows," Hallie told him as if she knew. "And Rik is going to need assistance. Aren't you, Rik?"

He wasn't going to argue with that. "I am, Jack." Signaling his best friend with every subtle nuance at his command, he willed Keaton to hang tight and stay close. "I really am."

Jack clapped his hand on Rik's shoulder and squeezed. "Sooner or later, old pal, a man has to fly solo. You know what they say…two's company."

"Oh, but Mr. Keaton," Hallie said brightly. "We need you to make a foursome. Me and you, Mr. Austin and Mr. Aloha."

This time, Rik was the one who gulped. He smiled, desperately at Jack. "Would you excuse us for a moment, please?"

Jack nodded and was in the hall before the last echo of the request faded down the stairwell. Rik frowned suspiciously into Hallie's audaciously innocent expression. "What in hell are you trying to do? I thought you were worried about your reputation? I thought you didn't want anyone to confuse you with a, quote, 'sex kitten,' unquote?"

"Me?" Her eyelids batted up and down, up and down. "You don't honestly believe anyone could confuse *me* with a quote, '*sex kitten,*' unquote?"

He wouldn't have believed his remark could have struck such a nerve with her, but she was obviously very protective of her image. He just couldn't figure out what image she was trying to protect…or at what cost. "I thought you had better sense."

She arched that saucy little eyebrow at him and his heart took a swan dive. "I'm only trying to make sure everyone, including Jack, gets his just deserts." She patted his arm. "It's a tough job, but that's what I get paid the big bucks to deliver. You might want to keep a close eye on your spark plugs, though. I yield a mean torque wrench." With a rebellious flip of her hair, she followed Jack into the hall.

Feeling a tad on the vulnerable side and a whole lot intrigued, Rik went after her.

Chapter Seven

Hallie approached the door of the hotel room, wishing she had never agreed to cross the threshold of this double-unlucky thirteenth room on the thirteenth floor in the first place. Technically, of course, she hadn't agreed. Rik had carried her over the threshold, dead drunk. Since then, she'd lost her clothes, gotten a new wardrobe, been kissed senseless—actually, she'd been half-senseless even before he kissed her—and been left with a phone that either didn't work or wouldn't stop ringing. Her clients thought she was a) not on the job, b) sleeping on the job or c) dancing on the job. But until a few minutes ago, when she had willfully, foolishly let Rik goad her into a silly charade of innuendo with Jack Keaton, her butt had been nicely covered. Babs Brewster might have her suspicions, but she couldn't prove it had been Hallie's derriere slung over Rik's shoulder last night.

But now, Jack could be forgiven for assuming she was the dancer hired for Friday night's entertainment and Hallie had no one to blame except herself. Well, Rik. But she couldn't just explain to him her aversion to being thought asexual. Hadn't she already paid her dues of frustration and indignities during her marriage to Brad? She'd be damned if she'd let any man say to her in that amused and astounded tone of voice, *"Sex kitten? You?"*

Rik had had no business insinuating that he had Friday night's entertainment in his room. He should have known it wouldn't be hard for Jack to locate exactly which room he was in. So this was all Rik's fault and it made her furious that she couldn't come right out and lay the blame on his doorstep.

"When is Mr. Aloha supposed to show up?" Rik asked as he stepped forward, pulling the key card from his pocket.

"He's here now." Hallie replied, oddly cheered by the thought.

"Here?" Rik glanced down the hall. He and Jack exchanged that peculiar, conspiratorial and very male look that men did when women were around. As if they had to humor her or something. "Is Mr. Aloha your invisible friend, Hallie?"

"Come on," Jack urged. "You can tell us."

"I'll just let you judge for yourselves." She smiled with sincere patience, knowing that in this instance, at least, she was in the clear. She hadn't been the one who invited Jack along on this outing and she had done her best to warn Rik.

"So how long before we can see him?" Rik asked.

"All you have to do is unlock the door and keep your eyes open."

"You mean he's inside?" Rik's teasing faded. "You let a stranger into our hotel room?"

"Our hotel room?" Jack repeated, his look of surprise swinging from Jack to Hallie and back again. "Are you two *sharing* this room?"

"Technically, yes," Rik said at the same moment Hallie uttered a definite "No!"

She arched a thunderous brow at Rik. "No," she said firmly, knowing Jack would only pretend to believe her. Men. If there was any conceivable way to put a situation into a sexual context, they'd find it. How would she ever be able to talk her way out of this? "We are sharing this room," she told Jack. "The hotel computers went down yesterday and put us together by mistake. They have yet to correct this mistake. But it will be corrected. So technically, yes, Rik and I are sharing this room, but don't make the mistake of thinking we are sharing anything else."

Jack processed that information with a sympathetic nod, but she saw the way his gaze sneaked to Rik and the look they exchanged, like two boys huddled under a blanket with their first *Playboy*. With a hearty sigh, Hallie grabbed the key card from Rik and inserted it into the lock. "I'm going in," she said.

"Oh, no, you're not." Rik took hold of the door handle and held it fast. "You're not walking into this room until you explain to me who this Mr. Aloha is and exactly how he happens to be running tame in our bedroom."

"You know, Rik, when I woke up this morning, I thought I had a hangover. But now I realize my head aches in direct proportion to how close I am to you."

"Whoa. She floored you, buddy." Jack sounded impressed and very understanding as he leaned forward to confide, "I've noticed the same correlation. Headache...Rik. Rik...headache. I've often remarked on how he can be a royal pain in the—"

"Neck," Rik said with an admonishing glare. He leaned against the doorjamb and crossed his arms over his chest. "Now that my faults have been clearly re-marked upon and you're both in agreement, let's hear your explanation, Hallie."

She was feeling better by the second. And in a few minutes, Rik was going to be so sorry he hadn't listened to her explanation the first time she tried to give it to him. "All right," she said graciously. "This morning I phoned the Honolulu office of Mr. Reynolds, who owns Mr. Aloha Formalwear. Someone else answered. Raoul. He's in charge of the business now, it seems. I asked him to check my original order and to send someone to take your measurements." She glanced at Jack. "Somehow, Rik was never measured for a tux and, as you know, time is short."

Jack's expression went from amused interest to dour resignation in less time than it took for him to blink. Hallie noted the change and filed it for later consideration. No bridegroom was going to look that unhappy in a Bernhardt wedding, that was certain. "So, Raoul said he had an associate already on Maui, checking out possible locations for another branch of Mr. Aloha Formalwear, and he'd send him right over. I said that'd be great and told him my room number. Not twenty minutes later, there's a tap at the door and our Mr. Aloha had arrived." She punctuated the end of the story with a that's-it shrug.

"You let a strange man just walk into your hotel room?" Rik asked, stressing practically every word.

"Yes," Hallie answered. "I did."

"Didn't it occur to you that you might be putting yourself in danger?"

"Come on, Rik," Jack intervened. "She's out here in the hall, isn't she? Give her credit for having good sense."

"Thank you." She smiled at Jack.

He smiled back. "You're welcome."

Rik scowled at them both. "What about all these theatrics, Hallie? Is Mr. Aloha someone I should or should not trust? Should I or should I not let him measure me for the tux?"

"Let me put it this way," she said sweetly. "If I hadn't believed he could be trusted to stay away from your clothes and personal possessions, I wouldn't have left him alone with them. And when it comes to measuring you for your tux—" she couldn't help but smile "—I think he'll do an admirable job."

"Then what are we waiting for?" Rik stepped back and Hallie pushed open the door.

"Hello?" she called. "I'm sorry it took me so long. Mr. Austin was a little more difficult to locate than I expected. But we're all here now."

The person from Mr. Aloha turned from the window with a shimmer of silver lamé, and Hallie fully expected to hear the thud of jaws dropping to the floor behind her as first Jack, then Rik, got a good look at him. Her. Whichever.

"I was beginning to think you'd deserted me, sugar." Tall, thin, as silver blond as a shooting star, the man in drag stepped into the middle of the room and smiled with an easy grace. He had beautiful eyes, very blue, very carefully lined with blue shadow, and an abundance of thick, long black eyelashes that couldn't be real but looked surprisingly natural just the same. In fact, other than his height and a suspicious broadness of chest and shoulders, he looked very much like a female. A tall, blond, curvaceous and quite lovely female.

Obviously, Rik and Jack were a little more stringent in their criteria for "female," because there was total silence from the peanut gallery behind her. Hallie could all but hear their testosterone screaming, "Get me out of here!" To their credit, neither one of them bolted from the room. Although she was pretty sure both wanted to.

"Celeste Sims," she said by way of introduction, "I'd like you to meet Jack Keaton, our bridegroom. And Rik Austin, the best man."

Celeste "Mr. Aloha" Sims obviously knew how to handle the male ego, because there was no offer or expectation of a handshake. Just a slight nod of acknowledgment and a comfortably confident renewal of her smile. "Oh, goody. Linebackers." With a zip of her retractable measuring tape, Celeste swept first Jack, then Rik, with a discerning eye. "Who wants to be first?"

"He does." Jack and Rik spoke at the same moment, each pointing unerringly at the other.

"Eager little campers, aren't we?" Held between the beautifully manicured fingernails of Celeste's thumb and forefinger, the retractable tape zipped in and out of its case. "Why don't I do you both at the same time? Just strip out of those old safari shorts and step over here into the light."

"Oh, gee, look at the time," Jack said in a rush. "I really hate to hurry off like this, but...I've got a tennis lesson."

"Me, too." Rik's excuse was hot on the heels of Jack's as they both backed toward the door. "I'm taking a lesson, too."

"We're taking it together," Jack confirmed.

"Doubles," Rik agreed.

"That's right." Jack reached behind him for the doorknob. "We play doubles."

"But, gentlemen," Celeste said in a husky and only slightly disappointed tone of voice, "I do doubles."

Not today, Hallie thought as the linebackers hit the door and kept on going, leaving her to console Celeste and pay her for her trouble. This was one fee that wouldn't appear on the Brewsters' final bill, though. Oh, no, this fee Hallie was happy to pay herself.

RIK SAT AT THE BAR, staring morosely at the lime wedge floating, rind up, in his glass. He barely glanced over when Hallie slid onto the stool next to him. "You look like you've lost your best friend in the world," she said.

"Nope. Not yet, anyway."

"Hmm. Well, that's good." Hallie settled more comfortably on the stool and looked around.

Behind the bar, a young man turned to greet her with a friendly smile. "What can I get for you?"

Her gaze dropped from that familiar smile to the more familiar name tag on his left breast pocket. "Hello, Kee-mo." She stressed the correct pronunciation of his name to let him know she remembered him and yesterday's conversation. "You're a long way from the front desk, aren't you?"

"I'm a jack-of-all-trades, Ms. Bernhardt. A little bit country. A little bit rock and roll. May I fix you a drink?"

She was a little bit leery of clichés and of men in general, but she *was* thirsty. In fact, her throat felt sorely in need of refreshment. "Thank you, Kimo, yes. I'll have anything you have that's clear, has no caffeine, sugar, artificial sweetener or preservatives and won't in any way affect my equilibrium."

Rik picked up his glass and twisted it so the ice

clinked. "She'll have what I'm having," he said. "Only be sure to leave out the acidic lime."

Kimo looked from Rik to Hallie, obviously uncertain whether this was a serious request or a private joke. Hallie took pity on him. "Water," she said, overruling Rik's order and explaining her own. "Just plain water, thank you."

"That's what I ordered," Rik said as Kimo turned away to get a glass. "Good old H_2O."

"Hmm. Why the sudden shift from orange juice?"

He twisted the glass some more and watched the wiggle of the lime wedge. "Since I met you, I've started having nightmares about the strangest things. Worms in tequila, panty hose in the wind, citric acid in my food."

"Measuring tapes?" she suggested. "Blondes of either gender?"

"Only one blonde, and only one gender."

"You can rest easy. Celeste left." Hallie thanked Kimo with a smile and a tip as he set the glass of water in front of her. "She gave me an excellent idea on where to shop for underwear, though. It seems the boutique here in the hotel is not the best place locally to purchase intimate apparel. But there's a little shop across town. If I have time and can find a taxi, I'm going to run over there this afternoon." The water tasted about as good as anything ever had to her, and Hallie paused long enough to take a second, soothing swallow. "Not that I don't appreciate the swimwear you bought. I mean, it was a really thoughtful thing to do. And spandex has its place in the world of fashion. It just isn't a very good substitute for silk."

"Thanks for telling me that."

She turned to look at him. "What's wrong with you? I know the incident with Celeste probably threw your testosterone levels out of sync, but that's no reason to drown your sorrows in a glass of water.''

His gaze slid sideways to hers, then back to the lime wedge. ''I think I liked you better when you had a hangover.''

''Hey, I can take a hint.'' Hallie was offended, although she tried not to let it show. She didn't know if she was responsible somehow for his mood now, and if by some chance she was, she didn't think she wanted to know that, either. ''I only came in the bar because I'm supposed to meet Babs Brewster in the lobby in a few minutes. If you don't want to talk, that's fine with me. I'll just sit here and go over my notes on the wedding.''

She made no move to open her planner, though. Suddenly, the Brewster-Keaton wedding was the last thing she wanted to think about. ''Don't mind me,'' she continued, because she wanted very much for him to reassure her that he did like to talk to her, that he did like to be with her, that he did, indeed, like her. ''I'm very good at pretending I enjoy being alone, you know. I get to practice at all these weddings I attend where I don't know a single soul except the person who hired me to coordinate the event.''

Bracing one elbow on the bar, Rik turned to face her. His bare, hairy and very warm knees slid against hers, pushing the sarong up and sending a row of goose bumps marching up her thighs. ''Celeste isn't the blonde who worries me, Hallie. You are.''

She blinked at him from behind the corrective lenses of her glasses, glad she was able to see him up close and personal, flattered by his admission despite his gloomy tone of voice. ''Technically, I'm not blond. Ash brown is what a hairdresser would call my shade.''

He twisted his glass in a slow circle on the counter as he took his time assessing the color of her hair. "Whatever you call it, it's nice. It suits you. And the haircut—" He took another moment to look it over. "The haircut is most becoming."

Surprised and intimidated by the compliment, she narrowed her eyes and flashed him a smile. "Have you been drinking? Something other than good old H₂O, I mean?"

"Are all the men in your life suspect, Hallie? Or is it only me you accuse of being insincere every time I try to pay you a compliment?"

She didn't know how to deal with Rik in this mood, didn't know how to restore his good humor, didn't know why it was important to try. "I think I liked you better when you weren't so serious. Maybe you should switch back to orange juice."

"Maybe I should go for a walk." He tipped the glass to his lips and downed the rest of the water in a long swallow. An action Hallie watched with an edgy kind of fascination. There was a dusky shadow of stubble covering his throat and jawline, a shade of concern just below his eyes. And there was a quickening in the area of her heart as she thought about bridging the space that separated them and touching his cheek. Nothing more. Just a touch. A connection of her fingertip to his skin. A contact to show her concern for whatever was troubling him.

Hallie sighed. Oh, who was she kidding? Why didn't she just grab him by the back of the neck, haul him close and plant one on him?

"What?" he asked.

"What?" she repeated, fearful that he somehow knew what she had been thinking.

"What are you sighing for? You have everything under control again. You know where to buy replacements for the clothes you lost, and you know exactly what you need to do to make Saturday's wedding a complete success." He set his empty glass on the counter with a clunk and it rocked in an unsettling half circle. "What do you have to sigh about?"

Obviously nothing, in his opinion. "I think the more pertinent question would be, what is it about Saturday's wedding that you find so upsetting?"

"It's not a good match," he said quickly, as if he had to get the words out before they choked him. "This marriage is a mistake."

"The Brewsters seem to think it's a great love match."

"Of course they do. They want their daughters to be wives and mothers, in that order, and sooner rather than later. They'd rather convince themselves Stephanie and Jack are a perfect fit than admit they might have pushed a little too hard for this marriage."

"Well..." Hallie proceeded slowly, wanting him to confide in her, hoping she was misreading his body language and tone of voice, telling herself he was simply concerned about his best friend's future happiness. "If Jack and Stephanie don't have a problem with marrying each other, I wouldn't think the state of their relationship is anyone else's business."

His lips tightened in what she perceived to be bitter disappointment, and her heart sank, dragging her hopes with it. "You're right," he said. "What business is it of mine if they want to go through with this marriage and ruin their lives? I'm just the best man."

An elderly man shuffled up behind Rik's bar stool and proceeded to sweep a speck of dust and a peanut shell off the floor and into his portable dustbin. "Darn honeymooners," he muttered. "If'n they had a lick of sense, they'd have stayed single!"

Rik looked over his shoulder and Hallie followed his gaze. The older man—his hotel badge read simply Dave—gave the floor another swipe with his broom, then snapped the lid of the dustbin and shuffled over to sweep under Hallie's stool. "Gettin' married was the biggest mistake of my life," Dave continued to mutter. "Worst mistake a man can make. I know. I done it five times. Five times! Same woman! Same goldarn, stubborn old woman every time!" He shuffled on, still talking to himself, still belaboring the institution of marriage and anyone silly enough to enter into it.

Whatever Dave's experience, his gruff interruption seemed to sweep away Rik's depression. Hallie would have liked to think it was her sympathetic ear, her ability to listen in a compassionate, soothing manner that had made him feel better. But she was pretty sure he'd just gotten tired of pondering the reasons Jack and Stephanie shouldn't be getting married, and with the uncanny faculty men seemed to possess as a gender-specific trait, he had simply decided not to think about it anymore.

"I think I'll go for that walk now. Want to come with me?"

She tried not to let her gaze shift past him to the rambunctious display of wind beyond the open bar. "Isn't it a little windy?"

"Not for a man among men like me." There was a hint of self-deprecation in the smile tugging at the corner of his lips and a trace of it in his voice. And for no reason she could fathom, Hallie felt like crying.

"Tell me something, Hallie?"

At that moment, she would have lied through her teeth if she'd thought it would make him happy. "Sure."

"How did you get that scar on your cheek?"

She touched it self-consciously and felt the old familiar rise of regret. "I got hit by a punch bowl."

He didn't laugh and she risked a glance at his impassive, expectant expression. Then, maybe because it had been a long time since she'd talked about it, or maybe just because he'd asked, she told him the story. "It was the wedding of the century," she began. "In terms of catastrophes, that is. The bride insisted everything had to be planned to perfection. Nothing unexpected should happen. No detail was too small to be overlooked. It would be perfect."

Hallie could almost laugh about the silliness of that now. Almost. "Needless to say, the wedding was planned to the nth degree. Nothing was too minor to rate attention. The bride and groom were sure of each other and of the forever quality of their love. But even the best-laid plans sometimes give way to disaster. And that's what happened."

Her hand strayed to the bowl of peanuts on the bar and she munched on one before she continued. "The wedding was utter chaos from the moment, only an hour before the ceremony, when the organist arrived, tripped over the bride's going-away case, fell and broke her wrist. No music.

"No problem. The bride's brother had a friend who worked at a music store across town. The friend was working and couldn't leave the store, naturally, but a tape of wedding music was available if someone wanted to drive over and pick it up. The brother volunteered, and on the way, he wrecked the groom's car. Luckily, no injuries, except to the car."

She glanced at Rik, wondering if he was bored beyond reason. He didn't appear bored at all. She sighed and ate another peanut. "Did I mention it was a new car? Brand-new, less than a hundred miles on the odometer, and the vehicle the happy couple had been planning to drive on their honeymoon. But as the maid of honor pointed out a little later, they could rent a car for their trip. Fine.

"No problem. So, minus the organist and the Wedding March, the bride headed down the aisle and the 'I do's' were said. Wedding over. Mission accomplished. All's well that ends well. Ah, but then we move on to the bride's family's backyard and the outdoor reception. There was a tent, an orchestra, and an entire wall of catered hors d'oeuvres. And a cake. My God, what a cake. Five layers high and thick with eye appeal. Everyone admired that cake. Every mouth under that tent was watering for just a taste of it. Next to the cake, the crystal punch bowl looked like an afterthought and the champagne punch barely raised an eyebrow."

Another peanut disappeared and she paused for a drink of water. "Did I mention that the rain started during the wedding ceremony? No? Well, a little rain. No problem. At least not until about twenty minutes into the reception, when the thunder and lightning started, followed a few minutes later by a good eight inches of rain, all within an hour's time. The wedding reception was buried in the deluge. The yard turned into a swamp. The canvas tent sagged, then ripped, then caved in. I dived for cover under the table holding the wedding cake. Unfortunately, the table legs sank in the mud just as I made my swan dive. I wound up sitting in a puddle the size of Georgia, covered by five layers of soggy, sickening wedding cake, while the punch bowl slid the length of the table and hit me on the head. The cut wasn't deep, but we couldn't get it to stop bleeding. My dress was ruined at that point anyway, but when Brad— he was the groom—tore off a bit of the sleeve to press against my cheek, it was the last straw. I started crying. At that point, everyone hastened to assure me the worst was over. What else could possibly happen? There wasn't anything left to go wrong. I should have known better than to believe them.''

"Did the family sue you?"

She shook her head, wondering how long it would be before she remembered that day with any kind of objectivity. "Since it was my wedding, there wasn't much point."

"*Your* wedding?"

He didn't have to sound so shocked, she thought, but she ignored the impulse to say so. "Ironic, isn't it? That horrible experience convinced me to open Bernhardt Bridal. I decided that since every possible thing that could go wrong at a wedding had already happened to me, I'd have a unique perspective to give to any bride who thought she had to plan the perfect wedding. And to everyone's surprise but my own, I'm quite successful at achieving perfection. The secret is—" She glanced over at him, then pushed away the bowl of peanuts. "Forget it. I'm not telling you my secret. You might move to Boston and open your own bridal service."

"I'm not into ceremonies. Weddings, perfect or otherwise, are not my area of interest." He gave her a strange, pensive look, then shook his head. "I would never have pegged you as a wife, though. You don't look married. You don't wear a wedding ring.''

She held out her hands, fingers splayed and unadorned. "I find rings just get in my way."

The memory of how bothersome Brad had found his wedding ring and how quickly he'd stopped wearing it altogether tightened around her and she shooed it away with a squaring of her shoulders. "So that's the story of my wedding scar, the sad tale of a true disaster."

"And a lesson in how good things can come out of bad."

"Here, here!" She lifted her glass in a silent toast to Brad, her ex-husband and one of the reasons she was happy today.

Rik pulled out his wallet and added a couple of dollars to Kimo's jar of tips. "Let me ask you one more thing, Hallie," he said as he slipped off the bar stool and stood beside her.

Don't ask, she thought, afraid he'd probe for the sorry details of her disastrous marriage. *Don't ask.*

"As it turns out, I'm not very good at pretending I like to eat alone." His smile developed slowly and took her heart by storm. "Ms. Bernhardt," he said formally, "would you care to have dinner with me tonight?"

Relief surged through her with the force of a flood. He was asking her on a date. Well, not a real date. Just dinner. A nice, friendly dinner. She had no reason to feel as if he'd just proposed they buy a sailboat and sail around the world together. She slid off the bar stool, brushing against him because he was standing so very near and there was no other way for her to be on her feet and standing except right next to him. Right next to his hard chest. Right next to his beating heart. Right next to a temptation she'd rather not feel. But what the heck. After all, she was standing knee-deep in Paradise. "I'd love to have dinner with you," she said. "As long as you promise not to notice I'm wearing the same thing I've worn all day."

"Lose the sweater and it's a deal. You have beautiful shoulders, Hallie. It's a shame to keep them covered."

Her heartbeat took off like a quarter horse, but she grabbed the reins and slowed it to a fast trot. "Flattery will get you nowhere, Mr. Austin." Reaching into the pocket of his sweater, she closed her fingers over a small, square instrument of torture. "I have plans for after dinner," she said, withdrawing the retractable tape measure and giving the tape a zippy little pull. "So don't even think about signing up for a tennis lesson."

For a moment, their gazes connected, and then he laughed. "It's hard to imagine anything could be more exciting than spending the night with you while you're passed out. The thought of you measuring me while sober will undoubtedly get me through the rest of the day." He raised her chin with a nudge of his thumb. "Eight o'clock tonight. It's a date."

A thrill of attraction rolled over her like a high-speed roller coaster and she swallowed hard, knowing he was only teasing her about last night, wondering how he could take her breath away with just one lazy smile. "I'll be the one in the red sarong and sweater," she told him. "You won't be able to miss me."

The corners of his mouth curved with a rueful frown. "Maybe that's the problem," he said. "I'm Jack's best man and you're Stephanie's wedding coordinator and I just wasn't able to miss you."

Then he walked out of the bar, shoving his hands into his pockets and bowing his head as he stepped into the full force of the wind.

Chapter Eight

Rik walked the beach until he was soaked to the skin and tired of fighting the relentless wind. Which took less than ten minutes. The last weather report he'd heard still put Hurricane Bonnie far out to sea and a long way from Hawaii's shores. The local meteorologist was predicting more of the same wind, rain and fussy ocean, but nothing worse. Rik was ashamed of himself for having even a half-formed wish that the hurricane would hit close enough to interfere with Saturday's wedding.

Not that he'd liked any of the thoughts he'd had in conjunction with this wedding. If the best he could do to rescue Jack was hope for an act of God, he wasn't much of a best man and even less of a friend. What kind of friend fancied himself in love with his best friend's bride-to-be, anyway? A desperate friend. A lonely friend.

Rik stooped, steadying himself with one hand while using the other to write "Rik loves Stephanie" in the wet sand. But the letters vanished as fast as he drew them, leaving nothing to mark his place, denying the message he had meant to write. He brushed the sand smooth and began once more, only to give up when the same thing happened again.

If he really loved Stephanie, why had he decided to come to Maui with Jack instead of heading straight to Honolulu and camping out on her doorstep? If he was really determined to stop this wedding, why wasn't he negotiating directly with her instead of wandering on this stretch of beach, trying to think of some way to interfere.

He wouldn't have even dreamed of making a protest if he'd believed for a single instant that Jack was in love with Stephanie. Or she with him. He'd watched the two of them during the time she'd visited their South American camp. She and Jack shared a history, certainly, but they acted more like brother and sister than friends who'd grown to be lovers. They weren't lovers. He knew he was right about that. He was right about this marriage being a sham, too. He just couldn't figure out why Jack would go ahead with it, couldn't understand why his friend was choosing to settle for much less than he deserved.

After Saturday, Stephanie would have her trophy husband who lived his life a world away from her, and Jack would have…what? The same life he had now, only without a hope of ever finding someone to share it.

Digging down, Rik brought up a seashell from its watery hiding place and brushed off some of the wet sand with the pad of his thumb. The action made him think of Hallie, dusting her hands in the stairwell, saying she washed her hands of him. The memory brought a smile and then a chuckle as he recalled how fast he and Jack had gotten out of the room when Celeste started snapping that retractable tape measure. What a spectacle they'd made of themselves.

Hallie had won that round in the battle of the sexes.

She had come out smelling like a rose. Why, she'd even tried to warn him and he'd been too obstinate to listen. He'd just kept on teasing her, flirting with her, enjoying the way her eyes got wide with excitement, then narrowed with suspicion, and the way her lips formed that little O when she was thinking.

Married. He still couldn't believe it. He'd have sworn Hallie was single...and apt to stay that way. She had an untouched quality, a certain candor about her that had made him think she was both inexperienced and distrustful of men in general.

Obviously, he'd overrated her innocence. Hallie was not only married, she was here alone, and she hadn't even batted an eyelash before announcing that she didn't wear her wedding ring because it got in her way. That had taken him by surprise. Knocked the wind right out of him.

How could a woman who was superstitious, wary of caffeinated and decaffeinated beverages, overzealous about the citric acid she did or didn't put in her stomach and afraid of everything from heights to hurricanes be on the lookout for a vacation affair? If she was—and he couldn't think of any other reason she would have made that remark about her wedding ring—she was a better actress than any he'd ever seen on film. And she didn't know the first thing about love...the faithful, rock-solid and honest love that gave marriage a foothold on forever.

He supposed he ought to be grateful she'd been honest with him. Not that he was actually considering her subtle offer of an affair. Sure, he found her attractive and he had enjoyed kissing her. But if he'd had any suspicion she was married, those kisses wouldn't have happened. There were unwritten rules regarding how to behave with married women, and he'd privately sneered at any male who wasn't man enough to abide by them.

So where did that leave him? Alone on the beach, congratulating himself on having principles before he'd even been officially propositioned, plotting ways to stop his best friend's imminent marriage, writing an invisible love letter in the sand to that same best friend's fiancée while thinking about kissing another man's wife. "You *have* been in the jungle too long, Austin," he said aloud.

The wind turned the words back on him, unimpressed by his claim to honor. Hell, he was no better off than Jack. He lusted—no, yearned—for a love of his own. He wanted a home and someone in it he wanted to come home to. But choosing Stephanie as his intended mate, based on little more than his own fantasies that she would turn out to be that someone, was every bit as bad as Jack choosing to marry her to fulfill whatever honorable promise he believed he had made.

With an underhand toss, Rik flung the tiny shell into the wind and watched it fall not a foot from where he was standing. There it would stay until either the tide carried it back out to sea or some romantic soul rescued it and carried it home to decorate a sunny windowsill.

He wondered what sort of home Hallie lived in and if it had a window that basked in morning sun and if she collected seashells. Not likely, he realized. The shell would remind her of the beach, which would remind her of palm trees, which would remind her of Hawaii's exotic fruits, which would remind her of citric acid, which would upset her stomach, which would pretty much take away any pleasure the shell might offer.

He thought about the perky way she'd asked Kimo for a glass of water and the face she'd made when he'd

told Kimo to leave out the lime. A smile began somewhere deep inside him but vanished like his scribbling
in the sand. What the hell was wrong with him? First
he kissed her. Then he kissed her again. And the moment she told him she was married, he couldn't utter
the invitation to dine with him fast enough.

Even now, all he could think about was the way she
looked in those duct-taped John Lennon glasses and the
way she squinted when she wasn't wearing them. The
way her hazel eyes looked green when she laughed. The
way her nose crinkled just a little and how the gesture
made him want to touch her forehead and smooth away
her worries. And he couldn't stop thinking about the
way she'd arched those sassy eyebrows and snapped
that silly measuring tape at him. And he liked the saucy
way she had of flipping that ridiculously flattering hair-
style.

So, okay, she was married, and that meant he'd keep
his distance. But it wasn't against any moral law he
knew of to have dinner with her.

Battling the wind, he bent to pick up the shell he'd
tried to toss aside. Brushing it off for the second time,
he dropped it into his pocket. He liked the thought that
Hallie might actually have a windowsill and that this
small gift from the sea might wind up sitting on it.

HALLIE LEANED FORWARD, her energy focused, her
sights set on her goal. "All right," she said. "A case
of Mallomars now and another at Christmas. That's my
final offer."

"No, no, no, no, no, no, no!" Jacques, the chef, waggled a finger in front of her face. "I am an artist. I
cannot sell my passion for such a price!" He rolled his
scornful eyes to the ceiling, as if he couldn't believe

she would suggest he could prostitute himself for his art.

"It's your decision, of course. If you don't want the goods, that's fine with me. I'm sure one of your assistants will make the cake to meet Mrs. Brewster's requirements. It won't be the masterpiece you would create, of course, but I'm sure it will be wonderful just the same."

His eyes narrowed on her. "Wonderful? Ha! You think it could be wonderful? A cake—" he pronounced it in a distasteful two syllables, *cake-cah* "—made by an assistant unskilled in the art of creation? Ha!"

Obviously, it was a rhetorical question, so Hallie smiled and upped the pressure. "I don't suppose your protégé—what's his name? Chef Charles?" She nodded, pleased by the dark scowl settling on Jacques's brow. "Does he have a sweet tooth, too? Would he make the cake as requested for a couple of pounds of chocolaty, marshmallow-filled, gooey-sweet Mallomars?"

Jacques slapped his fist on the desk, his Mallomar addiction lowering his bushy eyebrows into a fierce frown. At last, Hallie thought, progress.

Jacques glared, but she was unmoved.

He tried a pout, but she remained calm.

He caved in, and she was gracious.

"You drive a difficult bargain," he said. "But okay. I make this...this six-layer plain vanilla cake—" his lips curled in distaste "—as this crazy Brewster woman wants."

"With the champagne fountain in the middle."

He shuddered but still managed a snarl of agreement. "With the fountain."

Hallie stood and offered her hand to seal their deal.

"It's been a pleasure doing business with you, chef. Mrs. Brewster will be so pleased you've changed your mind."

"You will send down the box of cookies now, yes?"

"Jacques, you know I can't do that until after I see the cake on Saturday morning." She picked up her briefcase.

He followed her to the doorway. "It is sad that a proud man can be brought to his knees by a demanding woman."

Hallie gave him a commiserating smile and hoped he didn't find out that the promised box of cookies wasn't even on the island.

It was lost—God knew where—with her luggage. But the airline was bound to find everything before Saturday. She'd be sitting pretty by then. As she left the office, Hallie shuddered to think what he might do if the Mallomars failed to materialize. But she wouldn't think about that negative possibility. Positive. She would maintain her positive attitude. At least until after she'd spoken to Harold about decorating the hotel lanai.

"ORCHIDS ALL ALONG HERE." Her hand swept the length of the lanai. "And all along here. Across the front rail there and—" like a divining rod, her finger hovered, then specified the exact location "—all around the fountain."

Harold surveyed the scene with his hands stuck in his hip pockets. "That's a lot of orchids," he said. "But I can tell you right now they won't look so good after a couple of minutes in this breeze."

Hallie pointed to the side of the lanai that faced the ocean. "What if we hung a tarp across there?" she suggested. "Wouldn't that block most of the wind?"

Harold just looked at her. "You've never been this close to a hurricane before, have you?"

"No," she admitted, wishing he would talk faster so she could conclude this discussion and get back inside. The ocean was entirely too close, its roar too deafening, its salty mist too sticky. And she wasn't wearing a hat. "I avoid sun, storms, wind and rain whenever possible."

"You're not going to avoid this storm. I've already tried talking to Mrs. Brewster and I know what you're up against with her, but you'd be ahead of the game to just up and tell her now that this wedding isn't going to happen."

"If the wind hasn't died down by tomorrow afternoon, I'm going to suggest we move everything inside to the ballroom."

The groundskeeper guffawed, then shook his head in a slow, you're-not-listening-to-me movement. "I've lived on this island for sixty-odd years, Ms. Bernhardt, and I can tell you that the wind isn't going to die down. Not tomorrow. Not the day after. I like you, and that's why I'm gonna tell you for a fact there's a hurricane on the way and there isn't going to be any kind of wedding at this hotel come Saturday."

"The hurricane is moving away from Hawaii," she said with sheer stubborn confidence. "All the weather reports agree on that."

"You can take my word for it or not as suits you. But when my bunions ache like they have lately, I know there's a mother of a storm coming at me. Take my word for it, Bonnie isn't headin' out to sea."

Hallie did not want to hear a hurricane update from anyone who consulted bunions rather than scientific charts, but he sounded so sure, so depressingly definite.

"I appreciate your concern and your prediction, but I can't cancel this wedding," she said. "Not today, not tomorrow and certainly not Saturday."

"Suit yourself. I'm only trying to give you a bit of a warning." He rocked back and forth on his heels, hands still stuck in his pockets, his mind made up.

"So when the orchids arrive, you'll set them out as I've indicated, correct?"

"I'll make sure they're put just where you told me to put 'em, but I'm not giving any kind of guarantee they'll be there five minutes afterward."

"Thank you, Harold. I'll take my chances."

He shrugged. "Just so long as you know that whoever's footin' the bill may just as well kiss his cash goodbye and toss it into the wind."

Hallie couldn't think of a single positive thing to say except "Goodbye." Some people, she thought as she walked out of the wind, were just born pessimists. Obviously Harold didn't know that, between them, she and Babs had enough determination to carry off a dozen weddings, under circumstances much worse than this. He'd undoubtedly seen his share of hurricanes. He just didn't know the power of positive thinking.

HALLIE COULDN'T BELIEVE she had dressed for dinner. Well, really, she had only taken off the sarong, pressed out the wrinkles and put it on again. But this time she'd wrapped it around her and tied the ends over one shoulder, leaving the other bare. Amazingly, that had changed the look of the dress and her look right along with it. She'd experimented with her hair, drawing it up at the temples, then down on one side, then pulled back away from her face entirely, and finally left it alone to fall as it may around the single, fragrant plumeria flower she'd tucked behind her ear. Either she was getting used to the haircut or Rik's remark had altered her perspective on it.

She checked her image in the mirror, still amazed at how different she looked. Her eyes shone with satisfaction. No surprise there, really, considering the problems she'd handled like a pro that afternoon. Everything had turned out exactly as she wanted…with the possible exception of Harold's dour forecast. But the orchids would be delivered the day after tomorrow. Jacques had agreed to make the cake to Babs's specifications. The minister of Stephanie's choice had dropped by and surprisingly passed Babs's inspection with flying colors. The musicians, a three-piece combo, would arrive tomorrow to check out the Huki-lau Room, where the reception would be held. She hoped Babs wouldn't find fault with their contemporary mix of classical music.

Hallie smiled at herself in the mirror. This wedding was going to be perfect. There was nothing to worry about at all. Even tonight's weather report had been upbeat, predicting the hurricane would lose strength as it passed to the north of Hawaii, leaving Saturday's forecast as sunny and mild and a perfect seventy-eight degrees.

She'd spoken to Earlette at the front desk and found out the boutique would be open again by tomorrow. So even though she hadn't had time to check out the shop Celeste had suggested, and even if the airline didn't find her lost luggage, she'd still be able to buy something suitable to wear. Turning, she admired the drape of the sarong. Maybe she should consider changing her style. Wearing bright colors gave her confidence. Why, she wasn't even tempted to put on Rik's sweater again, even though she had a feeling that sitting across the dinner table from him, having her bare shoulder under his admiring eye might just give her goose bumps.

But she would risk it. A few goose bumps in exchange for this exhilarating sense of adventure seemed a fair trade. In fact, she was looking forward to seeing Rik's face when he saw her. His blue eyes would darken. He'd smile that really wonderful, exciting smile that made her feel as if she had a shot at winning the lottery. He'd say something terribly nice and complimentary like...

"Are you through in the bathroom yet?" A rap on the door followed his words and Hallie sighed. So much for romance. Sharing a hotel room and a hotel bathroom didn't make for the perfect date. Still, Earlette had assured her the problem would be corrected just as soon as the computers and the staff got their act in sync and located an empty guest room. So, for tonight at least, she and Rik would start and end their date in the same room. Which might be nice. Or awkward. Or awful. What if he wanted to kiss her good-night? What if she wanted him to?

Well, of course she'd want him to. His kisses had been very nice even when she hadn't been expecting them. To imagine a kiss she could plan for, anticipate... Goose bumps marched down her shoulder at the thought. So, okay, there would be a good-night kiss. She just had to decide if it should happen outside in the hallway before they came into the room. Or whether it was safe to have the kiss once they were already in. The hallway held the advantage of being semipublic and therefore ensuring that her hands stayed on his shoulders and his stayed circumspectly at her back. Kissing in the room had the disadvantage in terms of ready access to the bed in case things got a little overheated, but the definite advantage of being able to brush her teeth first.

"Hallie?" Rik's knock on the door settled the question in her mind. If possible, she'd kiss him both places. In the hallway and in the hotel room. What was the worst possible thing that could happen? He'd think she wanted to sleep with him? And if that was the worst...well, this could be a night to remember. He knocked again. "It's seven-fifteen and I still have to shower and shave."

After one last inspection in the mirror, Hallie took off her glasses and set them on the counter. She wouldn't be needing them tonight. If...when...Rik got close enough for her to require near vision, she planned to shut her eyes, anyway. Turning, she opened the door and stepped out.

Rik took a step back...only because he wanted to be sure he didn't need glasses. But Hallie was actually standing there, draped like a Grecian goddess in the poppy red sarong. One shoulder gleamed bare and creamy and seductive in the glare of the bathroom light behind her. And was it possible she really had a flower in her hair?

He swallowed hard, knowing he was in big trouble here. There she stood, smiling that soft, expectant little smile, looking at him with anticipation and pleasure in her eyes, waiting for him to say something about the way she looked. If he'd still harbored a doubt about her plans to seduce him, it died a quick and painless death. He may have spent the last thirteen years in the jungle, but he knew the look of the huntress and Hallie was wearing it.

"I'll, uh..." He tried clearing his throat. "I'll, uh,

just be a few minutes."

Then he escaped into the bathroom and shut the door.

HALLIE WAS WEARING his sweater when he came out. She was sitting on the edge of the bed, remote in hand and aimed at the television like a pistol at a target. The red light on the remote flashed every two seconds like clockwork and the television clicked from one channel to the next with precision. Rik hoped it wasn't a James Bond remote...the kind that changed the channels at the touch of one button and doubled as an automatic weapon at the touch of another. "Anything good on?" he asked, testing the waters.

"A documentary," she answered with complete disinterest. "Something about apes."

Okay. So he had a little fence-mending to do. Women were so difficult. If you complimented them, they took it the wrong way. If you didn't, they thought it must mean you found them totally undesirable. Rik frowned at his own generalization. He really didn't know if all women acted like that. He only knew Hallie did. "Ready?" he asked, moving toward the door and, he hoped, more neutral territory. "I'm starving."

She rose and followed him without comment, stepping past him and into the hallway, not even waiting for him to close the door before she headed toward the bank of elevators.

Rik caught up with her and just managed to beat her finger to the call button. He pressed it with sincere frustration and tried to figure out how he was going to get back into her good graces without flat-out rejecting her or unwittingly giving her the idea that he could be hers for the asking. "Did I mention how nice you look?"

Her glance told him he'd not only *not* mentioned it

before but he needn't have bothered to do so now.

"I like the flower in your hair."

It was jerked from behind her ear and crushed in her hand before the last word faded. "Now, look, Hallie," he began, determined to set her straight about the rules of seduction. "You're not being fair. I admit I told you up front that I didn't think much of rules, and I know I kissed you, not once, but twice."

He had her attention now. That was certain. She was staring at him with the same distasteful expression he'd seen on her face when he pulled out that bottle of grenadine and started to add it to her tequila sunrise.

"I thought you only kissed me once," she said.

"Once when you were a little the worse for tequila and once when I saved you from taking a dive off the balcony."

She sniffed. "Oh. That's right. I forgot for a minute about the chocolate kisses."

Now he knew where he rated...below Hershey's on the list of preferred smacks. "But kissing isn't the point," he said, beginning to wonder himself what point he was trying to make. "It's the other thing."

"The *other* thing?"

With a start, he realized what she might be thinking, and his ego had him blurting out a definite "No, not *that! That* works just fine."

"I believe you," she said hastily. "I never doubted for a second that everything you have works beautifully and that you don't have any problems with that...*or* any other thing." She paused, then hurriedly continued, "I mean, I didn't think you would. Really, I never even thought about it at all. Not until you brought it up." Her eyes got wide and looked green above the blush that stained her cheeks as she realized the double entendre.

If they'd been talking about anything less personal,
Rik would have cut his losses then and there and kissed
her until she couldn't pronounce the word *chocolate.*
Which brought him smack into the reason he'd begun
this disjointed conversation in the first place. How was
he going to handle this? *Hallie,* he could say, *whatever
you're thinking might happen between us isn't going to.
While I might be willing to be seduced if you weren't
married, the fact that you* are *married puts my partici-
pation out of the question.* Rik realized that he really
hated explanations and wondered why he'd decided that
living back in civilization again would be so great.

"Could we start this evening again?" he asked.

She frowned. "How far back would we have to go?"

"How about the moment you opened the bathroom
door and my heart fell at your feet?"

That did it. The color of her eyes switched from dis-
concerting green to a dreamy green gray and golden
hazel, and her lips parted in that little O he found so
appealing. "Oh," she said.

"Oh," he repeated, knowing he had just landed himself back in trouble. Big trouble. The temptation to
gather her close and kiss her senseless was very strong
and so tempting he was reaching for her before he
caught himself and brought his hands back where they
belonged—at his sides. "Now, if that elevator will ever
get here, we can go downstairs and have a nice dinner."
In the open, public surroundings of the dining room, he
added for his own benefit as he checked the arrows.
"Why do people always look at the indicator lights?"
he asked in a purposefully cheerful tone designed to
keep her thoughts, and his own, off the palpable silence
that had settled between them like an uninvited guest.
"As if that will give them some advantage on getting
into an elevator. I mean, there's not exactly a stampede

at the moment. There's no one here but you and me and it really doesn't matter when the elevator gets here, does it?"

She shook her head in agreement, and then, with some degree of fatalism, he watched her lift her chin and gather her courage with a deep breath. "We could stay in the room," she suggested on the exhale. "We could order from room service."

It was as near to an invitation as he was likely to get while waiting for an elevator, Rik thought, and wished the damn thing would arrive and get him out of this danger zone. "We could," he agreed slowly. "But I can't. I'd like to. I really would, but in the room we'd be...alone. And in the dining room we...wouldn't."

She looked down and her fingers uncurled around the crushed flower. A petal drifted to the floor, followed by another, but Rik saved them both with a sweep of his hand. "You don't want to lose your petals," he said as he dropped them back into her palm. "The fragrance will last even if the flower didn't."

The chime of arrival caught him by surprise, and when the elevator doors slid open, he motioned for Hallie to proceed him. Still holding the flower and petals, she stepped inside and, oblivious to the fact that there were other people present, turned to him with a troubled look. "Are you in love with somebody else?" she asked.

Rik shifted from one foot to the other, uncomfortably aware of how that must sound to the other occupants of the elevator. Couples, right down to the young man and woman who had watched Hallie do the bossa nova in the lobby last night. "I'm not sure," he answered in an aside. "But it doesn't matter."

"It matters to me." She did lower her voice, but she didn't stop talking. "You're only the second man I've even thought about...about...well, about sleeping with since... Well, for a very long time, and I'd just really like to know if your reluctance has something to do with me or if it's because of your feelings for somebody else."

"Believe me, I'm not that noble," he said tightly, and then had to slip his arm around Hallie and step close against her as the elevator stopped on the next floor and a couple in the back moved past on their way out.

She leaned away from him, planting a firm hand on his chest to keep him back. And then she lifted her chin and looked at him with a gaze that was thoroughly confused and uncertain, but definitely brave. "I understand," she said so softly he had to lean closer to hear. "I'm embarrassed I asked such a stupid question. I don't know what's wrong with me tonight. I usually don't indulge in this kind of fantasy and I hardly ever—"

"Excuse me." The elevator stopped at the next floor and someone pushed forward, squeezing past on Hallie's other side and pushing her even more tightly against him. Rik did the only thing he could. He pulled her into his arms and held her. And it felt good. And right. And he couldn't let her think for another second that he wasn't attracted and tempted by her uncertain proposition.

"High maintenance," Rik murmured to himself as he stroked her cheek with his finger and nudged up her chin with his thumb. "I'm not noble, Hallie, and I am flattered beyond belief that you're interested, but the truth is, you're married, and therefore out of bounds, even for a rules-are-made-to-be-broken guy like me."

"Married? You think I'm married?"

He blinked. "You mean you're not?"

"No." She sounded pretty sure about it and the floor

started to drop out from under him. The elevator had started to move again, but that wasn't the only reason. "I haven't been married for years. I don't feel like I was ever really married at all."

"But you told me all about the wedding, the cut on your cheek." He was losing ground but holding on to her. "And you said flat out that you weren't wearing your wedding ring because it only got in the way. What was I supposed to think?"

"That I don't wear any kind of ring because I've found they snag my clothes and are always either too tight or too loose and generally just get in the way?" The uncertainty in her eyes was giving way to a rekindled confidence, which he was in no shape to combat. "What did you think I meant, Rik?"

This conversation was taking an embarrassing turn, but he tried manfully to hold his own by keeping his mouth shut and not admitting to anything.

"You thought I was a married woman and I had set my sights on seducing you and making you the 'other man.'"

The amused glint in her eye should not have been appealing, but damn if it wasn't.

"So you've been struggling with, well, you know..." She lifted her shoulders in a sexy shrug. "That *other* thing."

Two could play at this game, Rik decided. "No," he whispered. "If I've been struggling, it's with the idea of your being unfaithful. There aren't many institutions I consider sacred, but marriage is one of them. Please believe me, I would never even have kissed you if I'd known you were married."

"I'll bet you wouldn't have taken off my champagne-soaked clothes and hung them out to dry, either, would you?"

His body was beginning to ache in all the wrong places. They were in the elevator, for Pete's sake. "No, I'm sure I'd have dumped you downstairs in the lobby and let Kimo wheel you up on the luggage cart."

"You're so gallant, Rik. Will it hurt your feelings if I tell you I'm a little surprised?"

"Because I thought you were married?"

"No, because it mattered to you when you thought I was."

A shifting, unsettling and very exciting feeling stirred within him.

"Excuse me," someone said. "This is the ground floor."

They'd landed, Rik acknowledged with a glance. Safely.

But he didn't make a move to exit the elevator. Neither did Hallie. Neither did anyone else. Rik looked expectantly at the only other couple still in the elevator with them.

The young man from last night spoke up. "We're sort of anxious to find out how this turns out."

"To tell the truth," Rik said with a smile, "so am I."

The young man's significant other caught Hallie's eye and shrugged. "So, he has principles. It could be worse, you know. I say order room service and be done with it." She pushed the button for the fourteenth floor, grabbed her young man's hand and pulled him through the closing elevator doors, leaving Hallie and Rik alone and going up.

Chapter Nine

Caught in the snare of Rik's arms and the speed of the ascending elevator, Hallie began to entertain some serious second thoughts. How had she gone from wondering where she would kiss Rik good-night to agreeing to have sex with him? In front of witnesses, no less.

She risked an upward glance but got only a blurry smile for her trouble. At least, she thought he was smiling. Without her glasses, she couldn't tell the difference between a considerate, patient, mature expression and a full-fledged, yippee-I'm-going-to-get-laid leer. How did a man look when a woman announced she wanted to sleep with him? Impassive? Gleeful? Would he display any sign of being surprised, or was surprise completely out of the question?

Her experience was extremely limited in these matters. And she couldn't exactly ask Rik. She'd already opened her mouth once too often in the past ten minutes, given away in an unguarded instant the reserve she cultivated like a reticent garden. In return, Rik had revealed next to nothing. Why didn't he say something? Tell her he really had no interest in her at all, admit he'd only pretended to accept her offer because rejecting her in front of those people wouldn't have been polite.

"You weren't just being polite, were you?" She couldn't *believe* she'd said that aloud. "Never mind," she said quickly. "*Don't* answer that."

But he tipped up her chin and forced her to look at him, anyway. "I've been living in the jungle, remember? I don't know how to be polite."

"Yes, you do. I understand perfectly that I forced the issue and that sleeping with me was probably the furthest thing from your mind, and I know that isn't the kind of thing a man would want to announce to an entire elevator full of people, so why don't we just go back downstairs and have dinner?"

"We'll order room service," he said calmly. "We'll start with dessert."

Hallie gulped. This was all Brad's fault. If he'd been half the man she'd thought he was, she wouldn't be in this situation right now. But if she wasn't in this situation right now—pressed so close to Rik there wasn't room for so much as a sliver of reluctance—she knew she'd be desperately trying to think of a way to get herself into a situation exactly like this. Rik was warm and solid and tantalizing. He was funny and handsome and desirable. And right now, she wanted him more than she wanted to keep breathing. "Rik?"

"Yes?"

"Are you sure you want to do this?"

"Go back to our room and order dinner? Yes."

"And the rest?"

"Let's take this a step at a time, Hallie, and see how things develop."

"You're not just saying that to make me feel better?"

"Hallie, there are a couple of things you should know

about me." He leaned against the elevator wall and she leaned with him. "I almost never say or do anything just because I think it would make someone else feel better. I'm not that thoughtful. And while I do hold to my own set of principles, I'm no saint."

The elevator stopped at their floor, but he didn't move to get out, and the doors slid quietly shut again. "A few minutes ago, you asked me if there was somebody else. I'm going to be honest and tell you I think there might be, but the relationship is sort of on hold at the moment. I'm telling you this because I want you to know I've made no promises or commitments to any woman and no woman has any claim on me."

That was unsettling, Hallie thought. What was she? Roommate of the hour? And if she hadn't just staked a fairly large claim on his commitment for the evening, she didn't know what he thought was going on here. Pushing back from his embrace, she jabbed the button for the ground floor and the elevator began a slow descent. "Are you always this romantic before a seduction, Rik, or do I just bring out the ape in you?"

He straightened. "You *did* ask, Hallie. Would you rather I lie and make believe I fell in love with you somewhere between the fourteenth floor and the lobby?"

"Thirteenth floor," she corrected. "Hotels only pretend it's the fourteenth floor. And for the record, I didn't ask you to lie, but I don't believe I requested the whole, unvarnished truth, either."

He stared. "You have to be the most confusing female I have ever encountered. One minute you're hot to get into bed with me and the next you're giving me the cold shoulder because I told you what you said you wanted to know."

"You weren't listening, Rik. I asked if you were in love with someone, but what I really wanted to know was whether or not I hold any sexual appeal for you at all...other involvements notwithstanding. And I don't believe I gave any indication I was *hot* to get you into bed."

He rubbed the back of his neck. "I may have been out of the dating scene for the past several years, but I haven't been isolated or celibate. I know the difference between casual flirtation and serious invitation, regardless of the subtle way it may be couched."

"And I suppose you think I was flinging serious invitations all over the place."

"Don't even try to deny that when you opened the bathroom door and stepped out with your bare shoulder and a flower in your hair, you weren't thinking ahead to the end of the evening."

"A kiss," she said. "I was thinking about a kiss. Specifically, whether I should kiss you good-night at the door or wait until we were in the room."

"Right, and you weren't thinking about how soon after that kiss you could rip off my clothes and get me flat on my back on the bed."

The elevator arrived back at the ground floor and she didn't even wait until the doors opened before she jabbed the button for the fourteenth floor. "Is that the best you can do in the fantasy department, Rik? Imagining that I want to rip off your clothes and have my wicked way with you? Frankly, I expected better from a man who's been, quote, 'out of the dating scene for the past several years,' unquote."

"I save my better fantasies for the second date." He braced his arms on the railing and crossed his feet at the ankles. "To be perfectly honest, I find it amazing that you, whose fantasy revolves around where a good-night kiss should take place, would be so picky about what is a fairly standard fantasy among adults of both sexes.''

"You, of course, would know all about standard, run-of-the-mill fantasies. *I* prefer to be on the cutting edge.''

"The cutting edge.'' A crooked smile tucked in at the corners of his mouth and made him look enormously desirable. "*You're* on the cutting edge of fantasy,'' he repeated with an amusement that squared her shoulders, brought up her chin and convinced her she was wrong about the enormously desirable quality of that smile. If she'd been wearing her glasses, he wouldn't have fooled her for a second.

"I guess you're going to have to educate me, Hallie. What kind of sexual fantasy would you consider to be 'cutting edge'?''

"Something more complicated than yours and infinitely more romantic. But you'll just have to fill in your own specifics. My fantasies are very personal and very private.''

He nodded, as if he respected that. Not that she thought he actually did. The elevator stopped and they stepped to opposite sides of the cubicle as Kimo stepped on. "Hi,'' he said brightly. "Where are you two headed?''

"Fantasy land,'' Rik said.

"In-your-dreams land,'' Hallie shot back.

Kimo glanced uncertainly from one to the other, then jabbed the elevator button for the very next floor and faced front. His foot tapped the floor until the elevator stopped, and then he was over the sill and into the hall-way. If he'd moved any quicker, he'd have had to pry open the doors with his bare hands. "Have a good one," he called over his shoulder as the doors closed again.

Hallie thought she'd enjoy a "good one" if she could ever figure out just what it was. She was fairly certain this wasn't it. Over the door, the floor numbers lit up and dimmed in sequence as the elevator passed by. At number eleven, she dived into the silence with a crisp, "Do you want to go to the room? Because if you do, I'll be happy to go back downstairs."

"I'm beginning to like elevator travel," he said.

"Perfect. I'll go to the room."

His gaze locked with hers and her knees began to tremble. *Must be anger,* she thought. She was so angry her knees were shaking. But they held her up until the elevator reached the fourteenth floor again, and this time, Hallie didn't wait to see if Rik was going to make a move. He could ride the elevator all the way to Christmas, but she wasn't going to hang around and make a fool of herself any longer. She stepped from the elevator into the hallway and walked briskly toward room 1413, head high, shoulders back, the hem of the sarong clipping her ankles, the hem of Rik's cardigan drooping low on her hips.

He probably thought she was an idiot. Hot. Cold. She might as well have the words tattooed on her arms so she could check them for reference and keep track of what she was running at the moment. Stopping in front of the room, she glanced at the numbers on the door and realized, with a sinking spirit, that she didn't have a key. She sagged against the door frame and wondered how she had gone from a successful afternoon of getting exactly what she wanted from everyone associated with the wedding to this disappointing state of affairs with Rik. How could she be so completely confident in business and so extraordinarily inept when it came to dealing with matters of the heart?

Not that her heart was actually involved. She'd just thought...wished...hoped... It wouldn't have worked out anyway. She'd tried this before and failed... miserably. Why had she entertained any thoughts that it might be different with Rik? Might be perfect. Might be better than perfect.

"I got tired of the same old view," Rik said as he came up beside her and inserted his key card into the lock.

He opened the door and waited for her to precede him, but she decided she wasn't moving. Not until she figured out how she could easily manage the myriad details of an elaborate wedding but couldn't coordinate the seduction of one reasonably willing man. "Thank you for bringing the key," she said. "Saves me a trip downstairs."

He leaned a shoulder against the doorjamb and held out the card. "You should keep this from now on. Put it somewhere...safe."

"I can think of only one place where it would be really safe, but I couldn't put it there." His gaze dropped in an oddly reluctant way to the curve of her breasts, when he lifted his eyes to meet hers, she regarded him skeptically. "It would be sort of pointless to lock the key card for the room in the hotel safe, don't you think?"

His sheepish glance darted past her into the room, dropped to the floor, then came to rest on the door frame just above her head. He cleared his throat. "Maybe I meant to say keep it handy, instead."

"Good idea." She dropped it into the pocket of his sweater and patted it flat against her side. "You can probably get an extra card at the desk. I'm sure Earlette will give you one. I think she likes you."

"She should. I'm a very good tipper."

"Then your worries are over. You can come and go as you please."

"From now on, I'll content myself with the go section of come and go. You need your privacy and I need..."

She waited, then prompted, "You need...?"

"My gear, clothes, shaving stuff." He shrugged. "You know."

Hallie sighed. He didn't need her. "Don't you need a place to sleep?"

"The couches in the lobby look comfortable enough. One of them will do."

"But that isn't fair, Rik. You had to sleep in a chair last night. You should have a real bed tonight."

"What makes you think I slept in a chair last night?"

"Because I slept in the bed."

"It's a double. A queen-size, in fact. You cuddled right up against me several times, but I had plenty of room."

She tried to get a good look at his eyes, tried to see if he was teasing her. But he was a little too close and her vision a little too untrustworthy. "I don't believe you."

He frowned and shook his head. "I suppose we could get back in bed and I could demonstrate."

"I suppose you could stop trying to make me think something happened last night when I know it didn't."

"Are you certain?"

"Absolutely certain." She might not be clear on everything that had happened last night, but she knew she would have remembered snuggling naked against Rik, tequila or no tequila. "You're wasting your time teasing me about it."

"Then I guess there's no reason to tell you what really happened."

"None whatsoever. Unless you want to hear me call you a liar."

"That would not be polite, Hallie."

Something in his voice sent a swirl of rich, warm anticipation through her. Maybe all wasn't lost, after all. "Rik?"

"Yes?"

"Can we go back and start this evening over again?"

He paused to consider. "How far back would we have to go?"

She took a deep breath. "How about the moment you kissed me good-night in the hallway and I said, 'Thank you, I had a wonderful evening'?"

"That would be one of those cutting-edge fantasy moments, I take it." She nodded and he pretended to consider the implications. "Well, even if this is your fantasy, I'm afraid I have to disagree on exactly what happened. I'm certain you didn't kiss me good-night until we were inside the room and the door was shut."

This was going to be all right, she thought as a thrill of excitement looped the loop around her heart. "The door was definitely open."

"No, you closed it. I remember because that's the moment I knew..." His voice trailed off and Hallie leaned toward him, wanting to grab the rest of that statement before it got away.

"You knew...?" she prompted.

"The moment I knew I was going to make love to you."

Her knees started knocking in earnest and she was

half-afraid windows all over the hotel were rattling in response. "That wouldn't be one of those standard, run-of-the-mill fantasy moments, would it?"

He shook his head. "Strictly cutting edge."

His smile was enough to set her shivering all over again. He wanted to have sex with her. They were going to have sex together. She was going to have a heart attack. Before anything even happened.

"I think I need to lie down," she whispered hoarsely.

He reached for both of her hands at once. "Come with me. I know just the place."

RIK KICKED THE DOOR closed and pulled Hallie into his arms in one synchronized movement. Not bad, he thought, for a man who was seriously out of practice in the art of being seduced by a determined woman. And as amazing as it was to him, Hallie seemed quite determined to seduce him. This wasn't the way he'd imagined the evening would end and it definitely wasn't the way he'd imagined the evening would begin. But here he was holding her, and here she was in his arms. And here they were together in their own hotel room. Complete with queen-size bed.

He didn't think anything Hallie might do after tonight could surprise him. Her proposition, however hesitantly uttered, had knocked the breath right out of him. And right now, she was doing it again...pressing her body against his, holding herself in a sensual juxtaposition, edging closer. And closer. When she cupped the back of his head in her hands and pulled his face down to hers, he wondered just how many days he'd have to spend with her before he stopped being surprised and fascinated and completely confused. A lot of days, he realized as she rubbed her thigh against his arousal. *Fantasy,* he thought, *thy name is Hallie.*

Just as he was getting into the swing of this particular fantasy, though, she brought the palms of her hands up and began bulldozing the material of his shirt back and forth across his chest. "Take your shirt off," she commanded.

"You first," he countered, a trifle concerned at her sudden hurry.

"I'm not wearing a shirt."

"Start with the sweater."

Her lips made a rapid sweep over his and then she was kissing him again while pushing and pulling and jerking at the sweater sleeves, and he wondered why she was in such a hurry. Not that he was adverse to getting naked and into bed with some degree of speed, but he did rather like to spend a little time working up to a frenzy. There was something to be said for slow, torturous kisses that sucked the energy out of a room and filled it with sheer anticipation.

The tip of her tongue limned his lips and he decided there was something to be said for frantic with passion, too. Hallie groaned as she struggled with the sweater, which was now off her shoulders but pulled inside out, the sleeves looped over and tangled around her hands. The more she wrestled with the sweater, the more anxious and agitated she seemed to get, and the more curious he became.

Even given the circumstances and the truly barn-raising kisses they were exchanging, he didn't think she'd had the opportunity to form a desperate passion and deep craving for his body. It was a good body, he thought. But in all honesty, he knew it wasn't this inspiring. Something was going on here that he figured he'd better investigate before she got him trapped into the sweater with her. "Hallie." He pressed a soft, let's-think-this-over kiss to her lips, grabbed the double helix knot of his sweater and began to untangle it. "Hallie?"

She stopped trying to kiss his cheek, lips, chin, neck and shoulder all at once and looked up, her eyes shining with excitement and nervousness and panic.

Panic? He double-checked the expression in her eyes and frowned. "Do you have a late date?" he asked. "Because I have all night, and, while it's very pleasant to be the seducee, I have a few moves of my own I think you might enjoy."

Her shoulders drooped and she sighed. "I knew this wasn't going to work."

"Now, wait a minute." He began to feel an edge of panic himself. "I'm not complaining. I just thought maybe you had a hidden agenda I ought to know about."

She shook her head miserably. "I just wanted to get it over with."

All right. So it wasn't his body she craved with a ravenous hunger. He could deal with that. But getting it over with as speedily as possible wasn't exactly his idea of mutually consensual, much less emotionally satisfying, sex. He moved his hands to her shoulders and pushed her to the full extension of his arms. She wasn't wearing her glasses and he wanted to be sure she was looking at him with as clear a vision as possible. "You've taken some pretty tight swings at my ego tonight, Hallie, but that one connected. I don't know what is going on inside that pretty head of yours, or who the hell you've been sleeping with before now, but for the record, I don't have sex just to 'get it over with.' I'm not that shallow. And I can't believe you are, either."

She blinked, several times in succession. She swallowed, once. She opened her mouth, closed it, then opened it again. "I'm...not good at this, Rik. I should have just told you right up front that this was an experiment."

Great. Now he was an experiment. "Hallie, you're killing me here. Please stop trying to put a good face on this. I'm a reasonably strong person. I can take rejection."

"No, you can't. I mean, this isn't about you at all." She stopped, and he could see her struggle to compose her thoughts. "I've been very unfair to you tonight, I know. So why don't we forget what just happened and watch movies or something." A tiny spark of hope flickered in the misery of her eyes. "We could order a pizza. Or popcorn."

Rik pursed his lips before slowly releasing his grip on her shoulder and putting his fingers back to work on the knot of sweater sleeves. "No popcorn," he said. "No pizza. And no TV. A half hour ago, I could have had a nice evening just having dinner with you downstairs in the dining room. Fifteen minutes ago, I might have been able to forget that you said you wanted to have sex with me." He paused, glanced at her pensive, troubled expression, then went on. "Okay, so I wouldn't have forgotten that you said it, but I could have had a nice time just thinking about it. But now we're stuck. We can't go back to a moment in the past and start over and we can't jump ahead to some imagined moment in the future and pretend this one never happened."

"I've ruined it. I knew I would, and I did."

"What are you talking about?"

She shook her head in abject misery. "Nothing."

"Nothing," he repeated just as miserably. If she'd slapped him, he could have walked out, good and mad, and slammed the door for his trouble. If she'd simply said she'd changed her mind, he could have told her it was all right and maybe taken her to dinner to show he was a sensitive, mature kind of guy. If she'd only stopped talking five minutes ago—right after that "let's-get-it-over-with" remark—he could have written off the evening he'd planned with her and spent a few mediocre hours commiserating with Jack, instead. But no, she had to sound so forlorn over *ruining* his evening that now he had no choice but to do something to convince her she'd done nothing of the kind. Hallie Bernhardt, he thought. Another way of saying high maintenance.

"Look, Hallie, you changed your mind. That's allowed. It's all right. Believe me, you haven't wrecked my life."

She frowned at him. "I didn't change my mind," she said. "You changed yours."

Amazing. "I don't think so."

Her frown turned pensive. "You didn't?"

"No. I objected to making love at the fast-forward setting, and I objected to being cast as the rat in your experiment, but I... On second thought, I did change my mind. Just now." He turned toward the door, turned back, warming to his newfound indignities. "This sounds like one of those made-for-television movies where the woman's biological clock is ticking and she tricks a man into sleeping with her so she can have a baby with minimal male involvement."

She stepped right up to him and glared, which would have had more of an effect if he hadn't known he was nothing but a blur from this angle. "I'll have you know my *clock* isn't even close to ticking. And what's more, I keep a condom in my billfold for just this kind of situation. I was not only *not* trying to trick you, I was actually trying to protect you from disappointment.''

Rik rubbed a pensive thumb across his jaw. "All right, Hallie. I surrender. Tell me what you want and I'll do my utmost to oblige.'' Then he was getting the hell out of this room. No matter what she said.

"I wanted a good-night kiss. Just a pleasant good-night kiss.''

He nodded. "Do we need to go back out to the hallway for that?''

"No. That won't be necessary. We can do it here in the room.''

"Okay. Just checking. Didn't want to cause a ruckus by kissing you in the wrong location.''

She stepped back and looked at him…and every instinct urged him to start backing toward the door. "So…?'' she questioned.

He managed to move one foot behind the other. "So,'' he repeated.

"So…maybe this wasn't such a good idea, either.'' She tried to gesture, but her hands were still caught in the silly sweater and her action only aroused his sympathy. He reached for the fabric knot, wanting to help, wanting to leave, wanting to kiss her for no good reason he could fathom. Intent on the task, he wasn't prepared when she bumped against him and planted an awkward kiss on the lower half of his mouth. And he wasn't prepared when she corrected her aim and nudged his lips with a determined kiss. And he wasn't at all prepared when she sighed into the kiss and his foolish heart changed his mind about leaving.

Chapter Ten

"Hallie," Rik whispered, his hands still on the sweater sleeves, his lips still distracted by hers, his body still interested, his better judgment on red alert. "Tell me, now. Is this your idea of a good-night kiss?"

She nudged his lips again. "I don't know yet. It might be just the beginning of a good night."

He freed the knot in record time and drew the cardigan from her hands. As it fell to the floor, he moved his palms over her forearms and past her elbows. "Next question...is this your idea of a seduction?" She tensed slightly. He hoped it was just his imagination, a little paranoia left over from the last time they'd been this close.

She confirmed his assessment with another ultrasensuous kiss. "If I say yes, what are you going to do?"

He tested her sincerity with a husky suggestion. "I'm going to kiss you," he said. "A long, slow, wet kiss that may last the rest of the night. And we're both going to enjoy the hell out of it."

"We are?"

She didn't sound overly confident. He tried again. "If I say yes, what are you going to do?"

"Worry."

Rik frowned, wishing now he'd gone while the going was good. "When a man suggests he's going to kiss you, Hallie, there are only two answers. Yes, no or a variation thereof."

"I'm not worried about the kiss, Rik. It's the—" She pulled away. "What did I do with my glasses?"

"They're in the bathroom, but unless you feel you just have to get a closer look at me, you don't need them. I can tell you, I look even more confused than I sound."

"Damn," she said, which didn't shed any light on the subject at all. "Damn, damn, damn, damn."

"My sentiments exactly."

She looked up, frowned and raised her chin with decision. "All right. I didn't want to have to tell you this, but I can't see any way out of it."

"You *are* married." He wouldn't have believed he could feel any worse, but suddenly, anticipating what she was about to confess, he felt terrible. Worse than terrible. Sick with disappointment.

"No." The brisk denial clicked with impatience and truth, and his spirits rebounded. "But I was married, and that's the problem. Do you remember my telling you about my disastrous wedding? Well, this may be hard to imagine, but the honeymoon was worse."

He ran through a mental list of the things that could ruin a honeymoon, avoiding anything that couldn't be classified as an act of God. "A hurricane?"

"No."

"Flood?"

"The weather was perfect."

Not an act of God, then. Maybe an accident. "Food poisoning?"

"No. Everything was perfect. Except the sex. It was…"

"Not good?" he suggested, hoping to spare her the embarrassment of confiding further details. Or maybe he only wanted to spare himself. To keep from feeling the sympathetic and protective pangs he was already experiencing.

"Worse. It was awful."

He didn't want to know this, Rik thought. He really didn't. "I've heard that happens sometimes. All the pressures of the wedding and the travel and—"

"It didn't happen."

"The excitement." He stopped cold. "You didn't have sex on your honeymoon?"

She shook her head no and repeated, "It didn't happen."

"Well, I can see where a couple might be overtired and decide not to…" Actually, he couldn't see any explanation at all. Not with Hallie. If he'd been there… That was a stupid thing to think, much less imagine. "So the honeymoon wasn't great," he finished. "There's more to a marriage than great sex."

She took a deep breath, which only seemed to accentuate the pain this subject obviously caused her. "You probably don't want to hear about this and I wouldn't even mention it except that, well, I wanted you to know I'm not a tease. That's the reason I've been wearing your sweater all day. I was self-conscious about baring my shoulders and—and advertising a product I couldn't deliver."

Rik suddenly developed an overwhelming dislike for her ex-husband, whoever he was.

"And there is a reason I'm having so much difficulty

getting past this initial awkwardness. I really do want to be with you, to…to…''

He reached for her then, wanting to hold her, comfort her, ease her past whatever awkwardness she felt, stop her from confiding in him about her past sexual experiences. But she stepped over to the bed and stood there, as if she were waiting for the ax to fall.

"There's no easy way for me to say this, Rik. If I could pretend it didn't matter and had nothing to do with what probably now isn't even going to happen between you and me, I wouldn't say it, but…'' She took a deep breath and exhaled with a rush of words. "Brad and I didn't have sex before the wedding. I wanted to wait and he didn't get a choice. Ironically, if I hadn't been so obstinate about being a virgin on my wedding day, the honeymoon wouldn't have been such a disaster. But I was, and it was, and the fact is, I had this small physical deformity that I didn't know about until…well, it prevented intercourse, and so, consequently, there was a lot of frustration and anger and upset and it ruined the honeymoon.''

She drew in another breath. "My physical problem was corrected with a single visit to the doctor's office, but sex was never very good after that anyway, and Brad found solace elsewhere and we divorced, but the reason I told you all this is because I'm terribly attracted to you and I really thought it might be different with you. But I can't help getting tense and worried and afraid that it won't be different and…'' She shrugged. "I thought you ought to know that even if I ripped off all your clothes and shoved you onto the bed, you're bound to be very disappointed when it comes to fulfilling the rest of the fantasy.''

Her shoulders drooped and she sank onto the edge of

the mattress, as if having to tell him had been so difficult she no longer had the energy to stay standing.
Which was all right with him. He was feeling a bit
shaky himself. "Hallie?" he said gently. "How many
men have there been since your divorce?"

For the first time since she'd begun telling her story,
she blushed. "Two," she said. "But only one who
made it past the...preliminary stage."

"Two," he said, shaking his head. "A woman like
you."

"I know. I can't believe it, either. You'd think I'd
have enough sense to run like a maniac the minute an
attractive man glances my way, wouldn't you?" She
looked up with a crooked frown that set his heart askew.
"But here I am and here you are and here's yet another
dismal episode in the history of my love life. I am sorry,
Rik. I should never have led you on as I did. I shouldn't
have advertised a product I couldn't deliver."

If he could have gotten his hands on her ex-husband
at that moment, Rik knew he would have gained im-
mense satisfaction from taking the guy on a scenic helicopter tour right into the jaws of Hurricane Bonnie.
He'd scare the living daylights out of the little twerp,
settle the score with the sorry excuse for a husband
who'd left Hallie in this condition, told her she *advertised* sex every time she bared her shoulders. And he
had a couple of extra seats in the copter for any other
man who'd added to her lack of self-confidence in the
sexual arena. "You don't owe any man an apology,
Hallie. Least of all me. Your experience is atypical at
best and just plain unlucky at worst. What I can't understand is why you've let it bother you for so long?
Aren't there counselors who specialize in this sort of
thing?"

She looked offended. "I'm not going to tell a stranger about this."

"You told me."

"Only because I thought you deserved an explanation."

"You didn't have to explain. You're not responsible for my sexual satisfaction."

"You have to admit we were heading for a frustrating and disappointing situation."

"I'll admit nothing of the kind."

"No matter what you say now, Rik, this evening would have ended just as badly one way or the other. I saved you from an embarrassing moment in the near future when you would have had to pretend you weren't disappointed and I'd have had to pretend it didn't bother me to have been the cause of it."

"Do you feel responsible for everything that goes wrong in the world, Hallie? Sex shouldn't be this big an obstacle in your life."

"Easy for you to say. You've probably never had bad sex."

"No, in my experience, there's no such thing."

"In my experience, there's nothing else. I ought to take a vow of celibacy and make the world a better place for the men with whom I come into contact."

He wanted to smile at the pointless melancholy in her voice, but he didn't. "That would be a tragedy. Especially for this particular male."

She sighed. "It's very nice of you to say so, Rik, but trust me. Weddings are as close as I ever need to get to fantasy. I figure that for every couple I send off on a wave of wonderful memories, it makes up a little for the disaster my own wedding was. And if they live happily ever after...well, it pleases me to believe I had a tiny part in launching them toward a long and fulfilling marriage.''

He thought she was selling herself pretty short, but it was obvious she'd made up her mind, and that left him with no place to go. He couldn't touch her. Or kiss her. Not now. Not when she was so thoroughly convinced she was the Medusa of sex, turning men to stone with her ineptitude. He wanted nothing more at that moment than to prove to her how wrong she was, but there were rules about that sort of thing, and now that she'd made him privy to her very personal, very intimate history, he couldn't make a move unless she made one first.

The silence stretched awkwardly and he glanced toward the window, where the night was peering in like a hungry man at a well-laid table. ''I guess I'll get my things together and go.''

''Where?''

''I'll bunk with Jack…until Stephanie arrives,'' he said, startled by the realization that since he'd met Hallie, he'd hardly given the woman of his dreams a fleeting thought. ''That way I can keep him out of trouble.''

''I thought you were the one who tried to get him into trouble.''

''Lately, I've just been trying to save his butt.''

''You're quite the rescuer, aren't you, Rik?''

''Some guys are born heroes,'' he said with a shrug. ''Jack, for instance. But me? No, I just sort of fall into it by default. Like with you. If I'd had any self-preservation skills at all, I'd have developed a passionate interest in televised golf the minute you walked into the bar. But you looked so bedraggled and lost and so determined not to show it, I all but leapt over a dozen rattan bar stools to rescue you from thirst.''

''Bedraggled?'' Her hand went to the feathery bangs

on her forehead as if the puppeteer had just pulled the coordinating string. "I told you it was a bad haircut."

"Yes, and I told you I liked it excessively."

"Oh, no, you didn't." Her unexpectedly saucy smile shook his resolve. "You said it wasn't that bad."

"But you didn't believe me, did you?" He shook his head in wry humor. "What would it take to convince you? Letting my hair grow out into the same style?"

"Don't do it, Rik. You'll be sorry."

His lips curved with wry humor. "I hate to be bothered with flyaway hair...that's a problem for helicopter pilots, you know."

"I can imagine."

"Hallie?"

Her gaze met his and his pulse quickened. "I think your haircut is tremendously flattering. You're a very lovely, very desirable woman and I sincerely hope you never take that vow of celibacy."

She looked, as forlorn as a single wilting rose. "Oh, I'll probably be tormenting men for years to come."

Rik watched her with a vaguely alarming resignation, realizing he had long since passed the point of wanting to leave, of being able to just walk away. He was suddenly, resolutely certain that sometimes rules were made to be broken. "Hallie? Could we start this evening one more time? Go back to talking about your haircut?"

She looked at him, frustration, curiosity and hope mingling in her hazel eyes. "Why would we want to do that?"

"So I can tell you how much I love the way your hair feathers around your face." He took her hands in his, and pulled her to her feet. "And how it wisps across your forehead and curves under at the back of your neck." He cupped her face in his palms and worked his fingertips into her hair. "And how it's all I can do to keep from burying my fingers in it." He drew her inexorably closer, letting his mouth descend slowly toward hers. "So I can tell you how desperately I want to make love to you."

"You're just saying that to cheer me up."

"Believe me," he whispered against her earlobe. "I'm not that unselfish."

"But, Rik, I—"

Her voice squeaked on the words and he pressed a fingertip against her lips, shushing her. "Hallie, unless the curtains catch fire or the glass in the window shatters, I don't want you to utter another sound."

"Oh...."

He took advantage of the rounded shape of her lips, and with every ounce of sincerity he could muster, he kissed her. A long, slow, wet kiss he hoped might actually convince her not to talk anymore. Gathering her protectively into his arms, he drew her with him, down into the soft, enveloping comfort of the bed.

Hallie fell hard. Oh, she landed on the mattress, sure. But her heart fell with a thump...halfway between hope and despair, squarely between the certainty of inevitable disappointment and the possibility a miracle could occur and save her from a lifetime of longing for something more than she could ever have.

Rik was solid fantasy, from the point where his breath mingled with hers to the weight of the leg he draped so erotically across her thigh. His body paid homage to the tremors of yearning that shimmered through her like pretty lies, and there was an overpowering intimacy in the provocative kisses he offered for her approval.

As his lips moved along the curve of her neck to sup

at the hollow of her throat, Hallie hung suspended between knowing she had to stop him and knowing she'd rather die than utter a word of denial. But she'd done everything in her power to give him fair warning. It was out of her hands and in his. Oh brother, was she ever in his hands. With every touch, he demanded her response, her absolute attention. There wasn't room for argument or fear or the memory of any other place or any other time.

Rik held her, and it was the way she'd always dreamed of being held by a man. He kissed her, and her heart leapt like a long-lost lover into his keeping. He touched her breast, and she ached to bare it to the massage of his seeking fingers. She wanted to bare her body and her soul to him, to lie naked in his arms, to invite him to explore each untouched, unclaimed, unbearably achy part of her. She wasn't afraid. Not with Rik. Fear of pain and disappointment was a conditioned response, something she could fight past, conquer. She knew, without knowing how she knew, that he would guide her through the jungle of intimacy to a place of mutual pleasure. A sharing place. A place of emotional communion. She trembled with that awareness, with the need to let this moment be the one she would remember from this time forward.

Her fingertips curled insistently into his shoulders when he pulled her against him and his tongue plied her lips, teasing, tasting and finally plunging deeply inside her mouth. Sensations ran rampant in a frenzy of impulses. Should she touch him? Where? She'd gotten this far before and... No, no, she hadn't. She'd never burned with such heat, never wanted anything as desperately as she wanted to please Rik at this moment.

She pushed back and reached for his shirt, fumbled

with a button, then made a mighty effort to rip off the
shirt. And wound up with her hand trapped and crumpled into a useless fist between their respective bodies.
He stopped kissing her...sort of. His lips were still
there, against hers, but his breath was warm on her
cheeks and chin. "Are you trying to rip off my
clothes?" he asked in a hoarse whisper as he nibbled
at the corner of her mouth.

"Yes, but it would be easier if you'd cooperate."

"Making love doesn't have to be rough, but it
shouldn't be easy. Fight a little for your pleasure, Hallie.
Claim what you want. Take it."

"Take your shirt off," she said with more confidence
than she felt. Could she just order him to do that? What
if he said no? What if he—

He unbuttoned the shirt, his large hands moving
down the row of buttons with amazing agility, his
knuckles brushing with sure intent against her breasts,
her stomach, her self-control. "There," he said as he
tossed the Hawaiian print aside and settled again beside
her. "Is this what you wanted?"

"Yes...for the moment." Her fingers splayed across
his bare chest, enchanted by the hair-roughened texture,
delighting in the power he had given her with his ready
capitulation. No other man had ever asked what she
wanted, much less told her to take it. "Kiss me," she
commanded.

He did...but not like before. No, this time the kiss
went longer and deeper, grew more demanding. She decided to get drunk on his kisses. She would command
him to kiss her until she couldn't remember her own
name. But for as long as she lived she would remember
the name of the man who kissed her until she was in-
toxicated with his taste, his scent, his touch.

"Rik." She didn't even know she'd whispered his name until he pulled back to stroke the hair at her forehead.

"Hallie," he whispered in reply.

"Don't stop," she said.

He propped his head on his hand and regarded her thoughtfully. "What will you do if I stop?"

For maybe half a second, she wished she had on her glasses, but decided this situation didn't call for twenty-twenty vision. Only twenty-twenty resolution. "I'll die," she said matter-of-factly. "Then I'll haunt you. You'll never be able to kiss another woman for the rest of your life. I mean it."

He smiled, a slow, lazy, seductive smile. "I believe you."

"Then kiss me again. And again. And—"

Pressing his finger to her lips, he let it slide with torturous lethargy down her chin to her throat, to the hollows of her shoulders, to the knot of fabric that kept her covered. "There's no hurry," he said, his gaze following the track of his fingertip. "No hurry at all."

Hallie hardly felt the tug that untied the knot, was barely aware of the sarong unwrapping around her. Her focus was on the ache inside her, the desire she knew was unfolding in her eyes and reflected in the gaze he returned to her. She was aware only that she wanted to make this experience as new and novel for him as she now knew it would be for her. His warm, willing flesh met her warm, willing breasts and she melted into the feel of his bare arms around her bare shoulders, the awareness of his lean, muscled body pressing against her with a tender but adamant request.

He slipped his hand under the elastic of the bikini

bottoms—the only bit of clothing between her and nudity. Hallie tensed. "I love spandex," he said.

"It's the new style," she replied, breathless. "Lingerie that goes from bath to beach."

"To the floor." He rolled the stretchy material to her thighs and then pulled the bikini pants down and off in a move she couldn't help but admire. She usually had to coax off anything so elastic, but Rik didn't seem to have a bit of trouble. He just manipulated her legs and the elastic and—

The fear encroached on her newfound resolve, the doubts clamored behind the closed doors of her memory. She couldn't do this. With every tiny step toward intimacy, she was growing more tense, remembering past attempts, past frustrations. She would freeze. Rik would get angry. He'd try to hide it, but she would know. He'd tell her to relax and she'd try. But it wouldn't work. Why had she ever started this when she knew how it would turn out, how nervous and anxious and tense she would be? How—

"Hallie?" His voice was close and comfortable against her ear. His hands stopped touching her intimately and pulled her into his embrace. "Tell me your fantasy. One you've never told anyone else."

She couldn't do that. Not even if she was fully clothed, much less while lying naked in his arms. But the words poised on her tongue and began tumbling out, precisely because she was naked. And vulnerable. And desperate to distract herself from the remembering. "I'm dancing," she began softly, letting the words unfold as they would. "And people are watching, but I don't care. I'm completely uninhibited, completely unaware of the admiring eyes on me. I feel wild, free, desirable. I'm a vamp, a seductress, a tigress awakening from a long sleep. Then one man steps out. He takes me in his arms and we dance together, our bodies so close it's impossible to tell who leads and who follows. We could be Astaire and Rogers, we're so good together, so perfectly in sync, so completely aware of every move the other makes." She stopped, blushing in the circle of Rik's arms, wondering once again how she could be so confident, so very secure in every area of her life except this one. "Sounds like *Fantasia* meets *Dirty Dancing,* huh?"

"It sounds very intriguing." His hand stroked her shoulder. Down to her elbow. Back to her shoulder. Elbow. Shoulder. Elbow. Shoulder. A long, smooth stroke that kept her from bolting up and locking herself in the bathroom. "Very cutting edge."

"It's silly. I won't even do the hokey-pokey in front of my friends."

His hand absently soothed a wayward tendril of her hair. "As long as we're fantasizing, cast me as your dance partner."

Hallie sighed. "I can't dance, but I'd be better at that than I am at this. That's for sure."

Rik shifted beside her, rolling her onto her back and pinning her with a tender gaze and a gentle pressure. "Who told you you can't dance? And whoever it was, I beg to differ."

She frowned up at him and was glad she couldn't see very well. Otherwise, she'd be half in love with him already. "Your turn," she said. "Tell me your fantasy...unless it's the same old run of the mill, standard—"

"Okay, okay," he interrupted. "Here's my fantasy. An updated one strictly for your benefit. I'm locked in a hotel room with a beautiful woman with a knockout

of a haircut. She's beautiful. She's smart. She's
hot…and she *wants* me. But she's been mistreated by
men in the past and she doesn't trust me, either. She's
afraid, which is understandable. But suddenly she stops
being afraid. She stops worrying. And she stops talking.
She kisses me like she really means it, and then she
kisses me again."

"And then…?"

His smile was warm and winsome. "That's up to
her."

"But it's your fantasy."

"Yes," he said. "Exactly."

"My purse is there." She pointed in the general vi-
cinity. "Inside my briefcase."

"Do you *need* your purse? Right now?"

"*We* need the condom inside my purse. Right now."
She couldn't believe she'd said that, couldn't believe
she was actually in need of the packet she'd carried for
God only knew how long. "Unless you carry one in
your hip pocket."

"No," he said, and she was charmed to see him red-
den a little at the thought. "I've been—"

"In the jungle. I remember. Well, I only have one,
so…"

"I'll get it," he said, and did so, shedding the last of
his clothes before returning to the bed and her.

He barely had both knees on the mattress before she
was reaching for him. She wrapped her hands around
his neck and pulled him down to her, her lips parted
with invitation and sheer, sensual yearning. Rik was different, she thought. She was different with him. It had
been a long time since she'd allowed herself to be held
and touched and desired. She wouldn't spoil it.

She sank into the mattress, into the welcoming hollows beneath her, his welcomed weight above her. Whatever happened was out of her hands....

No, it wasn't. Rik had told her to fight for her pleasure, to claim it, take it for herself. In the past, she had reached this point of arousal before and either plunged ahead with a wild, frantic hope that somehow all would be well, or withdrawn, letting sex happen to her, trying to ask as little as possible. But not this time.

When his hand grasped her breast and his thumb flicked the nipple to an aching peak, she took possession of her response and gave back kiss for kiss, touch for touch, need for need. She gave her lips, her breath, her heart. Where he touched her, she burned, and she made certain he felt her heat. She wanted him. She wanted nothing but him. She wanted everything he had to offer her.

Passion spilled over the edge of restraint and he hungrily took her breast into his mouth, bringing her arching up against him. His hands never slowed their steady, intoxicating, seductive sweep from one end of her body to the other. She cupped his hips in her palms, pressed his hardness to her and parted her legs to allow him entry as a terrible, wonderful anticipation flooded her senses.

He entered her with care, but no hesitation, taking her from the point of her greatest dread to the point of unbelievable pleasure in an instant. Their lips met and clung as he began to move inside her. Sensation followed pulsating sensation, and she could only cling to him, trusting him to guide her through the maze of emotions and desires. He was forever gentle, excruciatingly tender and desperately intent on fulfilling her fantasies. Fantasies she hadn't had the courage to share with him, but that he seemed to know anyway. When release came in great, gulping, wondrous spasms, Hallie called out his name, "Rik. Rik." His mouth came down to hers then, in a long, slow, wet kiss that lasted the rest of the night.

Chapter Eleven

"Oh, it's you."

Waking to the sound of Babs Brewster's voice was not Rik's idea of a morning in Paradise, but he did his best to be cheerful. "Good morning, Mrs. Brewster." He yawned into the phone as Hallie stirred to life beside him. "You're up bright and early."

"It's eleven," Babs informed him promptly. "And I was trying to find that wedding coordinator. The desk clerk rang through to you again by mistake."

"Hmm." Rik glanced at the huddled lump under the sheets and smiled. "The phone lines must still be messed up. I guess you'll have to try the call again."

"I'll do that." Her tone of voice was perfectly pleasant, so Rik figured he only imagined the word "moron" tacked on, by inflection, to the end of her sentence. "Do you and Jack have plans for the day?"

"Plans?" he repeated, distracted by the bare leg Hallie drew from beneath the covers and draped over the top of the tangled sheets. "Uh, yes. Yes, I do."

"Dan had planned to play golf, but with this nasty weather, he's going a bit stir-crazy. Would you mind if he joined the two of you?"

Rik tried to concentrate. He really did, but there was

an inch or two of bare hip emerging from under the sheets and he just couldn't focus on conversation. "What?" he said hoarsely. "He wants to join us now?"

Babs's sigh was classically impatient. "No, not this minute. Later. Whenever you and Jack do whatever it is you're planning to do."

Rik suddenly recalled Lynn, Sam and Big Bird and their places on his agenda...and Jack's. "Oh. My plans with Jack. That doesn't happen until later this afternoon and I'm not sure Jack will want company then. But he's probably not doing a thing now. You ought to call him, Mrs. Brewster."

"I tried. He wasn't in his room when I phoned a little while ago."

"Hmm." Rik smiled into the one eye Hallie had open, wanting to kiss her awake...and back under the covers with him. "I can't imagine where he might be."

"It seems to me no one is where they're supposed to be when I call," Babs said pointedly.

"Darn weather," Rik said with feeling.

"Humph," she said, and hung up.

Hallie stretched and slipped out of bed. Rik made a grab for her but missed as she headed for the bathroom. "Hey, come back here."

She tossed a sleepy, sexy smile over her shoulder and he went weak with wanting her. "No," she said resolutely. "I have things to do."

"So do I and you're at the top of the list."

She paused in the doorway, one hand on the frame, as she looked longingly back at him. "I have to work." But her tone waffled with lack of conviction. "Babs is going to be calling any second now."

"Don't answer the phone."

"I'm here to work, Rik, and I'm getting a late start as it is."

He stretched back on the bed, hands behind his head, content to watch her just standing there, her hair all tousled, her body language indecisive, her face tinted with the look of a woman well loved. "I'll help," he offered. "I have a luncheon appointment at twelve-thirty, but until then I'm yours to command."

"You're offering me a whole hour and a half of your day?"

He waggled his eyebrows. "It will be the *best* hour and a half of your day, kiddo."

The phone rang and she pursed her lips. Rik waited, willing her to ignore the insistent intrusion—and everything else in the world except her desire to be with him. The hesitant, uncertain woman of last night was gone, though, replaced this morning with organized, efficient and no-nonsense Hallie Bernhardt of Bernhardt Bridal. But he wasn't fooled. She had been magnificent, once she got past the idea she was inept in the art of love-making. He'd thought he would be her mentor, gently instructing her in the myriad pleasures possible between a man and a woman. But she'd developed her own style rather quickly and he'd spent most of the night marveling at her innate expertise. Early on, he'd made a fast trip to the hotel gift shop for a box of condoms, but there had been a couple of moments during the passion-filled night when he feared he'd underestimated her enthusiasm and endurance. At the time, he wasn't sure if he wished he'd bought the economy-size box or if he merely prayed she'd tire out before he was forced to confess that he wasn't really Superman.

"What are you smiling about?" she asked, then

added, "Never mind. I don't care what you say, I'm getting my glasses."

"The better to see me with?"

Her gaze dropped like a rock to the sheet draped across his lower body. "The better to get a good look at—"

"Now, now," he said hastily. "Remember my sensitive male ego. It may be large, but it's extremely fragile."

"I was going to say, the better to get a good look at the room service menu. Don't men think about anything but sex?"

"Well, sure. Let's see. There's football, basketball, baseball, soccer. Work, food, helicopters, electronics, the space program, politics..." He broke off with a frown. "No, basically, it's sex right down the line."

Hallie shook her head and disappeared into the bathroom, closing the door—firmly—behind her. Rik smiled, pleasure uncoiling inside him like the warmth of good scotch. Stretching lazily, he settled more comfortably against the pillows to consider what had happened to him somewhere between yesterday afternoon and today. Hurricane Hallie. She'd swept into the hotel bar, into his sights, and nailed him.

He'd been minding his own business—well, trying to mind Jack's, anyway. But definitely not looking for a relationship. And now he was in one. At least, he thought this had all the markings of a relationship, plus the added benefit of being with a real, live person. Not just an imaginary, maybe kind of thing, as Stephanie had been. Of course, being mostly imaginary, Stephanie had the advantage of being whoever and whatever he wanted her to be. Reality hadn't been a true consideration.

And until last night, Rik had preferred it that way.

He noticed in a glance a single plumeria petal on the pillow next to him and picked it up. There was no way of knowing where the rest of the flower was now. Petals were probably strewn from the elevator to the door of the thirteenth room on the thirteenth floor. But at least one petal had made it into bed with them, much the worse for wear, and the scent remained. He closed his eyes, inhaled the crushed fragrance and remembered Hallie, taking his breath away with a look, stealing his reason with a kiss, slipping into his heart when he wasn't looking.

HALLIE WIPED THE STEAM from the mirror and checked her appearance, wishing she had a hair dryer, real underwear and a book on the etiquette of postseduction small talk. Last night had been perfect, in practically every way. Rik had been fiercely tender, a wonderful lover. If she thought about it for ten seconds, she could imagine herself in love with him, could imagine a lifetime with him, home, family, the whole nine yards. But she mustn't let her imagination run wild. Just because she'd finally found a man with whom sex was good... Oh, okay, not good. Phenomenal. Well, that didn't mean she had to fall head over heels in love with him. Probably the best reason not to. Rik had his own agenda. She had hers. She was Boston. He was Tarzan. She had a wedding to plan. He might be in love with someone else.

Swallowing hard, Hallie scrubbed her freshly washed hair with a towel, then used one corner of the terry cloth to wipe more condensation from the mirror surface. Rik had been her brave, bold experiment, her fantasy come to life. She had no reason to be disappointed because it couldn't last.

With a frown at her water-streaked reflection, Hallie lifted her chin. It was this room, she thought. This unlucky thirteenth room. Where else would someone as unlucky as she find the man of her dreams?

Beyond the closed door, she heard the phone ring. Pulling her with shrill insistence to the reality of another woman's wedding, another bride's dream come true. In this instance, it was more like the mother of the bride's dream come true, but the point was, Hallie was merely a labor-saving device, a bridge between everything that could go wrong and the beginning of a happily-ever-after. And last night had been merely a perfect moment in a not-so-perfect life. It was just a good thing she hadn't been wearing her glasses then.

If she could have gotten Rik into focus at any time during their long, loving night, she might have believed, quite foolishly, that she was lucky in love, after all.

"YOU HAVE TO DO something about this." Babs gripped Hallie's arm with the strength of a determined mother. "I promised Stephanie a wedding cake with a fountain and you promised me she could have it. Now that horrible Jacques person is leaving because of the hurricane and the cake isn't ready and something will have to be done."

Hallie tried for a confident, leave-it-to-me tone of voice. "I'll take care of it, Mrs. Brewster. But you're going to have to trust me. Jacques is temperamental and he takes special handling. Let me do the talking. Please."

"All right, but when we leave his office, I want to

have that cake in my pocket. Not literally, of course, but you understand my meaning.''

''Perfectly,'' Hallie said.

Unfortunately, Jacques didn't understand the first thing about mothers of brides. Within two minutes of their arrival in his office, he referred to Babs as a fruit-cake—pronouncing it in four insulting syllables. Not an auspicious beginning. Two minutes later, Babs accused him of being a kitchen nazi with the IQ of an apple strudel, and it was all downhill from there. Hallie wanted to tell them both they didn't have a brain cell to spare between them. But diplomacy was her stock-in-trade and she jumped in decisively when the opportunity came.

''We're going to stop yelling and start talking,'' she announced. ''Mrs. Brewster? Let me talk to our chef in private. Jacques, sit down before your blood pressure hits the danger zone.'' Amazingly, they did as directed, and Hallie reopened the negotiations, resigning herself to the hassle of shipping chocolate-marshmallow cookies to the island for the rest of her life.

But Jacques's fondness for Mallomars had taken a back seat to his aversion to hurricanes, and when she left his office, she had nothing in her muumuu pocket except a recipe for disaster.

''YOU'D BETTER COME with me.'' Dan Brewster cupped Hallie's elbow and steered her in the direction of the lanai. ''Something will have to be done before Babs sees this.''

This was a huge, flapping, hulk of canvas mounded over a mass of perspiring orchids that took up the center portion of the hotel lanai. Harold stood, arms akimbo, ball cap pushed back on his head, lips pursed in a disapproving pucker. "Never seen anything like it," he said. "About an hour ago, a truck pulls up and the guy tells me he's delivering flowers. I didn't think much about it at the time, just told him to take 'em inside to the concierge and she'd take care of the delivery. Next thing I know, I'm bein' paged all over the place. Seems like your florist—" he looked at Hallie directly "—is closing shop today and heading inland. So your orchids arrived a day early."

"Babs isn't going to be happy about this," Dan said.

Hallie lifted a corner flap and was nearly jerked off her feet when the wind caught it and billowed the canvas like a giant balloon. Harold grabbed the canvas and Dan grabbed her and the three of them wrestled the thing back to its anchor. "This is going to end in a lawsuit," Hallie said, feeling the steel of desperation. "And before it's over, the Brewsters and I will own that florist's shop."

Harold shook his head. "Unless you were able to get a better contract than St. Peter, that florist is covered against hurricanes and such." He looked pointedly at the roiling gray sky and white-capped swells. "And whether you believe my bunions or the local weatherman, that there is about to be an act of God."

"MAYBE YOU SHOULD cancel your appointment." Rik looked up from admiring his nephew to frown at his sister. "That's a heck of a wind out there, Lynn."

"Since when did you develop this overweening concern about Mother Nature?"

"I didn't live in the Amazonian jungle for thirteen years without learning to pay attention to the weather. And this looks bad."

"I'll be back before either one of you has time to

miss me. Well, before Sam does, at any rate." Picking one last french fry off her lunch plate, Lynn popped it in her mouth, and began unstrapping Sam from the high chair. He kicked his feet and reached for Rik with a let's-blow-this-joint expression. Rik lifted Sam out of the chair and up onto his shoulders, where the little dickens grabbed a healthy handful of his uncle's hair and held on.

"You're sure he'll be all right with me?" Rik asked, still wavering between confessing his scheme to Lynn— thereby ensuring she would cancel her appointment and never let him baby-sit Sam again—and telling himself he was worrying way too much about a harmless little joke. A baby fist bopped him on the head and he opted for confession. "Sit back down," he said. "There's something I have to ask you."

"LET ME GET THIS straight." Lynn leaned across the table where they'd eaten lunch, no longer interested in the leftovers on her plate. "You're going to save Jack from a loveless marriage by depositing Sam on his doorstep and telling him it's *his* baby?"

"I'm not going to tell him," Rik hedged. "Big Bird is going to."

"And you think he's going to believe that?"

"Well, no, probably not, but he's going to have to give it some thought. And Sam is so darn cute, how can Jack help but realize what he'll be missing if he goes ahead with this marriage?"

"You may be overestimating your nephew's charm," Lynn said as she shifted her whining, wiggling baby from one side of the narrow restaurant booth to the other. She tried to put him back in the high chair and nearly provoked a tantrum for her effort. "He isn't always this adorable."

Rik wished he didn't care one way or the other what Jack did to screw up his life. But he did care. A lot. "I knew it was a dumb idea. But I thought…hoped…"

"It is a dumb idea, Rik, and if you weren't my favorite brother, I'd tell you exactly how stupid it is. But if you expect me to tell you not to pull this nutty scheme, you're in for a surprise. You understand, of course, that if I didn't love Jack almost as much as I love you, I'd never agree to the two of you passing my baby back and forth like a football. But I trust you both and I know how carefully and affectionately you treat a football. So as long as you promise me Sam will have constant, caring attention, a clean diaper and his bottle when he wants it, you have my permission to let Jack baby-sit."

Rik made a face and reached for Sam. "I won't let anything happen to him," he promised as he lifted the little guy across the table. "You can depend on that."

She scooted out of the booth, pulling the diaper bag behind her. "If I couldn't, believe me, he'd be coming with me." She waited until they were almost at the door before she hit him with the one question he should have expected all along. "Who's the girl?"

"Girl," he repeated. "I don't know any *girls,* Lynn. Except you, maybe."

"Woman, then. Come on, who is she?"

"Who is she who?"

"The person who put that sparkle in your eyes. If you've met someone, you'd better tell me."

"You always ask me this, Lynn, and I always answer the same way."

"Sparkling eyes are a result of clean living," she repeated dutifully.

"And B vitamins," he added. "I despair of ever getting you to remember that part."

"Well, I despair of ever having a sister-in-law." She wrinkled her nose in disappointment. "I'd hoped that since you're starting your new business here and looking for a house to buy that maybe there was a woman involved. I want you to find the right woman, get married and have cousins for Sam. He needs someone to play with, you know."

"He has Keanu." Rik raised the baby in the air and blew bubbles on his belly, causing Sam to laugh aloud. "And he has me. Why would he want some other baby stealing the limelight?"

"He just does," Lynn said. "So any chance he may get a kissing cousin anytime soon?"

Rik tried to look suitably shocked, although the idea was not without appeal. He could imagine a couple of cute kids with their mother's funny haircut and John Lennon glasses. Whoa. That was moving pretty fast, even for a take-action kind of guy like himself. "No chance, kiddo," he told Lynn firmly. "I'm already behind the production curve as it is. Even if I got married tomorrow, it would take nine months to deliver a cousin for Sam the Man here. And I'd want to spend a little time just being married before starting a family. That'll make Sam at least three or four and past the point of caring about a younger cousin, believe me."

"Which tells me nothing about the current state of your love life."

"Exactly what I intended." He held open the door and they walked out of the restaurant and into the sting of the tropical wind. Rik used his body to shield the

baby carrier—with Sam tucked inside—from the damp
air. "You're sure it's all right if Sam spends the afternoon with Jack?"

"You're the one who sounds uneasy," Lynn said
with a short laugh. "Trust me, Rik, Jack isn't going to
be fooled by this. He knows me. He knows about Sam.
It may take him a few minutes to figure this out, but I
can't believe it will take much longer than that."

"Jack hasn't seen you since you stopped wearing
braids and overalls, and the only picture he's seen of
Sam is the one where you and Keanu are in Washing-
ton, D.C., and the three of you are knee-deep in snow.
Sam was only three months old then and bundled up so
well he could have been a monkey. I don't think Jack
will connect the name with you, either, because I usually refer to Sam as Keanu, Too. So, there's a chance
it will take a while to discover just whose baby this
really is." Rik shrugged. "It's my only hope of getting
Jack to stop and think about what he's actually doing
with his life."

Lynn slipped her arm in his and pecked him on the
cheek. "I'm so proud you're my brother," she said.
"And I'm so happy you're going to be living here,
where I can see you more than twice a year."

"I bet you say that to all your brothers."

"Yeah, I do. You and all those other imaginary sib-
lings we never had." She caught the handle of the carrier and lifted the blanket so she could kiss Sam goodbye. "You take care of your uncle, you hear? Don't let
him get in any trouble and don't pay a bit of attention
to any story he tells you about me and a rock star,
understand?"

"Now you've done it," Rik said, turning the carrier
so the contact between mother and baby was lost.

"Now I'll have to tell him. Go on to your doctor's appointment. He'll be just fine."

She pinched Rik's side with firm affection. "You make certain he stays that way." Then, bowing her head against the wind, she jogged off to her car.

"Okay, Sam, my man," Rik said to his nephew. "This is our big adventure. I really hope you like Big Bird."

"WHAT ARE YOU DOING?" Hallie's voice echoed up the stairwell and Rik jumped a guilty foot. Spinning around, he let go his hold on the fire escape door, which clicked shut behind him as he watched her climb the last few steps to reach the landing.

"Babs isn't out there, is she?" Hallie asked in a conspiratorial whisper.

He shook his head, his vocal cords paralyzed by the start of surprise she'd given him. Or maybe it was the way she looked with her hair combed, but still tousled, her body disguised by the tentlike muumuu and her eyes clear and focused behind the duct-taped glasses. He would have cleared his throat then, but couldn't because his heart was in it.

"I came up the stairs—thirteen flights—just so she wouldn't be able to corner me in the elevator."

"Who?" he asked huskily, lost in the sudden wonder of being near her again.

"Babs. Who else?" Hallie looked at him with concern, then reached for the door, but he stopped her by putting his hand over hers.

"You don't want to go out there," he said.

"I don't?"

"No." He did not want her walking out and into the discussion going on in the hallway between Jack and a big yellow bird. A delaying tactic was obviously in order, so with no hesitation and a still-racing heartbeat, he kissed Hallie the way he'd been thinking about kissing her all day.

It was better even than he'd imagined. And when he drew back to share a smile with her, she sagged against him, obviously a little weak in the knees, as well. "Where have you been all day?" He caressed her cheek with a gentle stroking of his finger. "I missed you."

"I've been in the hotel all day. So, what are you doing in the fire escape? Are you hiding from Babs, too?"

He shook his head and thought quickly. "It's, uh…Celeste."

"Really?"

He nodded for effect and hoped she was buying this. "She…he…came back to get my measurements."

"That's odd."

"It is?"

"Mmm-hmm. She told me she'd fit Dan's and your tuxes Saturday morning."

"I don't see how she…he…can do that."

Hallie smiled. "It's only you that needs fitting. She can hem Dan's trousers and make what few adjustments are needed for you on-site."

"She…he…didn't measure me."

"She eyeballed it."

"What?"

"She said she has a good eye for size."

"If my tuxedo is too small, my size and I are going to be offended."

"You'll get over it." She reached for the door handle, then paused. "Is Celeste really out there?"

"Let me look." He cracked the door, checking for

Big Bird tracks and making certain Hallie couldn't see anything except him, blocking her view. "Whew! She's gone."

"I can't imagine what she was doing back here, anyway."

"Probably looking for her tape measure."

Hallie sighed. "I have her tape measure because I was supposed to measure you."

He closed the door. "You," he said, tapping her lightly on the chin, "may measure me anytime, anywhere, any way you want."

"Appealing," she said. "But not on my schedule."

"Cancel something." He reached for her. "Cancel everything for the rest of the day."

She came up on tiptoe to kiss him and make him all weak in the knees, then she pulled back with a frown. "Get out of my way. I have to bake a cake."

"What?"

"Jacques the chef has left the hotel. He's going inland before the hurricane hits."

"Would that be the hurricane that's going to miss the island by miles?"

"That'd be the one."

"Hasn't he heard the weather reports?"

"He's been listening to Harold's bunions." She tilted her head to the side to look up at him. "Have you ever baked a cake?"

"I've made cornbread in a skillet. Does that count?"

"I don't think Babs will be happy with a cornbread wedding cake. Charles will just have to do the best he can."

"Charles?"

"The assistant chef."

"Well, there you have it," Rik said, pleased to be

able to stand here and watch the expressions passing over her face. "You don't have to bake a cake. Chef Charles will be glad to do it for you."

"It's my responsibility to see that Stephanie and Jack get the cake they ordered, and if I have to supervise the entire baking process, then that's what I'll do." She bypassed him entirely and caught the handle, moving him aside as she pulled open the door and stepped into the hallway.

Rik followed her, practicing a speech in his head in case he ran a-*fowl* of his own plan and had to convince someone he'd never seen Big Bird before in his life. There was one lone yellow feather on the carpet outside Jack's room, and of course, Hallie saw it.

"Wonder where that came from," she said as she unlocked the door of their room and walked inside.

He picked it up and carried it into the room with him. "It's from a rare bird. A Storkus Rentalis. That's the scientific name for Hawaiian chicken."

Hallie laughed. "I suppose these Hawaiian chickens are migrating to the Big Island and stopped to spend the night at Paradise Bay."

He shrugged and closed the door. "Well, even chickens get a night out every now and then."

"And how do you know so much about chickens?"

"That's easy," he said. "I'm Superman."

Taking off her glasses in one seductive move, she sauntered slowly toward him. "Superman," she crooned, playing him like a banjo. "Something very sinful is about to happen to you."

"My mother warned me about women like you. She said you'd have Kryptonite in your pocket and lust in your heart." Hallie's march on his Atlanta didn't falter.

"I'd almost given up hope of ever meeting one, though."

With a determined look in her eyes, she put her palms against his chest and pushed him onto the bed. Grabbing the hem of her muumuu, she pulled it over her head and Rik lost what little reason he had left.

Lost it, that is, until he heard the faint, distant and unmistakable sound of a baby's cry. Sam. "Well, hell," he said.

Chapter Twelve

"You're supposed to fold in the egg whites, not beat them into a frenzy." Frowning fiercely, Chef Charles snatched the wire whip and the bowl of cake batter away from Hallie. He gestured toward the door, flinging the whip with wide, wild abandon and splattering her with tiny flecks of batter. "Go."

She wiped her face with the corner of her apron, feeling particularly useless and completely annoyed. Men, she thought. Powermongers, every last one of them. Give an assistant chef free rein, and he turned out to be a commando just like the one before him. Give a man a piece of your heart, and he decided he had better things to do. Rik had played her like a violin. He'd shown her a whole new world of feelings, made her hunger to explore them, then when she tried to do just that, *pfft*, he disappeared. One minute on the bed. The next minute, out the door. No explanations. One minute, *Bring it on, mama!* and the next minute, *Well, hell!* and gone with the wind. So she'd bundled her disappointment and come down to lend Charles a hand with the cake. Now he was showing her the door.

"Look, Charlie," she began.

"Charles," he corrected. "*Chef* Charles."

Hallie dusted her hands on the front panel of her apron. "Look, *Chef Charles*," she said, wondering where these guys came by their pompousness. "It's my job to make sure this wedding cake is made to Mrs. Brewster's specifications. If you don't want me to help, I'll just stand over here and observe." She scooted into an inconspicuous corner. "Think of me as quality control."

"Think of me as out of control," he replied snippily.

Hallie didn't see why he was so upset. "You know what a great opportunity this is for you to prove yourself. With Jacques gone, you can create your own masterpiece."

"A vanilla cake with a champagne fountain," Chef Charles said with a sneer. "I am an idiot to agree to make such a cake."

He was even beginning to sound like that *id-ee-ot* Jacques, pronouncing words as if he'd been raised in Provence instead of Iowa. "The hotel has a stake in this," she said.

"Hotel, ha!"

Hallie looked around the busy kitchen, noting the hurry and scurry of the staff, the shouted calls for a waitperson to take up a room service order. Then her gaze landed on a familiar face.

"Kimo," she said. Then again, louder. "Kimo!"

He looked up and gave her a frazzled smile. "Hello, Ms. Bernhardt. Is there something I can get for you here in the kitchen?"

"No, thanks. I'm just baking a cake."

He nodded, as if she had every right to be in the midst of the chaotic kitchen. "I hope you can find space in the oven," he said. "With the road washed out between the resort and the rest of the island, we've been swamped with food orders."

Hallie felt a sudden chill. "The road washed out? When?"

"A little while ago. Some of our employees are stranded on the other side and can't make it in to work, so we're a tad understaffed."

"The road washed out." She repeated the words as the ramifications began to sink in. "But isn't there another road?"

Kimo shook his head, slapped mustard onto a bread slice and mayonnaise on another and cut a tomato into thin sandwich slices with perfect precision. "We're stranded, too," he said. "Stranded in Paradise Bay."

"I'VE GOT IT under control, Lynn." Rik paced as far as the phone cord would allow. "Everything is fine. Sam's fine. I'm fine. We're all fine. The hotel is already battening down the hatches in case Hurricane Bonnie should come ashore. From the last report I caught, the worst scenario is that we'll catch the tail of the storm sometime later tonight. I swear to you, Sam is getting the best of care. Between me, Jack and the chicken, he's got the best nest in the hotel."

"Chicken?" Lynn repeated dubiously.

Rik paced back to the bedside table. "Just another way of saying you have nothing to worry about. Now, go on home before the weather takes another turn for the worse. I'll call as often as I can get a line out of the hotel, but if you don't hear from me, do not...I repeat...*do not* panic. Sam is in good hands." He heard the key card slide into the slot and looked toward the door. "I've got to go, Lynn. My roommate is back."

"Roommate?" his sister asked. "What roommate?"

"Your future sister-in-law," he said into the receiver, then hung up as Hallie entered the room. She looked great...for a woman who must have been standing in the path of a cake when it exploded. Her hair was dotted with flecks of batter and there was a clump high on her cheek and another on her chin. The apron she wore rode low on her muumuu, and a forensics expert would have had a field day with the stains.

Rik had never wanted to kiss a woman more than he did at that moment. "Hi," he said.

"Hello."

Cool tone. Standoffish manner. But not unfriendly. "Is the cake done?"

She leveled a very patient gaze on him. "No. The road's washed out."

"I heard. So, what happened to the pastry chef? Did he get stranded in town?"

"He banished me from the kitchen." She would have walked on past Rik and into the bathroom, but he caught and held her hand. "Bad day in Paradise?" he asked softly, and when she nodded, he squeezed her hand with sympathy. "Me, too."

Her hazel eyes came up to meet his, transfixing him with their compelling blend of colors. "Really?"

"Really. It's been a hell of an afternoon...but suddenly, things are looking up."

She sighed. "Maybe for you."

"Does that mean you aren't glad to see me?"

"It means the only person I'd be glad to see right now is the weatherman, and only if he was predicting sunny skies."

"We're only catching the tail end of Hurricane Bonnie, and although that's bad enough, it isn't as devastating as a direct hit would be. Things could be much worse, Hallie. Much worse."

"Nice try, but nothing less than sunshine is going to cheer me up."

"Ah, a challenge."

She pulled her hand free of his. "Forget it. There's nothing you can do to make me feel better."

"Ooh, a double-dog dare."

She resumed her trek toward the other room. "We can't even order room service."

"We can't?"

"You should see how crazy things are in the kitchen. Even Kimo's making sandwiches."

"That young man is going to wind up as employee of the month. He's everywhere."

"But never where you might expect. I wonder what his real job is."

She didn't sound as if she really cared one way or the other, and Rik cleared his calendar for the evening in one imaginary swipe. Not that he had had much to do, anyway. Certainly nothing as pressing as finding out if what he'd experienced with Hallie last night could possibly be as great as he remembered. And checking on Sam. That was it. Sam and Hallie.

"I'm going to take a shower," she said. "I don't suppose... No, never mind."

Surely she wasn't too shy to invite him into the shower with her. "What?" he asked, settling his fingertip just below the ribbon of cake dough on her chin. "You don't suppose what?"

"The airline found my luggage?" she finished.

Hallie was definitely tough on his ego. "No such luck."

"Thirteenth floor," she said.

"Thirteenth room," he agreed.

She sighed again, then, with a shrug, stepped inside the doorway.

Rik followed her, unwilling to be as far away from her as the other room. "You know, I was just about to take a shower myself."

"You just got out of the shower. Your hair's still damp."

"Rain," he said quickly, indicating the window with a wave of his hand. "It's raining out there."

Her glance confirmed it. "Rain is something of an understatement. You don't expect me to believe you were out in that, do you?"

"Maybe."

"Maybe not."

He leaned down to kiss the words right off her lips. "I'm lying. I just got out of the shower. But I'll happily go to the kitchen and dunk myself in cake batter if it means I can shower again with you."

Her eyes widened, and a slow, sensual smile punched him in the backs of the knees.

"But it's such a long way to the kitchen." She pulled his head down, brought her face to his, and the phone rang.

HALLIE SHOWERED ALONE, thinking of various—and not entirely painless—ways to tattoo "hot" and "cold" onto Rik's ears, so she'd have some way of knowing when he was going to rev her up and then dump her for the nearest distraction. All in all, things looked pretty bleak.

She wasn't going to be able to stop this hurricane from destroying Saturday's wedding. The hotel wall facing the ocean quivered from the knockout punches of the wind. Even inside the bathroom, there wasn't enough insulation to block the noise of the storm outside. The resort was under siege and Stephanie's wedding was the sacrificial lamb.

Even if Saturday dawned clear and sunny, even if the hurricane did no damage whatsoever, even if a miracle occurred at this minute, Hallie knew she could never put this wedding together again. Like Humpty Dumpty, it was cracked beyond repair.

On the other hand, she'd thought the same thing about her own heart. Until Rik kissed her, loved her, mended her mistaken beliefs. So what was she going to do?

All she could do about the weather was to admit she had no control over it, wait it out and do what she could when it was over. All she could do about Rik was enjoy what time the storm would give them and try not to lose her whole heart when it was over. That...and unplug the phone.

But when she came out of the bath, all freshly scrubbed, sweet smelling and as naked as the day she was born, he wasn't on the phone. He was standing by the window, as naked as she, holding a Hershey's bar in his hand. "I've solved our problem," he said with a smile.

"What problem?"

"The interruption thing." He gestured behind him at the locked door. "I put out the Do Not Disturb sign."

"That should put a stop to the walk-in traffic."

"I also unplugged the phone."

"Oh," she said softly, wanting this seduction to unfold like a slow-motion ballet, so the images of Rik would imprint themselves on her memory and she could have them to remember during the long, cold winter ahead. "What's the candy for?"

He looked at the naked chocolate bar in his hand. "I know how much you love chocolate kisses, so I thought maybe you might think of this as a substitute for cake batter."

"Oh," she said. "Oh, wow."

SOMEONE KNOCKED on the door. And knocked. And knocked.

"Someone's at the door," Hallie whispered, her voice raspy, her body heated with soft yearning. "Can't they read?"

Rik rolled out of her arms with an apologetic murmur. "Guess not. I'll get rid of them."

"They'll go away if we ignore them."

"I'm not taking any chances." He stubbed his toe on a chair and tripped over a shoe in the middle of the room before he found his clothes and hastily pulled them on. Hallie listened to his every move, smiling to herself in the dark, stretching a little as she heard his footfalls past the bed and the locks on the door being pulled back.

"Jack," Rik said, and then the door closed as he stepped into the hall, leaving Hallie alone in a bed already growing cold without him in it.

She had this bad, she thought. As bad as the wind howling outside the window. She wondered what Jack was doing and what time it was. And she decided if Rik left her for Jack, she would do something drastic, like enter a convent and become a singing nun.

But Rik returned a few minutes later, slipping into bed beside her and rescuing her from a dismal future. "It was Jack," he said, finding again the exact spot under her ear that, when nuzzled, drove her insane with need.

"Mmm," she said on a sigh. "What did he want?"

"A place to bunk for the night."

"What's wrong with his place?"

"He's allergic to chicken feathers." Rik nuzzled right on down to the hollows of her shoulder, then moved on to her breast, and Hallie was so glad she didn't have to sign up for singing lessons right away that she completely forgot to ask what Jack was doing with a chicken.

RIK LEFT EARLY the next morning to see what he could scavenge for breakfast and came back with a baby.

"I really just wanted a bagel," Hallie said as she stared, dumbfounded, at the infant. "Where did he come from?"

"See, Sam—" Rik directed his smile at the baby boy "—I told you she'd be delighted to have you join us for breakfast."

"Rik," Hallie said, keeping her tone pleasant but insistent, "where did you get this baby?"

"From Jack."

"Jack?"

Rik nodded. "Well, in all honesty, Jack got the baby from me. Although he doesn't know that."

"This is your baby?"

Rik extended one baby hand to her in a marionette kind of handshake. "This is Sam, Hallie. Sam, this is your aunt Hallie."

Hallie reluctantly wrapped her hand around Sam's, then discovered she was reluctant to let go. "He's so little," she said. "And so cute."

"That's his job. Not being little—he'll outgrow that

soon enough—but cute. Cute's his job.'' He made a clucking noise and Sam laughed. ''He does it really well, too, doesn't he?''

''Yes, you do, don't you?'' One baby smile and Hallie was in the cooing spirit, her face right in Sam's when he stuck out his baby tongue and blew a spray of bubbles at her. It was the sweetest thing that had ever happened to her. ''He's so precious. Can I hold him?''

Sam seemed a little unsure about the switch, but Hallie jostled him in her arms until his weight felt natural against her side. ''Where did you come from?'' she asked him, then turned the question to Rik. ''What are you doing with this baby?''

''Baby-sitting him so Jack and Dani can get some sleep.''

''Jack and Danny?'' Hallie suddenly felt a little nauseated. ''Jack's sleeping with Danny?''

''Remember me telling you about the chicken? That's her.''

''Danny is Dani.'' Hallie concentrated…hard. ''But Jack's marrying Stephanie, so why would he sleep with Dani? I mean, even sharing the same bed would be a bit risky at this stage.''

''Depends on what you believe the risk to be.'' Rik all but radiated delight.

''And you believe the risk is…?''

''Marrying Stephanie. But I'm hoping Dani and Sam, here, have changed his mind.''

''Jack's mind,'' she clarified. ''Changed Jack's mind about marrying Stephanie.''

''Mmm-hmm.'' He put his hands over his face and played peekaboo with Sam, who seemed much more interested in inspecting Hallie's haircut. ''Too early to tell, but there are definite signs of strain in the bride-groom."

"Are you telling me you set Jack up with another woman and her baby to change his mind about marrying Stephanie?"

Rik had the grace to look guilty. "No, I didn't. Not exactly. It's not the way it sounds. Not the way you put it."

"Then how is it, Rik? Because I don't see a positive angle to this…this prank."

"It isn't a prank. I consider it a rescue effort."

"For Jack? You think you're rescuing Jack?"

"Look, I didn't set up this thing with Dani. I called Patty's Party-Grams and ordered a singing telegram special delivery, thinking someone in a costume would drop off Sam and leave Jack holding a thought-provoking dilemma. That's all I intended. But somehow Jack talked Dani into staying and helping out with Sam and the road washed out and…well, she's still here."

Hallie grappled with the facts as he related them. "And what about Sam? He's still here, too, in case you haven't noticed."

"Now, wait a minute, Hallie. I know this sounds really nuts. Hell, even my sister told me it was crazy, but she didn't have a problem with it and I don't think you have any business getting upset over it, either."

"Your sister?"

"Lynn. Sam's mother."

"She let you use Sam as a bargaining chip?"

"I was baby-sitting, anyway. And she knows Jack. It's not as if she left him with complete strangers."

"No, just complete idiots."

Rik's lips tightened. "She'd have been here to get him last night if the road hadn't washed out, and besides, she knows Sam is okay. I've been in touch with her by phone.''

"That was considerate of you." Hallie felt the tug of Sam's little fingers in her hair and she reached up to gently untangle them. "Here, you'd better take him. He's been passed around to too many people in the last few hours as it is. He doesn't need another stranger in his life.''

Rik took the baby without comment, put him on the floor and gave him a set of keys to chew on. Then he turned to Hallie again. "Look, I'll admit this isn't the brightest idea I've ever come up with, but I was desperate to stop this wedding.''

"*My* wedding?"

"You're just the wedding coordinator, Hallie. It isn't your wedding.''

"It's a Bernhardt Bridal wedding, Rik. That makes it mine, and frankly, I can't imagine why you'd do something so stupid to try to stop it, no matter whose wedding it is.''

"Because it's a mistake.''

"Oh." She was conscious of being angrier than she had reason to be, but it didn't matter. He had no right to interfere. "In your opinion, Jack shouldn't marry Stephanie.''

"They're not in love.''

"Really? And how do you know that?"

"Because I know him. And I know Stephanie.''

Something in the way his gaze glanced off hers and dropped to Sam alerted her, and an uncomfortable possibility pinched her with annoying precision. "So, you're planning to rescue Jack *and* Stephanie from this disastrous marriage.''

"I'm doing my level best.''

"And once you do, then what, Rik? Are you sending Jack back to the Amazon to lick his wounds, leaving you to comfort Stephanie?"

His gaze came up and his shoulders went back in an angry affirmation, but Hallie had the pieces together now and could only wonder why she hadn't caught on before. Men didn't try to rescue other men from making a mistake. She'd observed too many best men who weren't crazy about the groom's choice of bride. They'd shrugged and minded their own business. Just as Rik would have done...if he hadn't had his eye on Jack's bride. "You're in love with Stephanie," she stated flatly, not wanting to make it a question and have to hear his answer. "That's why you said your own relationship was on hold. You're not trying to rescue Jack. You're in love with his fiancée and that's the reason you want to stop this wedding."

A reflection of her own hurt and anger flashed in his eyes, as fierce as the storm outside. He paced to the window, parted the drapes and looked out. "Maybe my original motives weren't entirely unselfish."

Sam tired of the keys and crawled after Rik.

"So what does that make me? Any port in a storm?"

"Hallie." He reached for her but she turned away. "I was wrong about Stephanie," he continued. "Not about stopping the wedding, but about my feelings for her. I only imagined I loved her. Until I met you and discovered what love really is."

Hallie would have liked to believe that, but the odds were against it being true, no matter how sincere Rik sounded. She was here. Stephanie wasn't. It was only natural he'd hedge his bets and try to keep his options open. Then, if Stephanie did marry Jack, Rik would have a backup woman to warm his bed and assuage his wounded pride. Maybe he did love Stephanie. Maybe he really believed she was the wrong woman for Jack. Either way, it made no difference now. Love didn't happen overnight and it didn't happen between two people who had nothing in common except the bad luck that had landed them in the same thirteenth room on the thirteenth floor of a honeymoon hotel.

Hallie gathered her courage before she looked back at him. "You don't have to say you love me, Rik. It's thoughtful of you to try and make me think I'm someone special to you, but it isn't necessary. I'm in the business of making happy endings for other couples, not for myself."

"Hallie," he said. "Listen to me. I love you."

"Oh, please, Rik. Be honest with yourself, if not with me. This has been a lovely affair, but that's all it's been. When the storm's over, we'll say goodbye and never see each other again. You know that as well as I do."

He looked thunderstruck as he bent to lift Sam into his arms. "I don't know anything of the kind. This isn't something that happens to me every time I check into a hotel. I'll admit I have no idea how we'll work out the logistics of this relationship, but—"

"This *is* the relationship, Rik. This room, this hotel, now. That's it. We're as much a creation of this damn hurricane as the havoc it's wreaked on Stephanie's wedding."

"Are you saying we're a disaster, Hallie? You and me?" His voice was tight with anger and Sam began to cry. Rik comforted him, and for a moment, Hallie wished she could seek solace in his arms, as well.

"I'm saying, Rik, that you're mistaking sexual satisfaction for deeper emotion."

Surprisingly, and without much humor, he laughed.

"Men don't confuse sex with emotion, Hallie. That's one of our charms."

"Well, women do. Which is why I'm telling you this now, so there won't be any misunderstanding when I leave. You don't love me, Rik. You don't even know me. I'm just someone you enjoyed being with for a few days during a hurricane. One of those, 'if you can't be with the one you love, love the one you're with' kind of deals."

"That's the way you see this?" he asked hoarsely. "That's the way you think of me?"

"Don't take it so personally." She tried to sound nonchalant, as if her heart wasn't throwing itself against her ribs in protest.

"Don't take it personally," he repeated. "I'm talking about seeing you for the first time and feeling a strange, compelling attraction. I'm talking about the way your hair feathers around your face and the way you pretend you have everything in perfect focus, even though you can't see a thing. I'm talking about what happened to me when you started dancing the bossa nova in the lobby. I'm talking about falling genuinely, deeply in love with you somewhere between the lobby and the thirteenth floor. And you're telling me I shouldn't take it personally when you say I don't know what I'm talking about?"

"Look, Rik. The truth is, I don't dance," she said in her best no-nonsense tone of voice. "Not the bossa nova or the Macarena. Not in the privacy of my own home and never, ever, in a hotel lobby. No matter how much tequila I've had to drink or how often you tell me it happened."

"What about your fantasy? You dance there. You told me so."

She shrugged. "I was lying."

"You're afraid." He said it with conviction. "You're afraid to risk an upset stomach, so you don't drink orange juice. You're afraid of ultraviolet rays, so you avoid the sunlight. You're afraid of failing, so you take no risks. Your wedding wasn't the biggest disaster of your life, Hallie. Neither was your marriage. The biggest disaster is the way you've focused on creating the perfect wedding for someone else, the way you've shut yourself off from discovering who you might be if you took that leap of faith and admitted you're in love with me, too. The forever kind of love, Hallie. The kind that doesn't fit a timetable or a schedule. The kind that happens to you when you're lucky enough to accidentally fall into it."

"Ah. There's your mistake, Rik. We had great sex and I'm really appreciative of how loving and tender you've been. But it had very little to do with luck and nothing at all to do with love."

"That's what you think." He started toward her, Sam in his arms, determination in his eyes, and Hallie held up a hand to stop him. Incredibly, regretably, he stopped. "I don't want to hurt you, Hallie. I just want to talk."

"Send me a singing telegram," she said, and walked out of the hotel room, leaving a resonant silence in her wake. Unless one counted the storm, Sam's baby gurgle and the plaintive cry of her own foolish heart.

Chapter Thirteen

"What do you mean, the cake is gone?" Hallie had spent the entire afternoon trying to salvage what remained of her painstaking plans for Stephanie Brewster's wedding. The orchids were gone, innocent victims of early delivery and no extra room, refrigerated or otherwise, in the hotel. The lanai was a wind tunnel, separated from the rest of the hotel by flapping canvas and the hellacious storm. The musicians had canceled, the minister had called in his regrets. Even the bride was stuck in Honolulu. The wedding wasn't going to happen. At least, not on the luxurious scale Hallie had planned. Certainly not on the extravagant one Babs had envisioned.

Rik would be thrilled, though. He'd sabotaged the wedding without lifting a finger—other than shuffling his nephew into the card deck. Superman to the rescue.

Hallie banned thoughts of Rik and turned her attention to Chef Charles, who lounged, loose-limbed and the worse for champagne, in his former boss's chair. "I made the cake," he said with a slack-jawed grin. "All six nillie-vanillie layers of it. Then we ate it."

"Who ate it?"

"The staff. By two o'clock this morning, it was

pretty evident the hurricane was heading this way. We were all exhausted and hungry and stuck at the hotel. I thought they deserved a treat, so when the cake was done, we ate it. So sue me.''

"You and the rest of the staff ate six layers of wedding cake.''

Under different circumstances, Hallie would have chewed him up one side and down the other. But frankly, she was glad the cake, at least, had served a useful purpose. Nothing else about this wedding had turned out pleasurably.

"So, what kind of dessert can you whip up for tomorrow?'' she asked. "On the outside chance this illfated couple decides they still want to get married.''

Charles smiled and leaned across the desk. "I can get you a heck of a deal on the cake they're using tonight for the party. It's mostly cardboard, but it's a *big* cake.''

"What party?''

"The bachelor party. There was supposed to be a stripper inside the cake, but she couldn't get here because of the road being out and all.''

Hallie did not want to know this.

"So, what about a dessert for tomorrow? What can you do?''

He grinned. "Not interested in the big cake, huh? Well, that's okay. Now, about tomorrow. Supplies could get a little low, depending on how long the storm lasts, but I think I could manage a fruit salad or maybe a coconut pudding.''

"Fine. I'll be in touch.'' She stood, suddenly angry about a lot of things, all of them having to do with Rik and the bachelor party and the big cake in the kitchen.

Hallie went straight to the kitchen with a half-formed idea of sabotaging Rik's plans for the bachelor party.

She found the cardboard cake and the scattered remains of the wedding cake. Pinching off a bite of one, she observed the other. Stuck back out of the way, the party cake was a good size and prettily decorated. Only a male would think of this setup, she decided. Putting a woman inside a cake for the entertainment of a group of otherwise sane men who pulled out their rowdiest, raunchiest behavior for the occasion called a bachelor party.

Brad had had the mother of all bachelor parties. At least, that's what he'd told her. And the stripper had had the body of a *Playboy* centerfold. Or so he'd said. Hallie winced at the memory, wondering why she'd thought it was all right for him to say such things to her, wishing she had had then the confidence she had now.

But for all her confidence, the Brewster wedding was one happy ending she couldn't deliver. Much as she hated to admit it, Rik was right. Stephanie and Jack weren't in love. She knew that simply because she knew Rik wasn't the kind of man who would betray a friendship. He would never have entertained thoughts of being in love with Jack's fiancée unless he'd been absolutely certain there was no love involved in the match. So why were Jack and Stephanie getting married? And what difference did it make? She'd been hired to deliver the wedding they'd bought and paid for and she was going to fail. Miserably.

"Darn newlyweds," grumbled a voice behind her. "Always kissin' and huggin' and leavin' cake crumbs on the floor."

"Oh, hello." Hallie smiled at Dave, who was sweeping cake crumbs off the floor. "I guess you're stranded here, too, huh?"

He looked up, seeming a little surprised to find anyone nearby. "Why would I want to go home, anyway?" he said. "No one there. Just a house. Like me. An empty, old house."

"I thought you were married." Hallie pinched off another bit of wedding cake and stuffed it all in her mouth at once when she saw him frowning at the crumbs that drifted through her fingers to the floor.

"Was." He angled the broom between her flip-flops and swept up the fresh crumbs. "Five times I married the same woman. Same stubborn old woman. She left me five times, too. Came back. Left. That was our whole married life. Darn stubborn old woman."

Hallie swallowed the cake and felt sorry for him because there didn't seem much point in feeling sorry for herself. "You don't like being alone," she said.

"Nah. I don't mind that. It's bein' lonely that bugs me. I see all these young couples kissin' and huggin' and it makes me wish..."

"Makes you wish...?" Hallie prompted.

He lifted his old blue eyes to hers. "I'll tell you, missy. If I had it to do again, I wouldn't get married five times to the same stubborn old woman. I'd do whatever it took to keep her."

"Oh." Hallie didn't know if there was any underlying wisdom in Dave's statement. He just kept on sweeping, grumbling under his breath. A lonely old man in a place swarming with couples young with love. Her glance strayed to the cardboard cake. Maybe it was only lust that brought these couples together. Maybe none of them had started out really in love at all. Maybe they only had the hope of love, the confidence that what they felt was enough to stake their dreams upon, enough to last a lifetime.

She wouldn't know. She'd thought she loved Brad and look how that had turned out. Now she loved Rik and look how that was ending. She'd go back to Boston, tail between her legs, her first—well, okay, second, counting her own—failure of a wedding under her belt, and he'd stay here. With Stephanie. Who probably wouldn't be married to Jack. Who probably would have Rik wrapped around her little finger in no time. Well, Stephanie could have him.

Wait a minute. Hallie stopped herself from nibbling on the remaining wedding cake. What was she doing? Maybe she didn't believe Rik could fall in love with her overnight, but why was she so ready to cast aside any chance that he might grow to love her over time? Why was she turning him over to Stephanie without so much as a whimper, much less a fight? Wasn't she as worthy of having a wonderful man like Rik in love with her as Stephanie was? She didn't even know Stephanie. But she knew Rik. She knew the tenderness in his touch, the fire in his kiss, the utter abandon she felt when she was in his arms. This might not be love, but it was a damn fine substitute.

So, what to do? Go back upstairs in the hope he was there? Apologize? Grovel? Say she'd been wrong to call him a liar, to throw his declaration of forever love back at him with a hateful remark about their lovely affair? She'd lied to him, too. She'd said she didn't dance, not even in her fantasies.

Her gaze strayed to the cardboard cake and she gulped. There was nothing like action to convey a message. Nothing like showing rather than telling. And sometimes there was nothing to do except take your pride in your hands, stuff it down the bra of your bikini and pop out of a cake. If that's what it took to keep Rik in the first place, what was she waiting for?

THE HURRICANE CHANGED course, lashing the Hawaiian Islands in a final, furious tail-whip of an attack. But as the wind wreaked havoc outside, the Lanai ballroom was awash with males determined to ignore the danger and enjoy the moment. Rik hadn't been keen on the idea of this bachelor party until Hallie had left him wrung out and utterly frustrated. Women made no sense, he thought. One minute they were all cuddly and lovey-dovey, the next minute they were telling a guy he knew nothing about commitment and less about how to communicate. So, what was a guy to do?

The obvious answer had come from an unexpected source. Dan Brewster had taken one look at Jack and Rik earlier in the day and pronounced that they needed a party. So Dan delivered a *party*. The room was decorated for a luau. Or maybe New Year's Eve. Rik couldn't be sure. There were long, polished canoes filled with hors d'oeuvres and a couple of bars stocked with premium booze. There were glittery hats and free-flowing champagne. He didn't see any good-time whistles, but there was plenty of bawdy behavior to go with the cocktail waitresses, who wore low-slung pareus around their hips and scanty bras over their breasts. As a bachelor party, it was a smash.

Except for the bridegroom and the best man.

"Hey, great party!" A stranger whopped Rik on the back and he spilled his beer. "Hell of a way to wait out a hurricane!"

The stranger moved into the crowd of unfamiliar faces. Who were these people? Rik wondered as he set down his empty glass and looked for the nearest waitress. He hadn't invited anyone. Dan had supplied the party, the guests and the introductions. The only person Rik remembered clearly was Carter DeHaven, Stephanie's sister's husband. Seemed like a nice guy, even if he had kept eyeing the exit with furtive glances.

Catching a glimpse of loose-jointed hips and the sway of long, silky black hair, Rik took off after the scantily clad waitress. It was pretty obvious that the only way he'd get through this party was to down a fair number of beers. Enough so he could sleep standing up, because it was a cinch Hallie wouldn't be inviting him into her bed tonight.

She was driving him nuts. One minute, a love match. The next, a sordid affair. No wonder he was confused. He'd wanted to talk to Lynn about it, but when he finally managed to get an outside line, the static was so bad he barely had time to assure her that Sam was doing fine. Truth to tell, he was just as glad he hadn't had the opportunity to ask her advice. It was embarrassing to have to admit he couldn't handle one petite, farsighted and totally unpredictable woman.

Lynn would have told him to do something dumb, like apologize for falling in love too fast. What the hell was wrong with that, he'd like to know. Some people took years to make a commitment. He could do it in an instant and be confident it was right. Some people would consider that a risky practice, but he considered risk an integral part of life and the only way he knew how to live.

Hallie obviously considered him an idiot. All because he wanted to stop her silly wedding. Her wedding. As if she had anything to do with Jack's future happiness. Or Stephanie's. She didn't even know them. The wedding—that was her focus. No wonder she didn't wear her glasses all the time. She didn't want to see things too clearly. She wanted to be a martyr to the perfect ceremony, a sacrifice to the gods of disasters, a casualty of the wedding she had failed to give herself.

And with that thought, Rik suddenly understood the reason she had banished him from Paradise. She had built her safe, insulated world to protect herself from risk, and he had leapt over the protective walls like Superman to the rescue, discarding her superstitions like pesky gnats, demanding her love because he deserved it, exposing her to a whole world of risks in one sitting. He was an idiot.

But now he was an idiot with a plan.

"Don't let Jack slip out of here before the main event." Dan Brewster laid claim to Rik's shoulder and attention. "I've never seen a man so determined not to enjoy himself."

"Jack's just nervous." Rik cast a furtive glance at the exit himself. "I'll talk to him."

"Good man." Dan started to move off, but Rik stopped him.

"Wait, Mr. Brewster...Dan. What main event?"

Dan smiled that uncannily aristocratic smile. "I took it upon myself to make sure Jack's party had *all* the essentials." He winked and turned away, leaving a parting sentence to hold the place he vacated. "They ought to be rolling her out any minute now."

Unless Dan had been able to get a roll-out bandstand and a female singer, Rik figured Jack was in for the routine, bachelor-party striptease. Hell. Jack would never forgive him for letting this happen. They'd agreed years ago that when the time came, they'd behave like dignified adult males and not embarrass the other with sleazy girl-jumps-from-cake pranks.

Oh, sure, Rik had teased Jack at every opportunity in the last few days with remarks designed to make a groom nervous. That, after all, was only fair, a traditional guy thing. But he hadn't booked a stripper for this gig, and if Dan had asked—which he hadn't—Rik would have vetoed his plan flat out. But now they were in for it. He'd better warn Jack. Casting one last, wistful look around for a waitress, Rik frowned and set his sights on finding his soon-to-be former best friend.

"Mr. Austin?"

Turning, he found Kimo beside him, holding out a glass of champagne. "Mr. Brewster..." Kimo indicated Dan with a wave of his hand, which Dan reciprocated with a smile and duplicate wave. "He asked me to tell you it's time."

Rik took the glass, although the last thing he wanted at the moment was champagne. "Time for what?"

"The cake," Kimo said. "They're bringing in the cake now, and Mr. Brewster wants you to get Jack up front."

"Hell." One look across the room brought Rik a thumbs-up from Dan. The trap was set. There wasn't going to be any escape. Not for him. Certainly not for Jack. "Thanks, Kimo," he said, then, squaring his shoulders, he headed for a spot close to the obscure door that provided access to the kitchen. He cleared his throat and pitched his voice above the chatter. "Could I have your attention, please? Can I have everyone's attention? Would the man of the hour step up here, please?"

Everyone turned to look for Jack, who was standing next to Kimo near one of the exits. Kimo? Rik decided that young man had to be on roller skates. "Jack?" he called. "Get your butt up here."

Jack's gaze was murderous as he approached, and

Rik figured this was not the time for lengthy explanations. Considering that a gigantic cake was already being wheeled into the ballroom by three scantily clad waitresses, it was obvious to Rik that any explanation at this point would be redundant. Jack knew what was about to happen, and from the look on his face, he was in no mood to be understanding. Rik felt sorry for him, but he took care to step aside and out of the way.

He watched the advance of the cardboard cake, idly wondering who had first come up with the idea of putting a stripper inside. Probably a woman, he decided, lifting his glass to his lips. Men didn't associate strippers with a wedding cake. The two things just weren't congruous. Stripper. Bride. Stripper...

The top of the frilly confection shook free, flicking vanilla frosting in all directions, even into Rik's glass of champagne. But he didn't notice. His attention was on the head of the woman emerging from inside the cake. Her hair was honey brown, but it wasn't the color that had him frozen in alarm. It was the haircut. The feathery, frothy cut.

Even before the bare shoulders topped the cake, even before the gold lamé swimsuit sparkled in the light, even before she wiggled around to face the rapt attention of the male audience, Rik felt the color drain from his face. The glass fell from his hands and crashed in silvery splinters at his feet, and from his throat came a stunned and raspy, "Hallie!"

HALLIE HAD NEVER BEEN hustled in her life. But when Rik met her at the bottom of the gigantic cake, hastily wrapped her in his Hawaiian shirt and hurried her out of the Lanai ballroom via the kitchen, she decided she'd been missing out. Being hustled by Rik had its good points.

Just as they entered the kitchen, the wind gave a mighty screech, the lights flickered and went out. Rik paused in the darkness, his silent anger as loud as any yelling Hallie had ever heard. Then, little by little, lights came on. A flashlight. A candle. Another candle. And another.

In the flickering lights springing up across the kitchen, Hallie saw Chef Charles, Grumbling Dave and Kimo. "Isn't this cozy?" she said, flushed with embarrassment, success and the exhilarating tautness of Rik's hands clamped, respectively, on her arm and waist. He might be angry with her—well, obviously he was—but at least he had been beside her when the lights went out, and he was with her now. They moved cautiously around a cooktop and wound up next to Kimo.

"Hi," Hallie whispered, afraid to say anything to Rik unless he spoke to her first.

"Hi," Kimo whispered back.

"How is it you manage to be everywhere in this hotel at once?"

"I'm a triplet," Kimo said. "It's just easier to use one name than to confuse the guests."

"Triplet," Hallie repeated, knowing if they weren't stranded in a dark kitchen surrounded by flickering candlelight, she'd have been thoroughly delighted by the explanation. "Did you hear that, Rik? Kimo is a triplet."

Rik growled something unintelligible, obviously unimpressed by anything less than quadruplets. Hallie took the candle someone—Dave, she thought—handed to her, and she held it steady while someone else—Charles, she thought this time—lit it from the one he held. She, in turn, held her tiny flame to Rik's candle and watched his face as the fire caught between their two wicks. For one breathless moment their eyes held, and every doubt Hallie had about their future together melted away.

"What the hell were you doing?" he asked suddenly, gruffly. "You had no business being at that party."

"I was there to prove a point," she told him, emboldened by the darkness and the tiny fires that flickered and bobbed all around them. "I wanted you to see that I'm not afraid to do something really stupid."

"And what does that prove?"

She swallowed. "I think I love you."

Someone jostled them, pushing them closer together. Rik cleared his throat. "When are you going to know for sure?"

"I don't know. Maybe a few weeks. Maybe never."

"So, what am I supposed to do? Wait until you decide?"

She lifted her shoulder in a plaintive shrug, her chin in a challenge. "It's a double-dog dare, Mr. Austin. A risk you'll just have to take."

Rik's candle bobbed as he ran his free hand through his hair. "We need to talk."

"Come on, people, let's get these candles out to the lobby. Get them distributed. You know the drill." A new voice permeated the congested kitchen, a commanding voice. A voice of authority. A vaguely familiar voice. "Hey, you two!" The voice turned on them. "Grab a box of candles and help. This is no time for mushy stuff. Get the lead out."

Dave moved past them, a box of candles under each arm and a stack of boxes in his hands. He was suddenly the man in charge, and Hallie couldn't stop staring at him, amazed that the candlelight cast him in such a different light.

Kimo clapped his hands near her. "You heard the boss, people. Let's move!"

"Boss?" Hallie whispered. "Dave?"

Dave gave her a wink in passing. "You didn't think I push a broom for a living, did you? Let's go! Move! Move! Move!"

Everyone moved, even Rik and Hallie. Caught in the can-do spirit of the employees, they were whisked out of the kitchen and into the lobby amid a sea of frightened, reassurance-seeking guests. Hallie handed out candles until her box was empty, then she touched her lighted candle to unlit wick after unlit wick.

A blanket of candlelight settled on the lobby as the storm screamed and beat against the shore. Someone had a radio that for a short while sputtered out reports on Hurricane Bonnie, then fell into a staticky silence. Across the room, someone sat down at the piano and began to play. Gershwin. *Rhapsody in Blue.*

As suddenly as she'd lost him in the crowd, Rik was beside her. "I believe this is my dance," he said softly, taking her hand.

She blushed, although no one could see. "Don't be silly. There isn't room to—"

"Ms. Bernhardt," he interrupted. "This is my fantasy and I don't care how crowded it is, I'm going to dance with you." He took her hand and started toward a vacant space near the piano, but she pulled back.

"I can't dance," she whispered tightly. "I don't know how."

He stopped and held his candle closer to her face. "You were about to do a striptease before the electricity went off."

"No, I wasn't. I was only going to make sure you saw how uninhibited I could be, and then I was going to kiss Jack and run out of the room. See? No dancing involved."

"Then it's time you learned." He led her around sitting guests and standing guests, around the front desk and behind the piano. There he blew his candle out and set it aside, took her candle and set it beside his. "We don't need candlelight," he said as he drew her into his arms. "We're Astaire and Rogers."

The music played and Hallie danced, held tightly in Rik's arms. When the music stopped, they didn't. They kept on dancing and dancing. In the silence. In the shadowed dark. "Rik?" she whispered. "I was wrong."

"Yes, you were."

"I mean about being in love with you."

"You were wrong about that, too. You already know for sure that you love me."

"I don't think so."

"Don't argue, Hallie." It was a tender warning and his arms didn't loosen their gentle hold of her in the slightest. "You love me and that's final. I'll spend the next five years shivering in the prim and proper winters of Boston convincing you that you cannot live without me. I'll fly those chintzy helicopter holiday flights around the city. I'll get a job training fresh-faced kids how to handle a chopper. I might even do traffic reports for the radio stations."

"You'd do traffic reports for me?" she asked, impressed.

"Yes." He shuddered, but only a little. And she loved him all the more for it.

"It won't work," she told him.

"Yes, it will," he told her.

She shook her head, liking the way her hair swung against her cheeks with the movement. "It won't work because I won't be in Boston."

"You won't?"

"Uh-uh. I'm tired of planning happy endings for other people. I've decided to plan one of my own."

He groaned. "A wedding?"

"Just a ceremony. A few friends. Family. Speaking of which, where's Sam?"

"He's safe with Dani. Why? Is he invited?"

"Of course. I mean, if I'm going to be his aunt Hallie, he should be there, don't you think?"

Rik hugged her close. The piano player picked them up in midstep with a softly romantic *Clair de lune.* "So, Hallie," he said, "if we're not going to live in Boston, where are we going to be?"

"Oh, offhand, I'd say Paradise. As long as you swear you won't rescue any beautiful women when I'm not around."

"What about ugly women when you *are* around?"

"Careful, now. I'm new at this. And I'm not entirely certain about my sudden career shift. What if I regret closing the bridal shop? What if we need the money? What if I open one here? Or go to work for Dave? What if—"

"What if you stop talking?" he suggested. "This is still my fantasy, you know."

"It's your fantasy to dance in a too small space, in a too dark room, surrounded by faces in shadow, with a woman who doesn't know how to dance?" She laid her head on his shoulder. "Now, Rik, if this is your idea of a cutting-edge fantasy..."

"It is."

She sighed with a happiness she'd thought was gone

with the wind. "Well then, I have no objection. Considering that I'm crazy in love with you."

"Are you wearing your glasses?" he asked.

"No. Is there something I need to see?"

He shook his head, rubbing his chin against her hair. "Just me, loving you."

"Lucky me." She tilted her face to his, delighting in the unfocused blur that was the man she would love for the rest of her life. "Be honest, Rik," she teased gently. "It's the haircut you love, isn't it?"

"It's the haircut," he agreed, and then he kissed her.

Epilogue

A tropical breeze zipped through the open lanai to puff the gauzy pink ribbons draped, ceiling to floor, over the main table. Above a perky ukulele tune, low-pitched conversations were interspersed with soft laughter and the soft *chink* of silverware on china. A baby blanket full of pastel-wrapped packages dangled from the wooden beak of a giant stork as it stood guard at the far end of the gift table. From an inconspicuous corner of the Lanai ballroom, Kimo supervised the wait staff as they removed plates, poured coffee and refilled glasses.

"I'd like to propose a toast." Danforth Brewster stood at the center table, dressed in sailor white, wearing a blue lei and a wide smile. "To my—" From the seat beside him, Babs tugged on his shirtsleeve and he bent to listen to her private whisper. With a nod, he straightened again and extended his glass. "In honor of the mother-to-be, I'd like to propose a *nonalcoholic* toast. To my son-in-law Mitch and to his son, my grandson, Carter. If not for them, I'd still be outnumbered by the women in this family."

The applause spattered, the toast was drunk, Dan sat down and was replaced by Mitch, who had his hands full keeping six-month-old Carter's fingers out of a tall glass of orange juice.

"I'd like to propose a toast," Mitch said. "To my wife, Bentley, the extraordinary woman who gave birth to this future Pulitzer prize-winning journalist." He held up Carter's baby hand like a referee at the end of a boxing match. Laughter followed Mitch's gesture and died down as he raised Carter's bottle in a salute. "And I also want to toast the one person who made this all possible...Hurricane Bonnie!"

Bentley tugged on his sleeve and he leaned down to hear her. Then, straightening, he hoisted Carter onto his shoulder.

"I've just been informed that Hurricane Bonnie is not a person and cannot be toasted. So I'll amend my appreciation and say a hearty, 'Hear! Hear!' to my sister-in-law, Stephanie. If it hadn't been for her eloping with Thomas on the eve of her wedding to Jack, Carter and I might not be here now. So, Stephanie—" he raised the baby bottle "—here's to last-minute escapes! And to the diapers you'll be changing for the next twenty-four months!"

Good-natured laughter swept the room as Stephanie pushed back her chair and levered her very bulky belly past the edge of the table. Her husband, Thomas, hovered beside her like a watchful mother hen.

"Thanks, Mitch," Stephanie said. "I have a couple of toasts to make myself...if I can stay on my feet that long. I know I look like I could go into labor any minute, but the doctor assures me it'll be another eight weeks." She smiled at Dan and patted her stomach. "He also tells me to paint the babies' room pink, so you'd better enjoy the next couple of months, Dad, because once the triplets arrive, you're going to be seriously outnumbered all over again!''

She accepted the glass of juice Thomas handed to her and lifted it in a toast. "Two years ago this week, Thomas Calhoun walked into the Honolulu airport and changed my mind about marrying my good friend Jack Keaton. I guess Hurricane Bonnie had a little something to do with it, too," she said with a smile for Thomas. "It took the full wrath of Mother Nature to bring about the happiness you see all about you today. And now, two years later, I'd like to say thank you to a very special man in my life. I can't begin to tell you what a wonderful person he is. He was always there when I needed a friend and I'll be forever grateful that I didn't break his heart. Jack, stand up."

Jack stood reluctantly and smiled down at the woman beside him. "Since we're being sentimental today," he began, "I'll toast the only woman in the world who could have broken my heart but didn't. Dani, you're one in a million and I love you." He bent to give his wife an affectionate kiss before he continued. "And in case there's anyone here who hasn't met my daughter, Bonnie..." He lifted his little girl out of her mother's arms and held her up like the proud papa he was. "Isn't she the most beautiful thing you've ever seen?"

There were oohs and aahs all around. Jack handed Bonnie over to the eager arms of her grandmother, Mona, then lifted his champagne glass in another toast. "When it comes to friendship, there's one person I have to acknowledge. He's been my partner, my conscience and my best pal for more years than I can recall. If he hadn't been so stubbornly certain that I wasn't in love with Stephanie or so doggone determined to talk me out of marrying her, I might not have met Dani. It was Rik's harebrained idea to borrow a baby and hire a stork. I have to thank Lynn and Keanu—'' he nodded across the room at the couple ''—for the loan of Sam. Dani and I will always be grateful for the thirty-six hours we spent with the little guy. And just between you and me, I'm convinced he's Cupid.''

''Hiya, Jack!'' Across the room, almost three-year-old Sam balanced between his parents' chairs and waved a model helicopter. ''Wanna see my *hopter?*''

''Later, buddy,'' Jack called back as he lifted his glass. ''As I was saying, let's drink to my friend through fair and stormy weather...Rik Austin.''

From her place at the table, Hallie watched, her heart bursting with happiness, as Rik acknowledged the toast with a modest smile. How could any man be so gorgeous, she wondered with smug satisfaction. Even the sunscreen he put on just to please her hadn't dulled the golden tone of his skin. And his eyes were still the heart-stopping blue of *Blue Hawaii.* He was successful, too. His tour business had exceeded even his high expectations, and her own event-planning service was thriving. Hawaii was home to her now. She'd even grown to love the ocean and couldn't imagine living anywhere else. Sometimes she told Rik that the island climate had cured her allergies, but she knew in her heart that happiness was the real remedy.

She'd had no idea love would be so lovely the second time around. But, then, that was the great thing about love. You couldn't believe in it until it happened to you...and then you couldn't do anything except believe in it.

Rik made her life rich with love and laughter. He was her happiness, her heart. And in a little less than eight months, he'd be her partner in the adventure of parenthood—a joint venture he'd been anticipating for a very long time. She hugged her bliss as her husband accepted Jack's tribute to their friendship.

"Thanks, Jack," Rik said. "I'd like to make a toast, too. Not to my wife, although she deserves one for bringing together such a great baby shower." His smile stole her breath away with its tenderness. "And not to the guest of honor, although I'm certain Stephanie would like a stiff drink every time she thinks about her impending multiple births. I'd like to toast all of the mothers and mothers-to-be in this room. May your children bring you joy and may love fill your lives."

"Hear, hear." The murmur moved through the room, and as Rik raised his glass to her, Hallie downed the orange juice in a long swallow.

"I'm sorry to interrupt." Kimo stepped forward and cleared his throat. "But I just heard that the tropical storm in the Pacific is now officially Hurricane Nicholas. It poses no threat to the Islands, but the wind is picking up and I wanted to assure you—"

The scraping of chairs drowned out whatever reassurances Kimo offered, and in the general exodus from the ballroom, Rik caught Hallie's elbow. "You weren't thinking you could get out of here without me, were you?"

"Don't be silly." She smiled up at him, oblivious to everything except the swell of love in her heart. "You know my fantasy about being stranded in a storm with you."

"I'll bet you say that to all your husbands."

"No. Only you."

"Then I'm a lucky guy." He reached out to give her stomach a reverent pat. "A damn lucky guy."

"Yes, you are." Hallie smiled at him, happier than

she'd ever dreamed of being. "Now, if we hurry, we can be safe and snug in our favorite hotel room before the crowd reaches the elevators."

"Mrs. Austin," Rik asked. "What do you intend to do in the thirteenth room on the thirteenth floor of this hotel?"

"Ride out the hurricane...and maybe, if you're lucky, try out a couple of new fantasies."

"Cutting-edge fantasies?"

"Is there any other kind?"

"Not with you, Hallie." He grinned and he swept her up in his arms and carried her quickly toward the waiting elevator. "Not with you."

COMING NEXT MONTH

#701 IN PAPA BEAR'S BED by Judy Christenberry

Once Upon a Kiss

In a cabin in the woods, runaway Jessica Barnes rested in a chair that was too big, ate leftovers that were too small, and slept in a bed that was just right. When Rob Berenson and his kids returned home, one look at the naked blonde between his sheets and as much as he had his own secrets to hide, Rob didn't want this Goldilocks to run away!

#702 A DARK & STORMY NIGHT by Anne Stuart

More Than Men

Katie Flynn sought shelter from a storm but on a windswept cliff she found a moody recluse named O'Neal. Trapped, she fought his sensuality, but she suspected that something haunted the man...something that only O'Neal himself could reveal....

#703 OVERNIGHT WIFE by Mollie Molay

Ditching her Christmas Eve wedding, Arden Crandall fled to the airport in time to take the honeymoon by herself, but she ran smack into a snowstorm and the mysterious Luke McCauley. The man was trouble, but she thought she could resist him—and then came the announcement that the airport would be closed all night....

#704 MISTER CHRISTMAS by Linda Cajio

The Holiday Heart

Holly had to help Raymond Holiday find his heart by December 25th or he'd lose it for good. He'd dodged love for years, from his family, friends, women—though he had a way with the latter, and with female elves like herself. She only hoped he found his heart before she lost hers....

AVAILABLE THIS MONTH:

Look us up on-line at: http://www.romance.net

HARLEQUIN®

A M E R I C A N ❖ R O M A N C E®

Everyone loves the *Holidays*...

Four sexy guys with two things in common:
the Holiday name and humbug in the heart!

PETER

the holiday heart

by Linda Cajio

MICHAEL

This year Cupid and his romantic cohorts are
working double—make that quadruple—time, not only
Valentine's Day but also Mother's Day, Labor Day and
Christmas—every holiday season throughout 1997.

Don't miss any of these heartfelt romances in:

May—#678 BACHELOR DADDY

September—#694 BOSS MAN

November—#704 MISTER CHRISTMAS

JARED

RAYMOND

Only from Harlequin American Romance.

The Gentleman & THE HELL RAISER

Don't miss these captivating stories
from two acclaimed authors
of historical romance.

THE GENTLEMAN by Kristin James
THE HELL RAISER by Dorothy Glenn

Two brothers on a collision course
with destiny and love.

Find out how the dust settles October 1997
wherever Harlequin and Silhouette
books are sold.

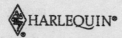 

As Seen on TV!

Free Gift Offer

With a Free Gift proof-of-purchase
from any Harlequin® book, you can receive
a beautiful cubic zirconia pendant.

This stunning marquise-shaped stone is a genuine cubic
zirconia—accented by an 18" gold tone necklace.
(Approximate retail value $19.95)

Send for yours today...
compliments of HARLEQUIN®

To receive your free gift, a cubic zirconia pendant, send us one original proof-of-purchase, photocopies not accepted, from the back of any Harlequin Romance®, Harlequin Presents®, Harlequin Temptation®, Harlequin Superromance®, Harlequin Intrigue®, Harlequin American Romance®, or Harlequin Historicals® title available at your favorite retail outlet, together with the Free Gift Certificate, plus a check or money order for $1.65 U.S./$2.15 CAN. (do not send cash) to cover postage and handling, payable to Harlequin Free Gift Offer. We will send you the specified gift. Allow 6 to 8 weeks for delivery. Offer good until December 31, 1997, or while quantities last. Offer valid in the U.S. and Canada only.

Free Gift Certificate

Name: _____

Address: _____

City: _____ State/Province: _____ Zip/Postal Code: _____

Mail this certificate, one proof-of-purchase and a check or money order for postage and handling to: HARLEQUIN FREE GIFT OFFER 1997. In the U.S.: 3010 Walden Avenue, P.O. Box 9071, Buffalo NY 14269-9057. In Canada: P.O. Box 604, Fort Erie, Ontario L2Z 5X3.

FREE GIFT OFFER   084-KEZ

ONE PROOF-OF-PURCHASE

To collect your fabulous FREE GIFT, a cubic zirconia pendant, you must include this original proof-of-purchase for each gift with the properly completed Free Gift Certificate.

084-KEZR

Don't miss these Harlequin favorites
by some of our bestselling authors! Act now and
receive a discount by ordering two or more titles!

HT#25720	A NIGHT TO REMEMBER by Gina Wilkins	$3.50 U.S. $3.99 CAN.	☐
HT#25722	CHANGE OF HEART by Janice Kaiser	$3.50 U.S. $3.99 CAN.	☐
HP#11797	A WOMAN OF PASSION by Anne Mather	$3.50 U.S. $3.99 CAN.	☐
HP#11863	ONE-MAN WOMAN by Carole Mortimer	$3.50 U.S. $3.99 CAN.	☐
HR#03356	BACHELOR'S FAMILY by Jessica Steele	$2.99 U.S. $3.50 CAN.	☐
HR#03441	RUNAWAY HONEYMOON by Ruth Jean Dale	$3.25 U.S. $3.75 CAN.	☐
HS#70715	BAREFOOT IN THE GRASS by Judith Arnold	$3.99 U.S. $4.50 CAN.	☐
HS#70729	ANOTHER MAN'S CHILD by Tara Taylor Quinn	$3.99 U.S. $4.50 CAN.	☐
HI#22361	LUCKY DEVIL by Patricia Rosemoor	$3.75 U.S. $4.25 CAN.	☐
HI#22379	PASSION IN THE FIRST DEGREE by Carla Cassidy	$3.75 U.S. $4.25 CAN.	☐
HAR#16638	LIKE FATHER, LIKE SON by Mollie Molay	$3.75 U.S. $4.25 CAN.	☐
HAR#16663	ADAM'S KISS by Mindy Neff	$3.75 U.S. $4.25 CAN.	☐
HH#28937	GABRIEL'S LADY by Ana Seymour	$4.99 U.S. $5.99 CAN.	☐
HH#28941	GIFT OF THE HEART by Miranda Jarrett	$4.99 U.S. $5.99 CAN.	☐

(limited quantities available on certain titles)

	TOTAL AMOUNT	$ _____
DEDUCT:	**10% DISCOUNT FOR 2+ BOOKS**	$ _____
	POSTAGE & HANDLING	$ _____
	($1.00 for one book, 50¢ for each additional)	
	APPLICABLE TAXES*	$ _____
	TOTAL PAYABLE	$ _____

(check or money order—please do not send cash)

To order, complete this form and send it, along with a check or money order for the total above, payable to Harlequin Books, to: **In the U.S.:** 3010 Walden Avenue, P.O. Box 9047, Buffalo, NY 14269-9047; **In Canada:** P.O. Box 613, Fort Erie, Ontario, L2A 5X3.

Name: _____
Address: _____ City: _____
State/Prov.: _____ Zip/Postal Code: _____

*New York residents remit applicable sales taxes.
Canadian residents remit applicable GST and provincial taxes.

Look us up on-line at: http://www.romance.net   HBKOD97